Save Me Once

a novel by Alana Terry

Note: The views of the characters in this novel do not necessarily reflect the views of the author, nor is their behavior necessarily condoned.

The characters in this book are fictional. Any resemblance to real persons is coincidental. No part of this book may be reproduced in any form (electronic, audio, print, film, etc.) without the author's written consent.

Copyright © 2020 Alana Terry

Scriptures quoted from THE HOLY BIBLE, NEW INTERNATIONAL VERSION®, NIV® Copyright © 1973, 1978, 1984, 2011 by Biblica, Inc.® Used by permission. All rights reserved worldwide.

www.alanaterry.com

Author note: Save Me Once *is a thriller by Christian suspense novelist Alana Terry. One of the characters you'll meet is a teen runaway involved in a life on the streets. Great care has been taken to avoid explicit scenarios or gratuitous violence; however, discretion is advised if you may be triggered by the above scenario of if you're considering sharing this book with a young reader.*

CHAPTER 1

How long had it been since the last time she ate? A day? Maybe more?

She rolled onto her side, forgetting for one single moment that she was bound.

Trapped.

Of course, even if the door was unlocked, she couldn't escape. The deadbolt was nothing but a symbol of her captivity.

A metaphor.

Her English teacher would be impressed by the comparison.

If she ever saw him again, that is. Mr. Daly once said she was his best student. Of course, with only fifteen members of his honors class to choose from, the competition wasn't all that fierce, but she'd let the praise float into her head just the same.

All that was gone now. Mr. Daly. The good grades. The

star pupil she'd once been.

She squeezed her eyes shut and for a moment was able to imagine. Imagine that none of this had ever happened. That she was home. That her mother was downstairs, sizzling bacon in a frying pan on the stovetop.

A sigh. Trying harder to recapture the memory. The smell of the bacon grease, savory enough to appease the hunger that gnawed very real in her gut.

The hunger that threatened to shatter her illusion of peace. Of home.

Squeezing her eyes even harder. Forcing her mind to remember. Forbidding the memories from vanishing. Not yet.

Not yet …

Where was the smell of bacon? She didn't want to let it go.

Xavier had come last night. But he didn't stay long. He rarely did anymore.

She told him she was out of granola bars. Hadn't she mentioned that? And he promised to get her more. Or had she misheard him?

He was mad at her. It wasn't his fault. Work was hard right now. Lean times. She saw the anxiety that draped over his shoulders like a hundred-pound mantle.

There. A simile. Mr. Daly had been a good teacher.

She curled her knees up toward her chest, turning her back toward the sunlight that was valiantly attempting to pry into her room through the thick curtains. The shackles chaffed her wrists, and her back kinked when she tried to inch away from the invasive sunlight.

Xavier had removed the clock from the nightstand, but she knew from the angle of the sun he should be here soon. She'd read in a history book once that dogs would rather be tortured than ignored. She couldn't recall which class she'd read that in or why such a random fact popped into her head now of all times, but she'd learned that random thoughts pop up at unexpected moments when you're chained to a bed.

She inched her heel away when she felt the prickles of sunlight land on her bare foot and counted the minutes.

Xavier would be back soon.

She hoped he remembered those granola bars.

CHAPTER 2

Perfect. Absolutely perfect. That's how this night had to go. For Caroline, there was no other way. She'd prayed too hard. Pleaded with God too much for him to allow a single hair on her graying head to fall out of place.

She stared at herself in the mirror. If Calvin's type was young, blonde, and buxom, he'd be disappointed. But then again, Caroline had never deluded herself into believing he'd married her for her looks.

Good thing, too. She sighed as she dabbed a little concealer over the wrinkles that spread out from the corners of her eyes like cracks in the desert sand.

A second later, her husband opened the bathroom door, announcing dryly, "We're late."

That was her Calvin. Always punctual to a fault. Punctual, stubborn, and looking surprisingly handsome in his navy-blue suit.

She gave him a slight smile, forcing herself not to react when he didn't return it. She'd promised herself not to get into any fights. Not tonight. She'd waited over half a year for this conference, and up until she and her husband actually passed through security at Logan Airport, she doubted he'd follow through.

And yet here they were. Truth Warriors Ministry held conferences at locations all over the country, many of them significantly closer to Boston, but over thirty years ago when they were just newlyweds, Calvin had promised to take her to Las Vegas.

So here they were.

And she wasn't about to ruin this perfect evening by fixating on her husband's stoic expression. This was Calvin, after all. When did he ever stop looking stoic?

"Ready?" he asked, twitching his upper lip.

She sucked in her breath. Gave herself one more tentative glance in the mirror. She didn't look quite as elegant as she imagined when she chose her outfit, but another thirty or forty minutes to primp and preen wouldn't make any significant difference.

Certainly not significant enough for her husband to notice.

She smoothed out her hair. Forced herself to meet Calvin's eyes.

"You look nice," she told him, her heart speeding up at such an unfamiliar set of words. Ordinarily, she would never say something like that, but today's speaker at the conference had convicted her. Caroline complained all the time that her husband didn't care for or appreciate her, but when was the last time she'd paid him a compliment?

Calvin cocked his head to the side. Maybe he felt as out of place as she did at this new conversational turn. Would he come back with something biting?

He cleared his throat and glanced at his watch. "Guess we're not that late." It wasn't exactly a compliment, but she decided it was the best she could hope for.

Small steps. Isn't that what this marriage conference was all about?

"Do you have the hotel key?" she asked as Calvin stepped aside for her to pass out of the bathroom.

He grunted a reply, and Caroline was ready.

She gave him another smile. Perhaps a tad forced, but considering where their marriage had been when she booked their tickets here, she was ecstatic.

Baby steps.

Small progress.

That's what today's speaker had said.

And that's exactly what Caroline was going to focus on.

CHAPTER 3

Drisklay hated ties. The only thing more insufferable than this four-day marriage seminar was dressing up in formal wear. The truth was he was only here because his wife begged incessantly. He swore he'd never go to a stupid marriage seminar, no matter how severely his wife nagged.

And yet here they were.

Las Vegas. With its neon lights, the so-called entertainment capital of the world.

Somehow, his wife had decided this was the place to renew their love for one another. Not exactly what he would have expected from her. Caroline was more the stay-in-a-cabin-and-read-a-dozen-novels kind of vacationer. Or hop on a flight to serve orphans overseas. The type who believed in prayer and miracles.

She could believe in that garbage if it made her sleep better at night. Drisklay knew better. Miracles were reserved for fairy tales and myths. Placebos at best. Delusions of madmen at worst.

But he wouldn't argue the point with her. In fact, he made Caroline promise that if he agreed to come with her to this silly Vegas conference, she wouldn't bring up religion.

Not even once.

No praying out loud before meals. No late nights in bed asking if he wanted to talk about the state of his soul. No Bible verses grotesquely inserted into random conversations, forced and awkward and full of hostility.

And surprisingly, she'd held up her side of the bargain. Granted, the conference wasn't over yet. But he'd been pleasantly surprised to find a refreshing absence of references to God, the Bible, and his wife's nagging reminders that he was a sinner destined to spend an eternity in hell.

Oh, Caroline.

Which brought him back to his curiosity that she picked a conference here of all places. Didn't Christians have to swear off all sorts of vices? And Vegas was dripping with them. Gambling, drinking, secondhand smoke ... weren't those all no-no's on God's holy list of not-to-dos?

Well, as long as Caroline didn't force-feed him Scripture, as long as Drisklay got a short reprieve from the constant barrage of Bible verses and morality lessons, he was happy.

Happy enough, that is.

Sure, today's conference speakers were just as inept as he'd expected them to be. If you followed their six steps to a happy marriage, you and your spouse could look as sappy and romantic as they claimed to be. But who wanted to live like that?

Here, sweetie, let me take out the trash for you tonight.
Oh, dearest, you're such a darling. I love you so much.
No, my love, it is I who adore you.

And so on and so on, *ad nauseum.* Literally.

He hoped Caroline didn't expect too much out of this week. Maybe if Drisklay was a stay-at-home dad or a day trader who worked in his sweats, he'd have time and energy at night to be Mr. Helpful around the house. But he had work to do. Real work. The people of Boston depended on him for their safety. Caroline understood. Didn't that new religion of hers teach her the concept of sacrifice? Well, here he was, sacrificing his own time every single day, not to mention his safety and physical health. He put his life on the line every single day so the people of Boston could sleep peacefully at night. And if that meant he came home tired and grumpy and in no mood to fix a faulty garbage disposal, his wife had no right to complain.

"Here's your stop." The taxi driver had a scruffy beard

and a slight accent Drisklay couldn't place. Probably not foreign, but an American dialect you didn't hear regularly out on the East Coast. Calvin swiped his credit card, and the cabbie smiled. "Have a good evening."

Drisklay grunted and waited for his wife to step out of the car before shutting the door behind her.

Caroline looked nice tonight. He'd give her that much at least. For a woman in her mid-fifties, she still knew how to take care of herself. She glanced over her shoulder and gave him a little timid smile. He hated that look, truth be told. The worry. The unspoken apology. The I'm-a-Christian-now-so-I-can't-have-any-more-fun look.

He let out his breath. "Well, you ready?"

She forced a smile and whispered, "I'm so glad we're doing this." He wasn't sure if she was talking about their dinner out specifically or their trip to Vegas in general, but at least she was happy. And that meant something to him.

Drisklay knew he was no real catch. He was rude. He took his wife for granted. He'd made her cry on more than one occasion.

But he did want her to be happy.

She deserved that much, at the very least.

CHAPTER 4

"Do you have to be on your phone while we eat?" Caroline regretted asking the question as soon as the words left her mouth.

Her husband glanced up sharply. "I'm working," he explained.

Caroline could have told him that. When was he not working?

"I just thought that ..." Caroline began but stopped when the tuxedoed waiter came to fill her empty water glass. At least this restaurant kept them hydrated. The casino joint where they'd had their lunch charged four bucks just for bottled water.

Caroline let out her breath, reminding herself not to argue with her husband. Not here. Not now.

Eventually, they'd talk about his manners at the table. She started rehearsing the most diplomatic way to explain to him how she felt ignored. Unappreciated. But for now, she'd give him some leeway. He was here, after all. That had to count for something.

Actually, it counted for a lot.

Last year, she and Calvin were fighting incessantly about church. He complained that she was brainwashed, that the pastor who baptized her only wanted her money, that Christians were all hypocrites. Self-righteous snobs, he called them. People who were convinced they're better than anyone else, totally oblivious to how foolish they look to the rest of the world. That was Calvin's opinion, at least, an opinion he shared with Caroline on a near daily basis.

Not that she had been all that much better. Calvin was disappointed in her. In a moment of perfect candidness, he admitted that he hated the way she'd drop Bible verses into their conversations. How it always made him feel like she was judging him. Like he'd never be good enough for her.

So she eased up. It wasn't easy. She still wanted to see Calvin saved, but she couldn't force him to believe the truths of God's word. Couldn't pressure him into a real conversion any more than she could force her students at Medford Academy to learn their history lessons.

And so she stopped sharing those Bible verses. Stopped asking Calvin if he wanted to go to church with her on Sundays or pray with her before meals. Sometimes she felt like the loneliest believer in the world, but things could be worse.

Much worse.

While they sat across from each other at the table, she studied her husband's face, trying to decipher if the message he'd been reading on his phone would help with his current investigation.

Calvin would deny it, but he never handled cases that dealt with children well.

And Caroline knew this case he'd been working on was hitting him particularly hard.

Hitting both of them hard, to be honest.

Calvin scowled at his screen.

"Is there news?" she asked quietly, scouring his expression for a sign of hope. Any sign of breakthrough.

He jerked his head up, startled. Had he forgotten she was there?

If he were working any other case, she might have demanded his full attention, but this case was personal to them both.

Becky Linklater, the girl who disappeared mysteriously last summer, had never been in Caroline's class, but she was well known at Medford Academy. A kind, bubbly, gregarious student. The sort who'd try out for the cheerleading team the second she reached high school and perform on the varsity squad by her sophomore year. A sweet little thing with adorably springy curls and dimples, a mix between Shirley Temple and one of those contemporary teenage pop stars.

Nobody in Medford was taking this missing person case easily.

Calvin shook his head.

"Nothing?" Caroline spoke the word quietly, as if by not giving full voice to the hopelessness of the situation, she might bring Becky back. Restore the missing teen to her parents.

The waiter came by with their food. "I hope you're both hungry tonight," he said, gallantly placing their dinners in front of them.

Calvin set down his phone. Finally. He gave her a brief nod before cutting into his steak. His version of pre-meal conversation. A second later, he was chewing a piece of meat so raw the juices stained his mashed potatoes pink.

"Where do you think she is?" Caroline asked. It was rare for Calvin to share anything about the cases he was working. Rarer for her to get personally involved.

But this was Becky Linklater they were talking about. Perfect student. Smiling, athletic, and kind. A charming thing, really.

Maybe too charming. Caroline wasn't blind. What if some predator saw those springy blond curls and decided ... She squeezed her eyes shut just for a moment. This wasn't what she'd hoped to be thinking about during Calvin's time off from work. She'd thought that getting him out of Boston would be good for them both. Maybe that explained in part why she'd booked their conference in Vegas instead of something closer to home. Maybe she hoped that if she put enough literal distance between himself and his office ...

Well, who was she kidding? Caroline knew Becky's mother. Margot Linklater was barely able to hold up under the pressure of her missing daughter. Caroline wasn't a mother herself, but if she were in Margot's place, wouldn't she want to know that Boston's finest detective was working on her case twenty-four hours a day instead of traveling for a vacation with his wife to the other side of the country?

There were plenty of times when Caroline hated her husband's job as a detective. The long hours, the endless stretches where he'd go weeks on only a few hours of sleep and dozens of pots of coffee a day. She hated the way his work made him so jaded, so distant.

But this was different. If answering a few text messages could do anything — and she meant literally *anything* — to restore Becky Linklater to her family, it would be worth the loneliness she felt.

"Aren't you going to eat?" Calvin asked, his mouth full of potatoes.

Caroline eyed her seafood salad, something the online travel bloggers had raved about, and realized she was no longer hungry.

CHAPTER 5

Last summer

My name is Becky Linklater, and this is my story. Wow, I didn't realize how scary writing this all out was going to be. Once I get into the groove, I'm sure it'll be fine. I'm really excited about that part. Because it really is, like, the best story I know, and it's totally true because it happened to me.

Or maybe I should say it's *happening* to me.

But that doesn't make it easier to figure out where to begin. Mr. Daly — he's my English teacher and one of the biggest inspirations in my entire life — told me once that I have a real gift for writing, but I need to do a better job with my opening.

Hook my readers, as he put it, because you only have a few paragraphs to catch someone's attention. Well, Mr. Daly, I bet that's really good advice. In fact, I'm sure it is because I read your novel, the one about the boy who's really a knight, and it was amazing. I'm not usually into fantasy. I like more realistic stuff, I guess. Either realistic or dystopian. I like that a lot too. But realistic dystopian, know what I mean? Your book wasn't like that, but it was still really good. And so whenever you give me writing advice, I try to pay attention because one day, I'm going to be a real writer. Just like you. Except I won't write fantasy. (No offense.)

Anyway, I think Mr. Daly was onto something for sure. I do have a hard time with my openings. It's not that I don't know what to say. I actually have the opposite problem. I have so many ideas swirling around in my mind right now, I literally have no idea where to begin.

But I have to start somewhere, and even though I'm writing this just for me and nobody else (not even my mom, even though she's great and I literally love her to death), it really is intimidating. I mean it. Like, I've got what's going to turn into the greatest love story, at least in this century, and I don't even know what to say in the very first chapter.

I guess I should start at the ice rink. I'm a figure skater. Well, I was. Mom even got Dad convinced to let me join the Troy Valley team, which is, like, super competitive. One of the girls even ended up trying out for the Olympics. That's how good we're talking.

But all that was years ago, before Dad took off. I promised myself I wouldn't start this story with anything sad, so I won't go into details of that. Bottom line is Mom ran out of money, and since Dad's basically a total deadbeat (seriously), I had to quit the team.

Yeah, it was a bummer, but that's life sometimes, right? You've just got to make the best of what you've got.

Or something like that.

I couldn't stay on the competition team, and even though it was majorly a disappointment, I have to admit I kind of have some mixed feelings about it. Like, on the one hand, my coach said I was really good. I know I shouldn't brag and stuff, but Mom told me once that being too humble is basically just as bad as being too proud. So I'm really and genuinely serious when I say I was that good. Best on my team, hands down.

Then I had to quit.

Boo hoo, life goes on, I got over it.

But I still skate. A lot. Not on a team or anything, at least not for competitions. Mostly now just for the love of it, which is why in some ways Dad being such a two-timing sleaze ball and Mom not making enough money to pay all my dues turned into kind of a mixed blessing. At least that's what Miss Sandy would say. She's my best friend's mom, but this story isn't that much about her, so I guess I don't really need to go into that.

Not right now, at least.

Anyway, I say quitting the competition team was a mixed blessing because it was so busy. Like, I had to be up at, like, five every morning to get to practice, and then after school I was either working out or back on the ice, and then three nights a week I barely had time to eat dinner before I had to meet my private coach, and ... Well, now I just get to skate when I want. Which is still quite a bit, and now there's not all the pressure of such a tight schedule and all those competitions.

That's just the way I am, I guess. Always looking for the bright side of things. Focusing on the good stuff. Which is why I wanted so bad to write this story out, because something *amazing* — I mean like literally amazing — just happened to me.

I fell in love.

If you're an adult reading this, maybe you're rolling your eyes. Maybe you're all like, *she's not even in high school yet. What's up with that, and how is she talking about true love?* Okay, I know it might sound sappy, but seriously, I may not be that old yet in years, but I swear this is the real thing.

Sometimes I feel so lucky and so happy it's like my heart is about to squeeze itself right out of my chest. I don't mean that exactly literally, by the way, and Mr. Daly's always telling me not to use too much hyperbole in my writing. Isn't that a cool word? *Hyperbole.* Four syllables. I won't ever forget that because I was totally embarrassed the first time Mr. Daly asked me to read something out loud to the class and I mispronounced it. I said "hyper-bowl," like a bowling team for really active kids or something, but nobody else in my class knew how it was supposed to be pronounced either, so it was all good.

But back to Mr. Daly. He told me not to exaggerate when I write, and if he were reading this, he'd probably tell me I'm using too many clichés, but the funny thing is he told me that exact same thing before I read his novel. So when I finally picked it up, I decided to count, and he's got, like, two or three clichés in every single chapter.

Ha! Caught him.

So you might think I'm exaggerating when I say I found true love, but seriously, I've never been more certain about anything in my entire life. I may be young, but I'm old enough to know what love is. Real love.

It was like we were meant for each other.

Like we were destined to meet, and when we finally fell

into each other's lives, the stars exploded overhead because this was the kind of encounter that only happens once a millennium.

Maybe less.

That's why I feel so lucky.

That's why I feel so blessed.

Because I'm loved by the most amazing, clever, considerate boy in the world. No, make that in the universe. And I'm not too shallow to admit it. He's totally gorgeous too, but that's just icing on the cake. (Oops! A cliché. Sorry, Mr. Daly.)

And it's one thing to be *in love* with someone like that, and it's a wonderful thing all in its own right. (Is that a cliché? I'm actually not entirely sure.) But it's even *more* amazing to be loved by a boy like this. A boy who always puts my needs and my feelings in front of his own.

A boy who would do anything — and I seriously mean anything — just to be with me.

A boy who knows me inside out and accepts me just as I am, no strings attached.

A boy like Xavier.

CHAPTER 6

Drisklay took a sip of cold coffee. He'd stayed up late working at the hotel last night and was paying for it this morning. It might be easier if this blasted conference speaker wasn't so boring. Drisklay would never be a vocabulary expert, but whatever the opposite of the word *misogyny* was, this guy had it.

Men, you must make certain that your wife feels completely safe with you. Safe and protected. She'll open up to you sexually if you open up to her emotionally.

Ha. If there was one thing Drisklay absolutely didn't need from a beta-male like this guy on the stage, it was bedroom advice.

Good grief.

So he gave himself permission to tune out from the conference and focus on his case.

Missing girl. Young teen. Pretty, blonde, suburban type. Which is why she was getting more media attention and fanfare than other runaways in his jurisdiction.

That and the fact that her mother was relentless. Drisklay had dealt with distraught parents throughout his career on the force, but Mrs. Linklater was a special breed. Voicemail messages every hour on the hour. Letters to him, to the department, to the editor. That woman would probably handwrite a ten-page treatise to the President of the United States every single day if she thought it might possibly help locate her missing daughter.

Well, what do you expect when you bring helpless creatures into a world as sick and twisted as this one? Drisklay felt bad for the girl, but all it took was one quick perusal of her cell phone records to figure out what happened. It was a clear-cut case of predatory grooming. An adult man posing as her teen boyfriend, expressing his undying love. She bought it hook, line, and sinker. And now she was gone.

Well, what did anyone expect? Why couldn't parents keep better track of their kids these days? And who in their right mind would even think of giving a junior-high girl a cell phone of her own? When Drisklay asked Mrs. Linklater if she ever checked her daughter's messages, she acted as if he'd insulted her.

"Becky's a good girl. I can trust her completely." Says the mother of the girl who ended up abducted by a child predator.

The boyfriend wasn't in Drisklay's database, at least not by the name he'd been using with Becky. But there were hundreds of men just like him out there. Thousands of Xaviers.

And thousands of Becky Linklaters, unfortunately.

He shook his head. Glad he and Caroline never had children of their own. Glad he'd never have to go through the guilt Mrs. Linklater was feeling now, knowing how pathetically she'd failed to protect her daughter.

The child was almost certainly out of state. Maybe even out of country, but that was unlikely. Why risk getting caught crossing borders when you can throw a girl in your trunk and drive unchecked from one coast to the other?

Becky Linklater was now one of the hundreds of thousands of child victims of human trafficking, whether or not her mom was ready to wake up and face the ugly truth. If the girl was still alive, she was living in a hell that a suburbanite like Mrs. Linklater couldn't possibly begin to imagine.

Mrs. Linklater went onto all the major news outlets, spouting off how she was holding onto hope of finding her daughter safe and alive. What she didn't realize was that some horrors were worse than death.

Drisklay knew that better than just about anyone.

CHAPTER 7

Last summer

Holy cupcakes, I can't believe I'm actually about to say this. Xavier loves me. He's told me so a ton of times before (and I know I still have to write out the whole story of the way we met), but something happened just today that I have to get out first. Mr. Daly told our class last semester that when he was working on his novel, he would sometimes write the chapters out of order. Said it was easier to focus on what he felt inspired to write and then splice the pieces together later. I thought it'd be hard to keep track doing that, but of course I hadn't started writing my own story yet.

Our story, I should say.

Me and Xavier.

Xavier. Cupcakes, I love that name. I really do. Because it's not so out there that you look at it and have no idea how to pronounce it or anything, but seriously. How many Xaviers have you met? It's not so strange it's, like, weird or intimidating, but he's totally one of a kind.

And I know that's a cliché, but I'm not just talking about his name here.

So anyway, here's what happened. Oh, but before I go on, I want to say something. Teen romances get this really bad rap, like even Mr. Daly once made fun of it and said that if he ever decided to write young adult love stories, he'd have to do it under a pen name or something because he'd be too embarrassed for anyone to know that's what he actually does, but I think most of the time when people make fun of teenage love, it's not the real thing.

Not what Xavier and I have.

I mean, I went out with Chuck Mansfield for a few weeks last spring. And it was all right, and sure, I probably thought it was something special at the time, but now that I've met Xavier, now that I know what true love *really* is, there's no comparison.

Like just today (this is the part of the story I was meaning to write from the beginning), it was the last day of school. No more junior high. Thank goodness. I'm so sick of these kids thinking they're, like, *so* mature, when really they don't know anything at all.

Xavier's older. That's one thing I love about him. (One of the millions of things, I should say!) He's seventeen, so he doesn't get caught up in all the drama, know what I mean? And junior high is full of drama. I'm so sick of it, which is why I'm so glad I'm done with eighth grade and ready to move on with my life.

Except this part of the story happened while I was still at school.

Xavier graduated high school a year early, so he doesn't have to waste his days sitting around the classroom. I envy him that. And some people might be worried about someone my age being with a person that much older, but it's nothing weird. And there are these Romeo and Juliet laws he showed me on the internet, and we're actually all right. It's not even something we could get in trouble for. (Good news!)

I mean, if one of my immature girlfriends like Carly or Megan started dating a seventeen-year-old, I would totally tell them to wake up and realize guys like that are only after one thing. But with Xavier it's totally different. And I'm different too. I'm way more mature than Carly and Megan (even though I heart them to death!). I'm not saying it to be mean. It's the truth. And I'm not just talking emotionally, although that's definitely true, but I'm talking about biology. I mean, I got my period two full years before Megan and about ten months before Carly, so there's that. I'm also old for my grade since my birthday's in the summer.

Well, speaking of school, like I said, today was the last day before summer vacation. Goodbye, junior high. (And good riddance too!) I'm going to miss Mr. Daly, although he gave me his email address so I can send him some of the stories I'll be writing over the summer. Not this one, obviously. That would be gross, writing to some middle-aged man about my love life. But you know, stories about other things. So we'll be in touch. Other than him, though, I'm really not going to miss anything about Medford Academy.

Other than Mr. Daly, the teachers weren't even all that great. I kind of wish I'd had Mrs. Drisklay for social studies because a lot of kids really like her, and I'd pass her in the halls sometimes and she'd always smile at me. But other than her and Mr. Daly, there really weren't any good teachers at Medford. Can't *wait* for high school.

I just hope Woong and I are in the same classes next fall. He's my best friend. Can't remember if I've mentioned him yet. He's Korean, which means he's got these adorable almond eyes (except he's kind of self-conscious, so I never say anything about them in front of him). But he's adorable, and his mom's just the best. Miss Sandy drives us around a lot of the time, and when I come over after school, she's like this baking machine and always giving us brownies and cupcakes and yummy treats like that. I honestly don't know how I would have made it through the school year without Woong, especially after Chuck dumped me for some eighth-grader all the way over at Worcester Middle. Can you believe it?

Well, Woong was right there even when I was feeling so depressed about Chuck, and I seriously don't know how I would have survived if it hadn't been for him. He's, like, the most adorable best friend you could ever have, too. I think it's because he grew up in an orphanage in Korea, and he's, like, a whole lot shorter than I am, and he's like having this cute little panda bear for a BFF, and I literally love him to pieces.

Except I haven't told Woong about Xavier. Not because he wouldn't understand. I know he'd be, like, super happy for me and all that, but he's kind of a talker if you know what I mean. Not like a gossiper, it's just that he's got all this energy and says whatever thing first pops into his head. Even though I know Woong would think everything that's happened with Xavier and me is perfect, he'd have a hard time keeping it quiet for his mom, and Miss Sandy is the sweetest thing but really old-school, and I know she wouldn't understand.

Come to think if it, I wonder if that's why I'm having so

much fun writing this story out. Because normally, if I was excited about something, I'd come home and text Woong. I used to tell Carly everything, but then she started bad-mouthing me when I broke up with Chuck because she's had this crush on him since sixth grade. Sigh. Why do girls my age act so immature?

Anyway, if I knew Woong wouldn't tell his mom, I'd be texting him right now, but since he's got this big mouth (and not in the bad way either; like I said earlier, I literally love that boy to pieces), I'll have to just write it down here. Which is better anyway, because once Xavier and I get married and start a family of our own, I'll want to have everything written out. So I can remember just what it was like.

Mom did that too. She had this whole box of letters she and Dad wrote to each other when they were dating and stuff, except she burned them in the fireplace after the divorce. And I definitely don't blame her. But Xavier isn't like that (thank God!). Not the type to leave his family for some supermodel wannabe. Ugh. Just thinking about my dad makes me so mad.

Which is what I absolutely adore about Xavier, because he isn't even into looks and all that superficial stuff, so I know I don't have to worry about him leaving me for someone else. Ever. And he is so sweet. Which brings me back to the point of what I wanted to write about today. It was the last day of school (I know I already mentioned that, but bear with me for a minute), and I was going to walk over to Megan's house and hang out there and then Mom could just pick me up on her way home from work. No problem.

Except while I was walking down the street with Megan, guess who pulled up next to me? Xavier (obviously!), and he said, "Hey, sweet thing. You two girls want a ride?" And he was being totally flashy and sweet and absolutely adorable, and he drove us to Megan's house, and when I got out to thank him, he said, "Where are you going?" so I said, "To hang out with Megan," and he said, "Oh, no you're not."

So he dropped her off at her place (sorry, Megs!), and he and I hung out the rest of the day. And you know what he did? He said, "This has been the best month of my entire life, and I always want to remember how happy we are right now." So he bought me this really fancy necklace. I mean *really* fancy. Like it cost over a hundred dollars. And it said *True Love* in what looks like diamonds (it's not real diamonds, but that's okay because we're not this superficial couple only looking for material garbage), and he put it on my neck, and while he was clasping it he whispered, "You're so beautiful." And it literally gave me goosebumps. Holy cupcakes. I hope it didn't make the hair on the back of my neck stand up because he totally could have seen that.

Okay, not going to think about that right now. Too disturbing.

So you'd think that necklace would be enough, right? Except there was more. Oh, yes. Way more.

First we got ice cream cones because he said, "Someone as sweet as you deserves something sweet herself," which I think is totally romantic. I mean, I guess when I write it out it might sound a little bit cheesy, and it would be if some kid like Chuck were saying it, but with Xavier it's different because he's totally sincere.

And gorgeous. (Duh!)

So we ate our ice cream cone. He got one just for me and said he wasn't hungry, but I made him take a few bites from mine, and he had this way of staring into my eyes the whole time he was licking the cone, and it was amazing. It was like this incredible connection, like he was looking right into my soul. I'm getting goosebumps again just thinking about it.

Which is what I mean when I say I know what we have is the real thing. Like the once in a lifetime thing. Because how many people can spend ten minutes or however long it takes to eat an ice cream cone just staring into someone's eyes without looking away once? Chuck and I definitely didn't have that when we were going out, and I'm guessing

Mom and Dad didn't either (and of course we all know by now how that story ends).

Let's see, what happened after ice cream? We held hands and walked outside for a while, and he wanted me to get a body piercing, except he knows my mom would totally freak out, so he was mostly just joking. But I didn't want him to think of me as a little kid who's got to do everything her mom says, so when we passed by this tattoo place, I asked him what he thought about getting matching tattoos one day, and we even picked the design out. It's these two doves, which surprised me because Xavier's the one who chose that, and in all honesty, I thought doves would be a little girly for him or something like that, but it was the one he liked most. Which is totally bizarre because I absolutely love birds. Not just doves, but all kinds of birds. Like when I'm an old lady, I'm totally going to have a parrot. Did you know there's this parrot that can use Alexa? Funniest thing ever. I literally could watch parrot videos all day. One guy even live-streamed his parrot for a whole week. Some of it was boring, though, like you could imagine, so now I just watch the condensed versions, but all that is to say is parrots are epic.

So I think it's revealing that the tattoo design Xavier chose was also a bird. Just another sign we're totally meant to be. (As if I needed any more signs!)

You'd think the day couldn't get any better than that, right? But then he took me ice skating. (Xavier says he loves to watch me on the ice.) He doesn't skate himself. Something about a bad ankle, but he just stood there watching me twirl, and I can guarantee that there's never been a single parent or coach or anyone else who ever watched someone skating that intently. It was almost like when he was eating my ice cream cone. Like, constant eye contact. (And here come the goosebumps again!)

After skating, I told him I'd better head home because I remembered that Mom had special plans for dinner to celebrate the first day of summer. She still thinks I'm with Chuck, believe it or not! I'm not trying to keep things from her, it's just that we don't really talk that much because she's been working late whenever she can. She's an LPN at a pediatrician's office, and he pays her really good overtime, which is important for her since Dad's basically never given her a dime in child support. Don't even get me started on that, or I literally won't ever stop.

But anyway, I knew today Mom wasn't working overtime, and I thought she might have even said something about going out to the Tin Trough, which is this huge all-you-can-eat buffet we like to go to on really special occasions, especially if it's a weeknight like this because even though I'm technically too old for it, sometimes they'll still give me the kid discount, which makes sense seeing as how I don't eat nearly as much as an adult anyway.

So I told Xavier it was time to go home, and he got all cute and pouty and had this adorable little whine to his voice, and he's like, "You're telling me you love your mama more than me?" and I'm like, "Don't be stupid. But she's my mom, and she'll worry about me if I'm not at home."

So then he said, "Well, what if I just take you away from home then? Wouldn't that solve everything?"

I laughed because I figured he was kidding, but then (you're literally not going to believe this) he told me he was serious. He's like, "What if we moved away, just you and me? I could help you study, and in a year or two you could get your GED."

I was already kind of worried about getting home late because I'd given him my cell phone to hold while I was skating, and so I lost track of time. But he looked so serious. Like *really* serious, so I told him sure. I'd run away with him, and then we both laughed, and he kissed me. Not right on the lips (we still haven't done that yet, which is another reason I know he loves me for me because Chuck wanted to make out with me, like, the first day we became a couple), but kind of on the corner of my mouth.

Can somebody please say *goosebumps*?

So, all that to tell you I just had the very best day of my life, and now it's summer, which means no school. Which of course means *way* more time with Xavier. I never thought I'd grow up to be living a real-live fairy tale, but that's exactly what I'm doing.

And let me tell you, I'm loving every single second of it.

Literally.

CHAPTER 8

Caroline leaned forward in her seat, soaking up every word.

"When a husband is cold or emotionally distant with his wife," the speaker said, "she'll have a hard time opening up to him. Women want to feel protected and emotionally secure before they can be vulnerable with their husbands physically."

Yes. Yes! This was exactly what Calvin needed to hear. He'd never accept it coming from her, but another man, a man standing on a stage with the authority of a conference like Truth Warriors behind him, and he was bound to get it.

Yes!

She was so thankful Calvin had agreed to come. She felt silly looking back on herself, how timid and scared she'd been to invite him here. This conference, these four days away from work, from life, from the force, were exactly what their marriage needed.

Exactly.

"When a woman feels safe to express her feelings and her emotions, and when she feels like her husband is courageous enough to reciprocate that emotional vulnerability, beautiful things can happen in their relationship."

Yes! She wanted to jump out of her seat and shout *amen*. The words the speaker said, down to the smallest of details, rang so true in her heart. Things she couldn't have found the ability to express to her husband without it sounding like she was nagging. But here was someone else, an expert in his field, a man singlehandedly responsible for saving hundreds of floundering marriages, and he was giving Calvin the blueprint he needed to be the husband Caroline dreamed of.

Her heart was pounding. She couldn't remember the last time she'd felt so much hope. Sheer relief that someone else was telling Calvin the things she'd longed to explain to him for years.

Their marriage problems had nothing to do with her conversion to Christianity. The root cause was Calvin's emotional distance, and this man, this speaker on the stage, held the key to unlock her stoic husband's heart.

Praise the Lord. She couldn't wait to tell Sandy back home everything she'd learned. Her pastor's wife was one of her closest friends and the woman God used to bring Caroline to the Lord in the first place. For years, Caroline had watched Sandy and Pastor Carl, had observed their marriage, their openness, their mutual respect and love.

What a lovely, godly family. And to think that maybe one day she might experience something like that of her own. A godly, loving husband.

A family.

Sandy was a few years older than Caroline and had raised three biological and several adopted children. She was already a grandmother and an empty-nester when God put it on her and Pastor Carl's heart to adopt little Woong from South Korea.

If Sandy could become a mother at her age, who was to say the same thing might not happen to Caroline?

One day.

One day ...

She glanced over at her husband, trying to gauge if he was as excited about this speaker's words as she was. Could he hear it? Was he listening? Did he realize that this right there, this simple, basic principle of opening up emotionally to one another was enough to singlehandedly revolutionize their entire marriage?

Did he hear?

Was he even paying attention?

It was so hard to tell. Calvin had always felt so closed off to her. For decades, she'd told herself it was because of all he experienced on the force. The hardness of human nature he witnessed first-hand on a daily basis. Of course it was enough to turn even the kindest person into someone who was hardened and jaded.

But it didn't have to be that way. Calvin could change. She knew he could. The morning's session began with testimonies from three couples who attended the Truth Warriors conference last year and had turned their marriages completely around. If following these basic principles could work for others, it would work for Caroline and her husband.

She had never felt so much relief.

She had never felt so much joy.

Change was around the corner. She could feel it in the depths of her very being. The core of her bones.

No more lonely nights, lying next to a man who felt even more distant than a stranger. No more shouting or tears. In fact, no more arguing in general. They could change.

Calvin could change.

If it worked for other men at this conference, it would work for him. A wave of love for her husband rushed through her soul. Love for the man he could become. For the life they might have.

A life of closeness. Togetherness. Emotional

vulnerability, just like the speaker described.

Yes.

Yes.

Yes!

Caroline was desperate. She was hungry for that kind of relationship.

And this speaker on stage was giving her husband the step-by-step breakdown of how to make it all happen.

She was so grateful to be here. She was so excited about putting these new principles into practice. If she'd been in church, she might have lifted her hands up to heaven and shouted *hallelujah!* for the entire audience to hear.

But that would raise a few eyebrows in this venue, she was sure, so she just sat, waiting. Waiting, expectant, and thankful.

One day, she'd look back on this session, this moment in her personal history, as the most life-changing encounter she'd ever experienced aside from becoming a Christian in the first place.

Three and a half years ago, she'd been born anew. Spiritually renewed.

Now, a similar rebirth was happening in her relationship with Calvin. She could feel it. She could sense it.

And Caroline — after years of crying, praying, and pleading for her marriage — had never felt so much hope.

CHAPTER 9

Last summer

Xavier is literally the sweetest guy I know. I mean it, too. It's only Saturday night, and we're not going to see each other for the rest of the weekend, but we've been texting for, like, two hours.

I can't wait for Monday to see you. I want you now.

It's such a good feeling to be that loved, to know that someone misses you that much. Mr. Daly told our class it was a good exercise to look for things throughout the day that are ironic, so here's one for you. The phone I've been using to text with Xavier all night is the cell my dad got for me so we could (as he put it) "stay in touch." Which basically means it's the phone I use to text Mom when I'm ready for her to pick me up from Dad's for my mandatory weekend visits.

So Dad got me this phone right after he left, except it's never so I can "stay in touch" with him because like I've already said, he's basically the worst father in the entire world. But there's a good side to the story, which is that Xavier and I can text now all we want, and since Dad's the one paying for the phone, Mom can't complain when I'm up late using it.

So I guess that's one good thing that came out of the divorce. I literally can't even imagine trying to convince Mom to get me a cell phone of my own. But I guess I can't complain, especially if I compare her to Miss Sandy. Woong's mom is super strict. In a way, it sort of makes sense because first of all, she's married to a pastor, so there's that. She even took Woong out of school for a year and homeschooled him, which stunk for both of us, but I guess he needed to catch up to his grade level after growing up in an orphanage. But anyway, not only is Miss Sandy a pastor's wife (which explains why she's so strict) but she's really old too. Like super old. Like she's got grandchildren older than me.

Kind of funny if you think about it because Woong is younger than a whole bunch of his nephews and nieces. All that is to say that it makes sense for Miss Sandy to be more cautious about things like technology. In fact, I couldn't text Woong at all until last year, and even now when I text him, we have to use a totally different app because he's only got an iPad. And seriously, the only reason he even has an iPad is because his parents agreed to get him one while he was being homeschooled so he could do some of his work assignments online.

I mean, seriously, what kind of eighth grader (now ninth grader!) uses an *iPad* to text?

So when I get to complaining about how uptight my mom is, I think about Miss Sandy. Now, don't get me wrong, I love her to pieces, but I seriously would go crazy if she was my own parent. I can guarantee you that if I were in Woong's family, I wouldn't still be awake at two a.m. waiting for texts from my boyfriend!

My boyfriend. I hate that word, actually. It does absolutely nothing to explain what Xavier and I have. Boyfriend sounds so, I don't know… So immature. Like, Chuck was my *boyfriend*, and all he wanted to do was keep me from talking with any of the other boys. He didn't even want me eating lunch with Woong! I told him that was absolutely ridiculous, but I later found out that while my boyfriend was throwing a fit because I texted Woong, Chuck was flirting with some girl in Worcester, so there's that.

I think that's another example of irony, don't you? Or maybe just stupidity.

Given what happened with Chuck and what I've seen my

mom go through with Dad, I could see how I might get all depressed and think that real love couldn't ever truly happen. But Xavier proved me wrong. You should read the kinds of things he's been saying. Like, when I was texting Chuck last year, all he'd do is want to know when we could meet up, which basically meant he wanted to make out, and other than that it was just like, *K. C U latr.* I mean, he couldn't even spell.

How pathetic is that?

But Xavier is totally different, which makes me wonder what I ever saw in Chuck Mansfield to begin with. I mean, he's not even all that hot, to be totally honest. And he has acne. Chuck does, I mean. Not Xavier. Xavier's skin is perfect. He told me when he was my age, he even did a little bit of modeling, and I can totally believe it.

Oh! Speaking of modeling, I *have* to tell you about one of the texts he wrote me tonight. It was so sweet. I mean, literally everything he does is sweet, but this one really outdid all the others. Blew them out of the water (to use a cliché).

Xavier wrote me, and these are his exact words here, *You're so beautiful it's a shame you're not a model.* And then he went on to say that he's got this friend out in Los Angeles who's this, like, model talent scout or something (don't remember the exact name off the top of my head), and on Monday while my mom's at work, Xavier's going to come on over and take a few photos of me to send to his friend to see if he thinks he can use them.

Can you imagine me on the cover of a magazine or something? I mean, I'm not totally full of myself. I know I'm not the best-looking girl in the world, but I'm not the worst either. Chuck said that he and his friends did that game where you rank the girls based on how hot they are, and the only reason I came in at number two and not at number one is because Carly is like a size D already, but that's literally all she's got going for her. I know I look okay, but I wouldn't have ever thought of sending my photos in to a modeling agency or anything, except Xavier thinks I totally should, and I know he isn't just saying that to make me feel good. He's totally honest with me, so he'd tell me if he didn't really think I could do it.

You might be reading something written by a future magazine star! Can you believe it?

I literally am the luckiest, most blessed girl in the entire world. I still can't believe out of everyone in Medford, Xavier even noticed me. I mean, all the other girls at my school are so immature (sorry, Carly and Megs!), but Xavier said the minute he saw me waiting at the bus stop that he knew I was different.

That's where we first met. At the bus stop. Can't remember if I told you that yet. It is such a sweet story, but I'm super tired. I only started writing in here because I thought Xavier was going to text me back right away, but it's been like thirty minutes, so I wonder if he fell asleep.

Sleep well, my handsome prince, and dream of Monday, when we'll be together again …

CHAPTER 10

Ruby tried to sit up in bed when she heard Xavier enter the room. Forgot momentarily about her chains. Smiled at him sheepishly.

"Sorry." She couldn't have said what she was apologizing for, but he sat down beside her and cupped her cheek with his hand.

He handed her a cup with a straw. "Got you some Mountain Dew."

Mountain Dew. Her favorite drink. He remembered.

He gave her a grin. "Favorite drink for my favorite girl."

She was parched.

"Slow down." He laughed at her as she gulped at the liquid. "You'll get yourself bloated."

He was right, of course. But right now, she didn't care. He was here. That was all that mattered. Xavier was here. He was sitting next to her, his leg brushing up against hers. And he was smiling.

"Let me get this for you." With gentle, tender hands, he

unclasped her chains then leaned over and kissed her on the forehead. Just like she remembered her father doing when she was very, very little.

"Thank you." She was lucky. Lucky Xavier was here. Lucky that he thought about how thirsty she'd be. Lucky that he was in a good mood. That he brought her a drink. That he was willing to take off her chains.

She rubbed her wrists and leaned her head against his chest.

"You smell good," he whispered, burying his face against the top of her hair. If she strained very hard, she thought she could hear his heartbeat.

Her Xavier.

"Did you sleep well?" he asked. "You were out like a light when I left this morning."

She smiled up at him, wondering what she'd done to deserve someone who cared for her that much. "Yeah. I slept really well. Thanks."

She let out her breath. This was the Xavier she remembered. The kind Xavier. The Xavier who wasn't worried about money. The Xavier who remembered what her favorite drink was and took care of her even when they were both dog-tired.

"Oh," she said, trying to keep her voice casual. "Did I

mention earlier we're out of snacks?"

A darkness passed over his expression. She sensed his body tense and hated herself for being so impatient. She should have realized. Should have known not to mention food first thing when he came back. She was as big of a nag as her mom, and if she wasn't careful, Xavier would leave her just like Dad.

Then what would happen to her?

Ruby picked up his hand and draped it around herself, trying to press herself farther into him. He was so strong, Strong and warm and protective and everything she'd hoped for.

He gave her another kiss on the head, his stress about money set aside.

Thankfully.

"I'll bring you something yummy tonight," he promised. "How does a burger sound?"

She tried to stifle her giggle. Xavier hated when she giggled. Said it made her sound immature, and he was right.

"A burger would be great." She tried not to let her enthusiasm show. Xavier was tricky that way. Sometimes he liked her young and excited and girly, but other times he wanted her to act grownup and mature.

The secret to their happiness together, Ruby knew, was

to always guess correctly what kind of mood he was in. Several weeks into her time in Las Vegas, she was getting used to it.

Really used to it.

There were some things she regretted. Sort of. And she missed home. A lot. But right now, right here, while her boyfriend ran his hand up and down her back, working out the hard knots near her shoulders, she relaxed. She melted into his strength. His closeness.

She felt perfectly at ease.

Perfectly at home.

CHAPTER 11

Margot Linklater woke up in her scrubs, her hair drenched in sweat. Another nightmare? If it was, she couldn't remember it.

She'd have to thank Dr. Harris for those sleeping pills he'd prescribed.

What time was it? She groaned and silenced her screeching alarm. At least she tried to. Then she realized it wasn't her alarm but her phone.

"Hello?" Her voice sounded awful. Awful and groggy and congested. She cleared her throat.

"Margot?" Paige. The office manager.

Uh-oh.

She jumped out of bed. "I'm so sorry. I forgot I was on the early shift today ..."

A pathetic excuse.

"I'm already dressed," Margot lied. "Just have to throw on my shoes. I can be there in ten minutes. Twelve tops. I'm so sorry."

"I know." There was a heaviness in Paige's voice.

"It won't happen again," Margot promised while she rummaged through her purse. Where were her car keys? Wait, she didn't need those yet. She needed clean scrubs. Clean scrubs, shoes, and then her car keys.

Hopefully, she could find a granola bar in her glove compartment to hold her over until lunch. And then at lunch break she'd call the ... Wait. Detective Drisklay was out of town. How could she have forgotten? Three more days before she could get an update. What did he say he was doing in Las Vegas?

Not looking for her daughter, whatever it was.

Margot grabbed a pair of socks. One was inside out, but she didn't waste time correcting it. That's what work breaks were for.

Dr. Harris was an understanding boss. When Becky went missing last summer, he'd given Margot two full weeks off. But now it was getting on toward the end of the month, mortgage was due soon, and of course Becky's father wasn't going to offer a dime to help with that, now was he?

No, not Jack. Margot was on her own, just like she'd always been.

Even though she hated to admit it, the routine of work was good for her. Giving her a reason to have to get out of bed each day.

At least, when she remembered to set her alarm.

The last thing she could afford was to lose her job, and so she threw on clean scrubs, slipped into her shoes, and raced down the hallway, digging wildly through her purse in search of her keys.

She was panting by the time she reached the driveway.

With her fingers on the handle of her car, she stopped. Jerked her head around so fast she might have just given herself whiplash. Which she definitely couldn't afford now that Dr. Harris's insurance policy no longer covered chiropractic services. He was a great doctor and a considerate person, but when it came to finances, he was almost as cheap as her ex-husband.

The vision that made Margot's head jerk around was a head full of blonde curls standing near the corner bus stop.

Becky?

Her heart leaping, flopping, and performing an impressive display of cardiac summersaults, Margot strained her eyes.

The girl turned, laughing as she talked with her friend.

No. Not her little girl at all.

And then came the expected, familiar crash.

The emptiness.

The certainty.

It wasn't her little girl.

Not Becky after all.

False hope in a situation that everyone else told her was hopeless.

Hopeless. That was what she was facing, right? It had been nine months since Becky disappeared. If that cynical detective with his stupid Styrofoam cups of cold black coffee could afford to take an entire week off the investigation to go vacationing in Las Vegas, did that mean he was giving up on Becky too?

It was ridiculous how quickly the world had moved on. The detective. Becky's deadbeat father. Sure, Jack had postponed his honeymoon with that twenty-something, one-hundred-pound walking box of spray tan, but that was probably because at the time Detective Drisklay still hadn't ruled him out as a person of interest. A few more weeks of somewhat intense scrutiny, a few more interviews spread out over the first month, and then he was a free man, able to move on with his life.

Just like everyone else was. Even Margot had to go through the motions. Wake up. Get dressed. Drive to work.

And nearly every day, something would catch the corner of her eye. A head of springy curls. A streak of blonde hair.

Or sometimes it was her other senses that taunted her. The sound of laughter, close enough that for a faint second she thought it was her daughter's precious giggle. The end of summer had been the worst, all the neighborhood kids running around outside, laughing and shrieking.

"Mom!" they'd call out at all hours of the day and night.

"Mom!" And each and every time, Margot's heart would race.

Why did these parents let their children play outside to begin with? Didn't they know what could happen?

A runaway. That's what that serious-faced detective had called her daughter. Her Becky.

A runaway.

"Were you aware your daughter was in a relationship with an adult male?"

She didn't want to believe it. The detective showed Margot the texts. But that was no relationship. It was brainwashing. Disgusting. To say Becky ran away was absurd. She'd been abducted. That was what happened. That pedophile, that miserable Xavier had kidnapped Margot's little girl and taken her to God knows where.

Margot shuddered.

Then blinked.

She was still standing outside her car, but something was

missing.

Why hadn't she moved?

Car keys. She must have left them in the house.

Sprinting now, still feeling somewhat sweaty and gross as she raced back up to the porch. She couldn't lose her job. She wouldn't. Not with Jack refusing to lift a pinky finger to pitch in and help with anything.

When Jack had been a person of interest in Becky's disappearance, Margot had vouched for him. No, she'd told Detective Drisklay. Jack wouldn't do something like that. Not because he loved Becky. If he loved their daughter, he wouldn't be so cheap. If he loved their daughter, he would pay the child support he owed so Margot didn't have to work sixty hours a week just to keep the electricity on.

If he loved their daughter, he would have never abandoned them in the first place.

Jack was certainly no father of the year, but he wouldn't have hurt Becky either. Not because he was a saint.

But because he was lazy.

Lazy and stupid.

Staging a kidnapping? That would mean Jack would have to keep his hands off that twenty-something trophy bride of his, get off his rear end, and do something.

No, she'd told the detective. Jack didn't have anything to

do with this. He wasn't the kidnapping, murdering, vengeful type. He was the type to get caught having an affair on Saturday and have all his things moved out the following day.

That was Jack in a nutshell.

Car keys now in hand, Margot locked the front door and threw thoughts of her ex out of her mind. Her heart was still racing as she sped toward Dr. Harris's office. It had now been 285 days since she'd cried. Yes, she was counting. Yes, she felt like a cruel, heartless monster.

For the first week, with all the media attention and the shock of Becky's disappearance, Margot had been the proverbial deer in the headlights, too stunned to leak out even the slightest hint of emotion.

Then came the texts. The records gleaned from Becky's cell phone. And all a result of the cell phone her father decided to buy for her even though Jack knew Margot could have used that money for something more practical.

Like groceries.

She'd never forget the day Detective Drisklay brought her into his office, poured her a cup of cold, black coffee, and explained that her daughter had fallen in love with some adult posing as her boyfriend. Someone who lured Becky away from the peaceful, safe home Margot had worked so hard to provide.

And Margot had cried. Man, how she'd cried.

But then the mortgage was coming due. Paige kept asking when she'd be back to work. Jack stopped returning any of her phone calls.

And just like that, the tears turned off.

At first, she thought it was because she was strong.

Now she wasn't so sure.

Not that she had time to think about that. It was hard enough to remember to brush her teeth. To eat her meals. To change her underwear.

Things that had once been routine, as natural as breathing, were now written out on tiny post-it notes left throughout her house so she wouldn't forget.

Buy groceries. Start the laundry. Pay the electric bill.

It wasn't until she felt a spasm in her forearm she realized how tightly she'd been gripping the steering wheel as she sped toward work. One day, she'd relax. One day, she'd focus on the self-care everyone around her (yes, even her cheapskate of an ex-husband Jack) told her was so important.

One day, she might even decide it was safe to turn the tears back on.

One day, she'd have her daughter back. Safe and sound. Even if Margot was the only person in the entire world who believed Becky was still alive, she would never stop looking for her. If that detective gave up the search, she'd work even more shifts or get a second job to hire a private investigator. If she had to, she'd show up on Jack's porch every single morning and drop down to her knees and beg until he gave her the money she needed to hire an entire search team, an entire army, to hunt for their daughter.

She'd raise funds. Offer a reward. A hundred thousand dollars. A million dollars for any information leading to her reunion with her daughter. That and the arrest, castration, torture, and then execution of this Xavier, this monster who'd stolen her little girl away.

I'm still looking for you, Becky, she whispered as she pulled into her usual spot in front of Dr. Harris's pediatric practice.

I'm still looking for you, and I'm not going to give up until we're back together again.

I promise.

CHAPTER 12

Last summer

Holy cupcakes, I just have to say that I literally can't imagine my life getting any better. So you know how yesterday I was waiting for Xavier to text me back? Well, something went wrong with the cell service or something. I eventually got tired of waiting and told him I was going to sleep, but then this morning I had, like, a dozen texts from him, all from last night.

While I was waiting to hear from him, he was waiting to hear from me! Must have been some weird delay in the phone service or something, but you know how technology is these days. It happens.

But he was so sweet. He's like, *Baby, are you okay? Are you getting my texts? I'm starting to worry.*

And then he said he doesn't know how he'd survive without me, and he said *If anything happened to you, I wouldn't even want to live anymore*, and all kinds of other super sweet things. I mean, I was kind of bummed when he stopped texting me last night, but I just figured he fell asleep because it was super late, but he was, like, really worried for me. I mean, the last time I remember anyone being scared for me like that was when I came home with a cold a few years ago, and this really bad virus had been going through town, and my mom was super worried and took me to tons of doctors and stayed home from work until she knew I was safe. But even that kind of worry was different. I mean, Mom's just Mom. She worries about everything, so I guess it felt kind of natural for her to be freaked out. And seriously, this virus was super bad (a few people even died), so I can see why she was so uptight.

But then this morning I called Xavier because I just felt so bad to get him anxious like that, and at first he was mad. Like, I've never heard him talk to anyone like that, let alone me, but when I explained none of his texts came until this morning, he sounded so relieved I almost thought he might be about to cry. That's seriously how worked up he'd gotten.

He thought I'd been ignoring him. He said he stayed awake all night, picturing all the bad things that might have happened to me, and he made me promise that I'd always respond to his texts right away so he didn't have to get scared like that again, and it just felt so good to have someone be that concerned for me.

And then we spent like an hour just talking, and it was one of these really special moments. Because sometimes when we talk it's like, *So, what's new with you?* and then the other says, *Oh, not a whole lot. How about with you?* And sometimes I have such a hard time figuring out what to talk about that I'll literally tell him the things I'm learning at school. Like I'll recite some of Mr. Daly's lessons about allusions or allegories or things like that, and I think it's totally boring, but Xavier says I'm the smartest girl he knows, and he loves to listen to me talk, so that's what we do.

But this morning on the phone, we didn't even come close to running out of things to say. Because after I finished telling him I was totally fine, and he realized he'd been worried about me for no good reason because sometimes texts just get delayed or every once in a while they don't even send out at all, we just talked about our future.

He was like, *It's gonna be so nice when we've got a place of our own because then if I'm worried about you, all I'll have to do is roll over and see you in bed with me and know you're perfectly safe.* Okay, talk about goosebumps. Because this may totally fall into the realm of TMI, but that's okay since nobody's ever going to read this (at least not for a super long time, like maybe when Xavier and I have kids, and our girls are grown up and they want to hear what it was like with me falling in love with their daddy or something). But seriously, I just want to get it out there that I'm still a virgin. I mean, hey, I haven't even started high school yet. And Xavier is like this perfect gentleman. I mean, not like in Woong's family where they're super strict and he's not even allowed to date until he's twenty-one or something ... But still, I love Xavier because he isn't pressuring me. That thing he said about rolling over and seeing me safe, that was the very first time he's even mentioned us sharing a bed or coming even close to talking about that sort of thing.

I was telling Megan about him once, and she got all jealous and said that he just wanted to get something out of me. Obviously she has no idea what kind of guy he really is. But I do.

And he's amazing.

I could go on and on because it was so fun just talking with him about our future. One day he wants to move to Los Angeles. He says maybe I can earn enough money as a model that we can buy a house in Beverly Hills. Sounds fancy, right? And I'm like, "Oh, that'd be really expensive," and he said, "Yeah, but you're worth every penny."

I just can't believe I could have ever felt happy at all,

even a little bit, before we met. It's like my life hadn't even started until Xavier came into it.

Anyway, I could write pages and pages more, but I've got to get ready. Woong and his mom are on the road now. They're picking me up so I can go to church with them. I know it might not sound super fun, but actually it is. And like I said, Miss Sandy is like a saint, and I love spending time with their family. So I'm off to church with Woong, but I guarantee I'll be thinking about Xavier the whole time.

Xavier. Have I mentioned lately how much I love that name?

Here come more goosebumps.

Talk to you soon!

CHAPTER 13

Margot's fingers trembled as she removed the thermometer from the little boy's mouth.

"Does he have a fever?" his anxious mother asked.

Margot remembered the time a few years earlier when an elevated temperature was the scariest thing she had to worry about. Back during that Nipah virus outbreak when Becky came home with a cough, Margot had taken her temperature every single hour to make sure she wasn't getting any sicker.

But this little boy in Dr. Harris's office didn't have Nipah. He most likely had an ear infection, which would explain the lethargy and 99.8-degree temperature. Nothing a generic antibiotic couldn't cure.

Unfortunately, there were no antibiotics to fix a mother's anxious heart. No bandage Margot could wrap around her soul to stop the hemorrhaging that had started the day her daughter disappeared.

They'd been fighting. Becky wanted a card for the subway, but Margot was out of money. Words were exchanged. Words Margot never had the opportunity to take back.

Becky moved in with her dad.

Two weeks later, she disappeared.

Can you ask Becky if she's seen my credit card? It was a text from Jack's new wife. Why would she be asking Margot about a credit card if Becky was staying there?

She's not here, Margot wrote back. *It's been a few days since she's stopped by.*

Jack's wife said Becky moved back home three nights earlier. And that's when Margot knew. Up until then, she'd never heard of Xavier. But she knew a boy was involved.

She called her husband. Her ex-husband, that is. Then Becky's friends from school. Nobody had seen her in several days.

And then she called the police. She hadn't allowed herself yet to revisit that first day. The interviews. The insinuations. The questions.

"And she was missing *how* long before you called?"

The weeks that followed were no better. And now, nine months later, Margot's body still hadn't learned how to discard any of that stress. She'd gained fifteen pounds since Becky disappeared. She didn't care about her appearance, but it was clear that her body wasn't made to carry around this degree of anxiety. Margot was in her mid-forties but felt like she was one panic attack away from a cardiac arrest. During her first week back at work, she was overcome by heart palpitations so terrifying she rushed into Dr. Harris's office, convinced he'd need to start CPR on her any minute.

Panic, he suggested. Anxiety. *Have you thought of talking to a therapist?*

Sure, she'd love to talk to a therapist. If that therapist could show her the easiest way to find this predator named Xavier and teach Margot the cruelest, most painful way to make him suffer.

That, and if her appointments were covered by Dr. Harris's insurance policy.

Which meant therapy was out. Margot had lost track of the people who told her that getting outside, being active were good for her mental health. Because when your daughter's been kidnapped, it makes perfect sense to go strolling through the park in the bright sunshine. She let out her breath and forced a smile at the mother in the triage room.

"How long did you say he's been like this?"

The woman furrowed her brow. "Since Tuesday. I wanted to bring him in sooner, but my husband's working on this big project at work, and we've only got the one car, and this was the first day I could get down here. Is he going to be okay? Should I have come in sooner?"

Margot was running out of patience. Patience and energy.

Which she hated about herself.

Did she love being a nurse? No. Would she have been happier as a stay-at-home mom, baking cookies for Becky and all her friends who'd come over after school?

Absolutely.

If money grew on trees (or if Jack got off his butt and finally signed the check for all those back payments he'd missed), Margot would love to tell Dr. Harris *adios*, pack her things, and retire.

She didn't love nursing. But she was good at it. Dr. Harris trusted her with the more difficult parents, and Margot had been respected around the office for her warmth and efficiency.

Until her world shattered. Since then, she'd left three patients in wrong rooms, waiting for a doctor who had no idea they were there. But that wasn't the worst of it. Not even close. Last month, in the course of one week, Margot botched a phone message about an important inhaler refill and gave a mom wrong information about how much Tylenol her baby needed, forgetting they were talking about the infant drops and not the less concentrated children's formula.

Thankfully, the mom had called back when she realized Margot had instructed her to give her four-month-old nearly half the bottle. Margot tried not to think about the fatal consequences that her neglect might have caused.

Margot hated herself. Hated the way she treated her patients these days, the way she despised the parents who brought them in. *Why are you worrying about a stupid fever?* She wanted to scream at this nervous mother. *At least you know your kid's alive and not being tortured by some ...*

She sucked in a deep breath, stopping the thoughts before they ran her into a brick wall of panic and paralysis. Thankfully, the triage form on the screen in front of her gave her the exact script of questions she was supposed to ask.

For the first few weeks after returning to work, Margot was thankful that her job gave her something to focus on. Something to do besides calling that detective and talking to his voicemail twenty times a day. But the work proved physically and emotionally exhausting. Even when Dr. Harris let her cut back to six-hour shifts, the time she spent on her feet, the time she spent interacting with parents and their relatively healthy and perfectly safe children, bled her soul dry.

"I'll just feel so bad if he gets sicker and it's all because I didn't bring him in sooner."

Margot didn't look at the young mother but made a sympathetic sounding noise. At least, she tried to make it sound sympathetic but had no idea whether or not she pulled it off. "I'm sure he'll be just fine."

"I worry so much," the woman answered with a smile.

Margot was forced to smile back. "I know," she replied. "I know. Now let me go tell the doctor you're here. He'll be in as soon as he's ready, just a few minutes I'm sure."

Margot glanced once more at the little boy, who looked sad and tired but inherently safe in his mother's arms, and she hurried out of the exam room. All she wanted was for her shift to be over, even though there was nothing to go home to tonight except for a silent, empty house.

CHAPTER 14

Last summer

Hey again. It's me. I just got back from church with Woong. I should have warned you. Going to church with his family is like this whole-day affair. Since his dad's the pastor, Woong and his mom stay for all the different services. So for the first hour, Woong and I go to church like regular, and then after that we go to Sunday school. This was our first week going to the high-school class, not junior high, and I like this teacher way better. His name's Scott, and he's really cool. Like super funny. He was actually a missionary for a long time, and so he's got these really neat stories.

I wonder what it would be like to become a missionary. I could totally see Woong doing something like that. I asked him if he'd want to go and be a missionary in South Korea, since that's where he got adopted from, but he said he doesn't remember Korean anymore. I told him that's impossible. He's only been in America like four years or something like that. You can't just forget an entire language, but he said he did. And I only know English, so seriously, who am I to argue?

Anyway, Sunday school with Scott was fun, like I said. I think I'm totally going to like being a high schooler. Junior high never really felt like that good of a fit for me. I mean, I had friends and all. I just never really got into all the drama.

I'm glad to be back home now. It sounds silly, but I felt pretty bad because I couldn't text Xavier at all. I didn't want Woong to get all suspicious and want to know who I was talking to, so I just turned my phone onto mute. I warned Xavier. The last thing I wanted to do was get him as worried as he'd been last night, but still, I got home and ran upstairs and texted him, and now I'm just waiting to hear back. And it's only been like ten minutes since I got in, but I totally get now how he felt last night. I'm sitting here staring at my phone, waiting for it to beep, and inside I'm wondering, like, *Did he get into a car accident? Is he okay? Do I need to call the police?*

All this because he doesn't text me right back. Haha. When we're a little old lady and a little old man with, like, a hundred kids and grandkids and great-grandkids, we'll look back and be like, *remember how silly we were when we first fell in love?* And we'll laugh because by the time you get to that age and you've stayed together that long, you probably stop worrying if someone doesn't text you back right away.

And speaking of texts, there's the ding! Xavier said he was in the shower. Ha. Should have known.

Obviously I've got to go now, but I just wanted to write and say what a perfect day I've had and what a perfect boyfriend I have and how happy I am to be alive.

CHAPTER 15

Another day. Another shift. Another never-ending march toward her next paycheck.

Margot walked through the front door, tossing her purse onto the couch and slipping out of her shoes with a sigh.

She shivered when her bare feet touched the cold laminate flooring. The clock ticked at her in greeting, a constant reminder of the relentless, merciless passing of time.

Time since she'd seen her little girl. Margot couldn't even think about that. Where was Becky? Every once in a while, Margot liked to imagine that her daughter and this Xavier really were in love and had run away and were doing their best to live out their happily ever after.

Drisklay couldn't tell her with certainty that this Xavier guy was a criminal, but all the signs pointed that way. Margot didn't have the stomach to read through the hundreds of pages of printed texts, but even a quick scan revealed a man who was controlling and manipulative. If Becky didn't respond to one of Xavier's messages in half a minute, he'd be sending her a dozen different notes, demanding to know where she was. *Don't you know I can't live without you?* A bunch of stupid nonsense like that.

And her girl, her Becky, her straight-A student, bought into all that?

It was her father's fault. Jack should have never gotten her that phone. Didn't he realize what could happen when you gave a girl that age access to the outside world? At the very least he could have realized the thousands of texts she was sending a month weren't to her girlfriends at school.

But no. Jack was totally inept at fatherhood. At marriage. At life. What was even worse was the way he was handling Becky's disappearance just fine. In fact, only a month after Becky went missing, he told Margot she didn't have to keep calling him. That he was getting the same information from the detective she was, so there was no reason for her to pass it on to him a second time.

What? Did he realize this was their daughter he was talking about?

It was probably Candy. Jack's new wife felt threatened. Didn't want Jack and Margot talking every day. Didn't want to risk Jack waking up one day and realizing that he already had a family he loved and that Candy was nothing but a midlife mistake.

Margot hadn't eaten since a quick lunch break at eleven, but her feet and legs were too tired to stand up and try to cook. She opened her freezer, hoping to find something quick and easy.

No such luck. She was supposed to go grocery shopping last weekend, but she'd been too tired. She reached into the cupboards and pulled down some cereal. There wasn't any milk, so she'd have to eat it dry.

It still beat standing in the kitchen sweating over a hot stove.

She plunked herself down in the dining room. The couch would be more comfortable, but that would add an extra ten feet she'd have to walk. Instead of dirtying any more dishes, Margot grabbed a handful of corn flakes, spread them out on the table in front of her, and popped a few pieces into her mouth at a time.

With imagination, she might be able to pretend it was popcorn. Most of the time since Becky's disappearance, Margot's imagination had become her arch nemesis. Lying awake, picturing every horrible thing this Xavier might have done to her baby. Might be doing. Might continue to do for years if nobody caught him or intervened.

Run away, she whispered into the darkness. *Run away from him. Don't do anything he says.*

At one point, back when Margot was still in regular contact with her ex, Jack told her, "At least there's still hope. Until someone tells us otherwise, we've just got to hold onto faith that she's still alive and still out there."

Was he seriously that obtuse? He acted as if he was glad for the uncertainty. As if no news really was good news.

Goodie, we haven't found her body yet. Let's throw a party.

A few years ago, the daughter of one of Margot's coworkers was hit by a car. The child died instantly. "There's nothing worse than burying your child." Margot had listened to Paige sympathetically. And at the time, she believed it was probably true. Nothing could be worse than Becky dying.

Except, of course, for Becky being kidnapped by some pedophile or pimp or whatever this Xavier was. At least Paige knew where her daughter was buried. She could go and leave flowers whenever she wanted. Comfort herself in the knowledge that her child's passing was quick. Mercifully quick. Perhaps even painless.

Sure, you'd grieve. But that was the point. You'd grieve. You'd cry. Margot couldn't do any of those things. Maybe Becky was dead. Maybe she wasn't.

And if she wasn't dead, what kind of torment and

suffering did she have to endure?

That was the worst question of them all. Not if Becky would ever come back to her. But what was she going through right now? While Margot was on her way to work this morning, was Becky being attacked? Assaulted? Passed around like communal property?

While Margot was eating her dry corn flakes, was Becky starving? Was she sick? What if this Xavier monster had given her some kind of disease? What if Becky was gravely ill and Xavier refused to get her any medical treatment because of all the questions it would raise?

Some days Margot thought the uncertainty would kill her.

She would have traded places with Paige any day of the week.

Nearly as crippling as the uncertainty was the guilt. While Margot slept in a soft, warm bed, was her baby girl out on the streets, drenched by rain and catching pneumonia in some germ-infested alleyway? While Margot complained about her aching feet after a long day at the office, was Becky's body torn and beaten and battered beyond recognition?

The reality was too grisly too imagine. The future too bleak. Too uncertain.

And so Margot thought about the past. Christmases before the divorce. Where to anybody looking in, the Linklaters looked like a loving family celebrating a happy, uplifting holiday.

Watching Becky twirling on the ice on her skates, so graceful. So beautiful. So free.

She might have gone on to the Olympics. Her coach said she had the focus and determination to make it. She just needed a little more confidence. Needed to believe in herself, push herself a little harder.

Then of course Jack decided to rip those dreams right out from under them both. It had been his idea to get Becky into skating in the first place. The least he could have done was continue to pay for her lessons, but apparently that was far too much to ask.

Margot could only immerse herself in these memories for a few minutes at a time before dwelling in the past became just as painful as picturing the present or the future.

Which left nothing. No safe place. No comfort. No balm.

Each and every day, Margot's wounds were as raw and as open as a freshy dissected specimen. Nine months already. Nine months and no word.

If Becky was safe and happy, she would have made contact by now. Margot knew it.

Which meant that her daughter wasn't safe or happy.

The worst part was that there was nothing, absolutely nothing, Margot could do.

She didn't want to stand up again.

Didn't want to walk all the way over to the cupboard.

Didn't want to pull down the bottle of vodka she'd stashed up there for nights like this.

But she was tired. Most evenings a glass of wine was enough. Tonight, she needed this.

She didn't have any clean cups, so she drank right out of the bottle. She let out her breath and wiped the corners of her mouth. She'd have to be careful not to drink too much. Just enough to take the edge off.

Just enough to help her sleep through the night.

Tomorrow, she didn't have to be at work until ten. She'd tidy up the house, dump the rest of the vodka down the sink so she didn't grow too dependent on it, and then she'd go to work feeling slightly more rested than she was right now.

It was the most she could hope for.

Just another few drinks. If she made herself tired enough, she wouldn't even notice how hungry she was. She could go right to bed.

Margot hadn't slept through the night in a very long time.

CHAPTER 16

Last summer

Hey there, it's me again. Funny thing happened. I just spent like an hour holding three different text conversations at once. I mean, I'm pretty good at it, and I never send anyone the wrong note like what can happen if you're not paying attention. And besides, texting's, like, super fun. It's not sitting around talking, where you always have to wonder what you're going to say next and worry about people thinking you sound dumb. With texting, if you don't know what to say, all you've got to do is put in a few emoticons, and then the conversation just keeps going from there.

So, I was talking with Xavier. I mean, I'm guessing that part was totally obvious. And I'll have to look back and find some of the things he wrote because they are so sweet! That's the one problem with texting him as much as I do because I'm always like, *aw, that's the nicest thing he's ever said*, and I want to save it, so I figure I can always just scroll up and find it. But when you're sending as many texts a day as us, it gets hard to find the ones you want. I really should start taking screen shots or something. Hey, how cute would that be? I can take screen shots of some of our sweetest conversations and have them printed up. Woong's mom knows how to do that because once Woong wrote about what it was like to be adopted and how life was when he was still at the orphanage, and his mom got it printed into a real book, which I think is super cool.

So I can ask her how to do it and then turn it into a present for Xavier. There aren't any major holidays coming up, not like Valentine's Day or Christmas or anything, but maybe I can do it on our one-month anniversary or something like that. Wouldn't that be adorable?

Anyway, while I was texting with Xavier, Woong and I were writing too because he wanted to know what I thought about Sunday school. So I told him it was great and I really liked Scott, and then we talked about what it would be like to be a missionary. I told Woong again I can totally see him turning into a missionary one day. He's really good with people. Like, when I met Woong in elementary school, I was really self-conscious. Carly and I had just gotten into this major fight and hadn't talked in weeks, and half the girls at school were mad at me because Carly told them it was all my fault. It was totally stupid. She was mad because I didn't invite her to go camping with me and my dad. But the reason I didn't invite her was because she told me once my dad kind of freaked her out (and I honestly don't blame her), so I invited Megs instead. And I couldn't tell her I would have rather invited her than Megan anyway because then Megan would be mad at me, so anyway, when Woong and I met I wasn't in a very good place.

But he was super cute (not in the I-like-you-and-want-to-be-your-girlfriend kind of way, but just like this adorable little baby panda bear or something like that) and he was trying really hard to get better at English, and Mom says I'm a really good teacher. Sometimes I figure I'll grow up and become an English teacher just like Mr. Daly. I guess you could say that's how Woong and I became friends.

One of the reasons why I say I could totally see Woong as a missionary is that his dad's a pastor and his mom's always talking to people about God and inviting them to church. I can't tell you how many times she's asked my mom to go, and sometimes she does, but honestly, Mom's so tired after working all week she doesn't like getting up early on Sundays, which are her only real day off. But I don't mind it. Church, I mean. I probably won't ever get into it as much as Woong or Miss Sandy or anything like that. Like, I'm not going to become a nun or a missionary or a pastor's wife, but I totally believe in God, and that gives me a lot of comfort, especially since Dad left.

Miss Sandy and I talked about it once. I was really mad at my dad (because seriously, who wouldn't be?), and so she talked to me about forgiveness and how Jesus forgave me for all the things I did wrong. It was super encouraging, although I do have to point out that even though Jesus may have forgiven me for certain things like maybe being grouchy or being jealous of Carly for her parents' pool and big house, at least I never abandoned my family and basically forgot about my own daughter and married someone half my age. So there's that.

But Miss Sandy and I talked some too about God as our heavenly Father, and I'd heard that kind of stuff as a kid. Even before I started going to church with Woong, I knew a lot about Jesus because my grandma used to go to church all the time before she went into the nursing home. Took me to VBS and sang Bible songs in the kitchen together and all that. So I knew about God being my father, but somehow hearing Miss Sandy put it in just this special way made me feel way better.

So yeah, I'm a Christian even if I'm not going to go around like Miss Sandy inviting people to church and asking to pray for strangers in the grocery store. I mean, some people just aren't comfortable with that, you know?

Anyway, Woong doesn't get to text all that much because like I said, his parents are super strict, but we talked some about church and summer and things like that. One day I really should tell him how glad I am to have a friend like him because honestly, it's so much nicer to have a guy friend. Woong and I have only gotten into one fight in our entire lives, and that was because Woong gave me this note and Chuck saw it and got jealous and thought we liked each other. Which is totally hilarious because Woong's like my brother, and I absolutely love him but never to where I'd, like, date him or anything.

I still haven't told Woong about Xavier, which kind of makes me feel bad, like I'm keeping something from him, but some things I just don't feel like I can share unless I know someone's going to understand. But it is nice to have a friend like him just to talk to and know that there isn't going to be all that drama and stuff.

Oh, and speaking of drama, guess who else I was texting with all night? Carly. Miss Drama Queen herself. I guess Megan told her that I told her I'm dating Xavier. And so Carly asked me why I didn't tell her first, and she was all mad. But I didn't want Megan to say anything because I knew Carly would only be jealous, so I had to pretend like it was no big deal. I told her Xavier and I went out once but then I just stopped texting him because he was so much older and it was freaking my mom out.

Which isn't a full lie because if my mom ever did find out, that's exactly what would happen.

So now I have to tell Megan that if she and Carly talk about it again, Megan's got to tell Carly the same thing, except I've been trying to get a hold of Megan all night, but she isn't answering. So I hope Carly hasn't gotten hold of her first because then things have the potential to get really ugly.

Why do girls have to act so immature? Ugh. I can't wait until all the drama ends. Middle school really stinks, to be honest. I'm definitely not sorry to see it go. High school's going to be so much better. In fact, everything's better now that I'm with Xavier. I still can't believe I've fallen in love with such an amazing guy, and I know some people would think it's impossible to be in love at my age, but they've never experienced what Xavier and I have. They've never seen the way he looks at me like I'm all his and only his. They don't read the notes he sends and the texts and the way he calls me out of the blue just to make sure I haven't stopped thinking about him. It's so romantic.

He can get jealous too, which with someone immature like Chuck can be super annoying, but with Xavier, he's only jealous because we don't see each other enough. That's why I'm so excited about summer. Mom's got this neighbor I'm supposed to babysit for, but that's only two mornings a week, and honestly, the little girl's, like, addicted to the iPad, so all I have to do is make sure her batteries don't die and that she goes to the bathroom every so often. I can definitely still text Xavier while I'm there. The rest of the time he can come over or we can go shopping or we can just do all those things that people do in the summer when they're in love. He even talked about going one weekend to this BNB on Cape Cod, which honestly kind of freaked me out a little bit because, um, hello? Overnight? But maybe I'll feel differently by the end of the summer. I know my mom would never allow it anyway, so I can use that as an excuse, but then if I change my mind, I can just tell my mom I'm going over to Megan's or something.

It is absolutely an amazing feeling to be so loved. I feel sorry for anyone who hasn't gone through something like this. And I'm especially mad at my dad right now, because at one point I'm sure my mom loved him as much as I love Xavier. The only difference is I made a better choice because Xavier's not about to go and find someone half his age and move in with her the same week he leaves his wife and daughter.

Ugh. He's so disgusting. My dad, I mean. Not Xavier (obviously).

Speaking of Xavier, I told him I'd call him before I go to bed. He likes to talk until I'm so tired I'm basically falling asleep. He tells me he likes to do that so I can be sure that I'll dream about him and only him.

Can someone please say *romantic*?

I've got to get into my pajamas now, so talk to you later and good night!

CHAPTER 17

"Hello?" Margot fumbled for her cell phone, cursing her splitting headache.

The voice on the other end of the line was deep, masculine, and grumpy. "Margot, what's going on?"

"Jack?" She didn't know what to say. Why was her ex calling her so late at night? What if it had something to do with Becky? She tried to jerk herself awake.

"Margot." Jack's voice was strained. Angry. As usual.

"Yeah." She rubbed her eyes with her free hand, immediately regretting that vodka last night. "I'm here. I'm awake."

"Margot." Deep in the recesses of her memory was the hint of the time when she loved to hear him speak her name. But that was before. Before the divorce. The barely-legal other woman. The disappearance.

"I'm here," she mumbled. "What do you want?" If Jack was going to call her at this time of night, the least he could do was try to sound a little more apologetic. But no. All he cared about was himself. Himself and that twenty-something blonde woman …

"Margot!" He was snapping now. As if she owed him some sort of apology for daring to be asleep when he called her at three in the morning.

"I'm sorry," she muttered. At least she wasn't slurring her words. That would be awkward.

"How many drinks have you had?" There it was. The softness she'd longed to hear in his voice. The edge of sympathy. You couldn't feel sorry for someone you hated, right? So there was still something there. Something between them after all these years.

Wasn't there?

"I'm not drinking." She was telling the truth. If she remembered right, she'd put the bottle down hours ago and come to bed. The bed that they used to share together.

Before.

She let out a giggle.

"What's so funny?" There he was snapping again at her. It didn't matter. He was the one who woke her up, not the other way around. And now he was acting angry and uptight just because she was so tired the littlest thing set her off laughing?

"I was just thinking about that time we took Becky to

Disney World." Did he remember?

"Margot …" His voice was soft again. Soft and strong and everything she remembered.

A fumbling in the background. Had he dropped the phone? She pictured him in his stupid plaid boxers, hunting for his cell in the dark, and another laugh escaped her lips.

"Margot, is that you?" The masculine voice was gone, replaced now by a grating, piercing shriek.

"Hello, Candy," Margot answered. Now she understood. None of this seemed funny anymore.

"Margot, you really need to stop calling us. I know you're having a rough time, but seriously, Jack's got to be up in two and a half hours, and he can't have you waking him up like this."

Margot rolled her eyes. Candy had no idea. "He's the one who called me." If she'd just give Jack his phone back, everything would be fine. Exactly how it should be. Why wouldn't she let Margot talk to her husband?

"I'm hanging up now." Candy's voice was curt. Not just curt but downright rude. Margot had a name for women like her.

"Don't go," Margot interrupted. "Just let me talk to Jack. He had something to tell me."

"No, he didn't."

"Then why'd he call me this late?" Margot heard the panicked edge rising in her unusually calming voice and suddenly had to fight the urge to throw up.

"You need to get some sleep." Candy's voice was condescending. Demeaning. The tone a jaded nurse would use to calm down a neurotic mom. "Get some sleep," she told Margot, "and stop calling us."

"But Jack wanted to tell me something." Margot was whining now, but she couldn't help it. Why had her husband given this woman the phone in the first place?

"You can't call him when you're like this." Candy's voice dripped with disdain, sharp enough to pierce through the fog of Margot's sleep-deprived headache. "You're drunk. You're upsetting Jack, and he needs his rest."

The line went dead. Margot waited. Waited for a silent moment even though she had no idea what she hoped would happen. That Jack would call her back and apologize? That he'd tell her he remembered that day at Disney World when Becky was just a little girl and so overwhelmed by the crowds she started screaming when Winnie the Pooh wanted to give her a hug? How they were all so tired and hot by that afternoon that they just rode and re-rode that silly boat ride for hours?

Hot hatred seared through her body as she thought about

Candy. What right did that woman have to interrupt their conversation? Interrupt their life?

Had Candy ever taken Becky to Disney World? Had she woken up every morning at five for years in a row to take her daughter to ice-staking lessons? Was she the one losing sleep, aging a decade every week while she waited to hear from a stone-cold detective who never had any good news to pass on?

No. Candy didn't care about Becky. In fact, it was probably convenient for her now that Becky was gone. No more weekend visitations to juggle into her busy social schedule. Candy had Jack all to herself now.

Just like she'd wanted from the beginning.

Cruel, heartless woman.

Margot had heard the hint of triumph in Candy's voice before she hung up the phone. But why had she said that Margot was the one to call Jack? Margot swiped her phone's screen. Outgoing calls. It didn't make sense. Why did it show that she'd called him? It was some kind of mistake. Some sort of accident. She couldn't remember exactly now …

She'd text him. That's what she'd do. Text Jack and explain everything.

Her fingers fumbled on her screen. Words that appeared

made no sense when strung together. Stupid autocorrect.

She'd wait until morning. She'd text Jack while he was at work. That'd be better anyway. No half-clad trophy wives staring over his shoulder, intent on interrupting their conversation.

She'd explain everything to Jack later. Yes, maybe she'd had a little bit too much vodka. She'd made a simple mistake. Thought he'd been the one to call her.

A simple mistake. Nothing more.

And the only reason she'd laughed in his ear was because of something he'd said, something in his voice that reminded her of Disney World. Of a little girl crying at the sight of an oversized Pooh Bear coming at her to give her a hug. A pair of exhausted parents riding around in a tiny boat all day.

If Candy hadn't interrupted them, Jack would have laughed too.

She just knew it.

CHAPTER 18

Last summer

Well, now that the weekend's over, I can officially say summer is here! Today didn't go quite as planned. I was a little bummed about that, but it's okay. Xavier was going to come and pick me up this morning, and we were going to hang out together. He even said if he had enough money, he'd treat me to a half hour at the massage parlor, and I've never had a real massage before. Sometimes Mom will come and rub my back for a minute, but that's about it. So I was really disappointed when he texted me around ten and said his car stopped working. Sad face.

I could tell he was pretty upset. He's not the kind to get angry easily, but when he does, it's so hard. Because he's so different from the guy he is normally, and all I want to do is make him happy. So I told him I could take the T, but he didn't want me riding the bus alone, which is super sweet of him. I love how worried he gets. It isn't like I haven't ridden the bus by myself before, but he didn't want me to do that today.

So then I told him he could come over here, and I was a little nervous about that because most of the time we've been together it's been, like, going shopping or driving around in his car or hanging out some place a little more public. He hasn't been at the house before, but you know, it's probably stupid for me to be nervous about something like that. I mean, we've been going out for over a month now, so it's not like I have anything to be afraid of.

So I told him we're right off the bus stop and I could meet him there if he was worried about getting lost, but he didn't text back right away, and for a minute I was afraid he was mad at me. I wasn't sure what I did. Maybe he didn't like me suggesting I'd walk to the station alone, but it's literally, like, three minutes away, so it isn't like anything could happen to me in that short a time.

I kept waiting for him to respond, and I was getting more and more worried I'd done something to upset him, but I didn't want to be one of those nagging girlfriends who's always just like, *why didn't you write me back? Are we okay? Do you love me?* Because I'm not needy like that. I just wanted to make sure he wasn't angry. I know it's because he's worried for my safety, which is adorable, but it does kind of get a little annoying. I really don't mind taking the bus by myself. I do it all the time. Sometimes even at night. Like once I was visiting my dad, but his new wife had the car, so Dad and I rode together to our stop, and then I just walked myself home, and that was, like, last year sometime. So yeah, not a big deal.

But I didn't want to go into all that with Xavier, especially if he was mad at me, so I just waited for him to text back, which in the end I think turned out to be the best thing. I mean, it was a really rough half hour for me because I've got this problem with my imagination getting carried away, so when something bad happens I immediately think of all the worst things that could go wrong. But Xavier actually called me, he didn't just text. He apologized and said, "I know we were going to spend the day together, but I'm having some problems right now with money."

I guess what happened was Xavier's cousin was falsely accused of something, and it totally wasn't his fault, but he needed help with the bail and lawyer fees, and Xavier is so sweet and generous that he just gave him everything. I mean, I didn't ask for details because it's not my business, but I kind of think it must have been a lot of money because it was literally everything Xavier had.

Of course, at the time he didn't know his car was about

to break down either, and this is so sweet, but I think what disappointed Xavier the most was that he wouldn't be able to buy me a real massage after all. And I told him that was totally not something he had to worry about, and I even made a little bit of a joke that he could just do it himself once he came over. I thought it might cheer him up, you know. I wasn't being totally serious, but then he got upset all over again and was like, "I don't have money to take the T, remember?" That's when I realized how bad it really was. I mean, I know what it's like to be out of money. Dad's rich enough that he has no excuse not to be making his payments, but that's the ironic part. He's got the money, so he can afford the good lawyers to keep Mom off his back. And she's got this, like, lazy attorney who doesn't do anything to help and still sends her a bill for doing absolutely nothing, so finally Mom just gave up trying to get anything.

All that is to say, I know what it's like not to have money to take the T, but I had no idea Xavier was that bad off. So I asked him what I could do. Mom gets paid this Friday, and she always takes out a little cash on payday so we can use it for groceries when things get tight before her next paycheck comes in. I know right where she keeps the money, and she's really bad with using her coins, so they'll just sit there for months and pile up until we go and take them to one of those automatic counter machines at the grocery store. So if it was just the matter of getting Xavier a few dollars so he could come over, I told him it wouldn't be a problem, especially not once Friday rolls around.

But of course, that's five days from now. Sad face. And it would totally stink to have to wait that long to see him at all because that's why I was so excited for summer break to begin with. I know some men get really proud about asking for money and stuff, so I was glad that Xavier wasn't too embarrassed to tell me about his problems. Plus, it made me realize he wasn't mad at me after all. It's just that Xavier is way too nice and he couldn't say no to his cousin. And in another week or two, once his cousin gets everything sorted, Xavier will get all that money back plus interest, but until then it might really stink if we can't get together at all.

Sigh. I really wish Xavier would let me take the bus and visit him. I tried to hint that I could come over to his place if he wanted, and he could give me a massage there. Call me silly, but I'm actually starting to worry that Xavier hasn't wanted to do all that much more than just give me a quick peck on the cheek. I mean, I know we're attracted to each other because my stomach literally flips when we're together, and I can read him well enough I know the same thing happens to him. And I hope it's not because he's worrying about scaring me away or something, because I'm definitely mature for my age. I'm not a little girl. I just don't want to be the one begging him for more because that's going to come across as super desperate, and that's not the kind of person I am. But seriously. When Chuck and I went out, he waited, like, all of five minutes before he wanted to French kiss. And part of me loves that Xavier's such a gentleman, but come on. He's an adult. I'm at least mature enough to be an adult.

And I'm kind of ready to start acting like one.

CHAPTER 19

Ruby closed her eyes. What had she done wrong? She couldn't remember how or when it happened. Did Xavier even need a reason anymore?

"Stop!" Since she came here, she learned how to scream the word in her mind so she wouldn't make him angrier. *This is just the way he is*, she told herself. *He's stressed out about money.*

Always the money.

She should have worked harder. It was her fault, really. If she'd earned her quota, he would have all that he needed.

She deserved this.

His feet smacked into her head. Her back. Her sides. She cradled herself on the floor. A lullaby floated past her on a tenuous breeze. Something her grandma used to sing. How did it go?

Jesus loves me this I know. For the Bible tells me so ...

Snippets flashed in her memory. Grandma singing hymns in the kitchen, the smell of home-baked cookies wafting through her tiny flat.

A little girl at Vacation Bible School giggling when the pastor wore a clown's suit as part of the opening skit.

Holding onto her shiny new quarter before she put it in the offering plate, her black dress shoes pinching her toes, her white tights itchy on her skin, Grandma swaying slightly in the pew next to her while the elderly pianist played *The Old Rugged Cross*.

"I told you not to text anyone," Xavier shouted.

She hadn't been texting. Hadn't seen her phone in months. Hadn't talked to anybody except for Xavier.

And the clients, of course, but they didn't count.

Only Xavier counted.

He was the only one who loved her.

The only one who provided for her.

Didn't he bring her a Mountain Dew just this morning? Didn't he remember that was her favorite drink?

Favorite drink for his favorite girl.

She wished he didn't get so worried about money. Wished that all those years ago she had saved some of Grandma's shiny quarters instead of putting them in that offering plate every time it came around. Wished she could buy her boyfriend a little peace of mind.

Then he'd stop kicking. Stop yelling.

And he'd hold her. Love her. Comfort her.

Like before. That summer when everything was perfect. When they were so in love. Making promises to always be together. Nothing could come between them.

That's what got her through times like these. Remembering that this man — this one right now, the one standing over her, calling her ugly names, the one making her cower on the floor — wasn't the real Xavier.

The real Xavier was kind. Caring. Adoring.

The real Xavier would never hurt her.

And she would never disappoint him.

Their love was like a fairy tale. He'd told her so himself.

And as soon as he got his money problems in order, as soon as that stupid cousin of his paid him back, they'd be out of here.

No more dates. No more hunger. No more hotel rooms.

Just the two of them in a nice apartment in a quiet part of town.

Her and Xavier. He wouldn't call her Ruby anymore, either. He'd use her real name again.

"This isn't the life I want to give you," he whispered the first night she went to work. "This isn't the woman I want you to be."

It wasn't going to always be like this. And in a way, the

fact that he changed her name was a blessing. A cloak of protection.

When she curled up on the floor, shielding her head from the heel of Xavier's boots, she was someone else. A woman named Ruby.

The kind of woman who'd never gone to church or Sunday school, who never wore unbearably stiff dresses and itchy tights, swinging her legs in the pew while the congregation sang about an old rugged cross.

Any sense of protection, any sense of solace came from this one simple realization.

Ruby wasn't real.

Which meant that Xavier wasn't kicking *her*. He wasn't beating *her*. He didn't hate *her*.

And one day, as soon he got the money he needed, as soon as his deadbeat cousin repaid him everything he owed, things would go back to the way they were. She could stop living this life.

Stop going on so many dates.

Stop being Ruby.

The thought allowed her to survive his kicks until Xavier got tired and plopped down on the bed. Allowed her to find the courage to stifle her tears so he'd never know how heartbroken she was. Allowed her to continue to hope for the life he'd promised her. A life together. Just her and her Xavier.

She thought about Grandma's church again. What was that song about heaven, the upbeat one where even the old men started to clap?

When we all get to heaven, what a day of rejoicing that will be ...

God wouldn't let someone like Ruby into heaven. Not now. Not with all the horrible things she'd done. But it wouldn't always be that way. Once Xavier got that money, once they could move into a nicer part of town, she'd discard her old life. Trade it in. Forget about these past few months, like a nightmare that vanishes by morning.

She and Xavier would be happy. They would be together.

And he'd never call her Ruby again.

CHAPTER 20

"Another work call?" Caroline asked tentatively when her husband returned to their hotel room.

Calvin grunted in response.

"Any more news on the girl?"

Calvin didn't like talking about work. Their marriage worked best when Caroline pretended he wasn't a detective. Didn't ask about his cases. Didn't request any updates.

But Becky's disappearance had impacted everyone in Medford. Caroline still remembered seeing Mrs. Linklater at the supermarket a few weeks after her daughter went missing. Becky's mom was carrying an empty shopping basket down the aisles, and she stopped in front of the snack section. The raw pain on Mrs. Linklater's face was palpable, like a furnace blast. Caroline hadn't wanted to intrude. She'd been a teacher at the same school, but Becky had never been one of her students. She didn't feel she had the right to say anything, and so she kept to herself, only whispering a prayer for the broken mother in the aisle.

Mrs. Linklater was staring at the boxes of crackers, cookies, and granola bars. Most likely the kind of snacks a middle schooler would come home and eat after school. Mrs. Linklater reached out her arm, almost as if she were going to select a box of granola bars, then let her hand fall and continued past the shelves, her basket totally empty.

"It was heartbreaking," Caroline had told her husband that evening. "Absolutely heartbreaking. I want to cry every time I think about what that poor woman must be going through."

Calvin just shrugged. "Kids disappear every day."

"This is totally different," Caroline objected.

Calvin glared at her. "Why? Because she's white? Because her dad's rich?"

"Because she's a student at my school," Caroline snapped. She should have known better than to even mention it. "No parent should have to go through anything like that."

Calvin hadn't responded. He wore that same stoic, impenetrable expression on his face now when he returned to their hotel room. They were supposed to be getting dressed for tonight's formal dinner. Caroline had actually bought herself a brand-new dress. Not even a thrift store treasure. A real dress right straight off the rack. Red satin, with sleeves that dropped down her shoulders at the slightest hint of an angle.

While her husband took a call from his partner, Caroline had spent half an hour staring at herself in the mirror, trying to figure out how to best expose the right curves and hide the wrong ones. She didn't have her jewelry or makeup on yet, but her hair was probably about as good as she could manage without a professional styling.

Calvin shoved his phone into his pocket and fixed his eyes on her. It was impossible to tell if he was pleased with the way she looked or not. Caroline reminded herself what the counselor had said in one of today's breakout sessions just for women. "Your husband isn't as comfortable with emotional displays as you want him to be. Instead of trying to change that, you need to develop your own sense of confidence. There's nothing more alluring than a woman who's deeply convinced of her own beauty and worth."

Her own beauty and worth. Caroline glanced at herself once more in the mirror, digging deep in search of that part of her psyche where her confidence might be hiding. She gave a hopeful smile to her husband. Calvin still hadn't mentioned the new dress, but he hadn't taken his eyes off her either.

That had to count for something, right?

Finally, she couldn't stand the silent scrutiny. "Well,"

she asked, "What do you think?"

She angled herself slightly in a move that she'd rehearsed a dozen times in front of the mirror already. And then she waited.

"Well?" she prompted again.

Calvin was staring at her shoulders. Had her husband forgotten she possessed a collarbone? Two of them, actually.

She licked her lips and breathed in, getting a strong whiff of the spay-on deodorant she'd used right after showering.

Calvin finally pried his gaze away. "You ready to go?" he asked.

Caroline couldn't wait any longer or mask the slight whine in her unusually calming voice. "You still haven't told me what you think of my new dress."

Calvin gave her one more cursory glance before he said, "Looks expensive. Hope you got it on sale."

CHAPTER 21

Drisklay wished he was back at work. Why had he ever let his wife talk him into flying out to Las Vegas of all places? And right now of all times. It wasn't just the Linklater case he was working on. His desk back in Boston was covered with files of missing persons and murdered victims.

Did he ever ask Caroline to take an entire week off of teaching? Of course not. She had no idea what kind of mental energy it took to do the kinds of things he did.

And he did them well.

At least, he could when he was at his office.

He'd been on the phone that evening with Alexi, his partner back in Boston. Apparently, Margot Linklater had called 911 in the middle of the night, drunk as the mascot in a St. Paddy's Day parade and claiming that her ex-husband's new wife had murdered their daughter. Of course, it was the ravings of a madwoman, but Drisklay and his team still had to document everything.

Which meant more paperwork.

Always the paperwork.

Wasting time he didn't have when he was here in Las Vegas traipsing around town. Thank God his wife hadn't asked him to go to one of those stupid circus shows while they were here. At least she knew him well enough to realize how miserable that would have made him. As it was, they had to walk the Strip each and every night so she could take his arm and croon, "Isn't it beautiful?" as if she hadn't said the exact same thing five minutes earlier. Caroline would stop at each and every gaudy display, pull out her camera, snap photos. It was a wonder the two of them hadn't gotten themselves crowned Tourists of the Year.

"I'm glad we get to eat at the hotel tonight," Caroline said as they followed the sign leading them to the part of the restaurant reserved for conference attendees. "I've enjoyed walking the Strip," she continued, "but it's so depressing seeing all those driving billboards for call girls. It's so degrading."

Drisklay shrugged. What did she expect him to do about it? Call the number the next time one passed and when a girl showed up to his hotel room ask her if she wanted to have an hour-long conversation about her life choices?

Caroline was an idealist. That was her problem. What

she didn't realize was that for every Vegas call girl being advertised in neon signs for any passerby to see, dozens of girls back in Medford were doing the exact same kinds of things for the exact same kinds of people, except there it was everybody's dirty little secret. Las Vegas was no more vile than any other city of its size in the States.

It was just more honest.

"I just can't stop thinking about that poor girl being trapped in a life like this." Caroline sighed again.

Drisklay knew which girl his wife was referring to. Knew that Caroline was harboring unspoken resentment since he hadn't solved the case yet.

Well, maybe if he were back home where he could actually continue on his investigation, the case could progress more quickly.

Caroline was an idealist, but she was right about the runaway. It didn't take a professional criminal profiler to figure out what happened. Teenagers like the Linklater girl were wooed away from their homes by men like Xavier on a daily basis. Some were promised fame as models or Hollywood stars. Others were trying to escape chaotic home lives. Then there were the ones like Becky, girls who needed some guy to tell her she was beautiful and she'd go with him anywhere.

Do anything for him.

Disgusting.

Drisklay would be more than happy to find this Xavier and see him thrown into a general population prison cell. It was exactly what scum liked him deserved. But for every Xavier that Drisklay caught, a hundred more were ready to rise up and take his place.

It was never-ending, this cycle of crime. And Drisklay was caught up in the middle, like a man trying to stop the tide with a bucket.

That's why he needed to be home working. When you're interviewing witnesses and perusing files fifteen hours a day, you don't have time to wonder if what you're doing really matters. If you're making any amount of difference whatsoever.

Once Drisklay caught the Linklater girl's kidnapper, at least her mother would gain some measure of peace. He'd reunite the girl to her family, if she was still alive at least, and then the very next day show up to his office ready to solve more cases just like hers, or even worse. Except hopefully his wife wouldn't drag him along to any more of these dumb marriage retreats. The last thing he needed was even more time away from the job.

Time to spend thinking about the futility of his calling.

About the senselessness of it all.

Time he could be using to catch Becky Linklater's kidnapper and finally bring the monster to justice.

CHAPTER 22

Caroline stared at her husband and offered a smile. "How's your food?" she asked quietly, trying to gauge his emotional state from across the table.

Calvin grunted a reply.

"My salad's good too," she offered, this time to no response.

She bit her lip. All around her, underneath these gaudy chandeliers, were nearly a hundred couples. Tonight's dinner was put on by the Truth Warrior's conference, and everyone in this section was here to work on their marriages. Husband and wives leaned toward each other, their faces illuminated by soft candlelight. Smiling couples. Laughing couples.

Talking couples.

The setting would be absolutely perfect if it weren't for the overwhelming stench of cigarette smoke and her husband's usual silence.

"What'd you think of your breakout session?" she finally

asked.

Calvin looked up as if he was surprised she was still sitting there. "Huh?"

"Your session this afternoon," she prodded. "I already told you what I learned in mine. What'd you guys talk about in yours?"

He swallowed a huge chunk of steak then shrugged. "I was on a call."

"You were working? The entire afternoon?" When he came into their hotel room that evening on the phone, she thought he'd been squeezing in a quick meeting before dinner. She'd had no idea he skipped the afternoon sessions completely.

Calvin took a noisy gulp of coffee. "Alexi had to fill me in. We've had a few developments."

As upset as she wanted to be with her husband, she felt her body lean forward expectantly. "Any new leads?"

He shook his head. "No. Just the mom being melodramatic. Now she wants us to look into her ex-husband's new wife. I swear that woman will do anything she can to avoid the truth. Her daughter is out now on some street corner, waiting for some john to come up to her and …"

"Just stop." Caroline couldn't believe that her husband

could speak so callously about a real girl, especially one as young as Becky Linklater. Calvin had always been crass, but this felt intentionally spiteful. Was he mad at her reaction when he admitted he'd worked straight through the afternoon session?

He gnawed at a chunk of bread. "It's ridiculous," he said with his mouth full. "This woman wants us out there searching under every rock, but she's too fragile to admit the truth. Her daughter's been taken by a piece of trash who knew exactly what to do and what to say to get an impressionable underaged girl to follow him anywhere. You should have seen the gifts he gave her last summer. Over three thousand dollars' worth. Diamond jewelry, high-end shoes, you name it. It's all there. It's all documented. You know why he spent that much, don't you?"

Caroline set down her fork. She'd lost her appetite. "I don't think you need to tell me."

Apparently, Calvin didn't care what she thought. "He spent that much," he went on, "because he's a businessman. A *businessman*," he repeated more slowly, as if Caroline hadn't caught the words the first time. "And the first rule of business is to earn more than you spend. That's what making a profit is all about. That's what every good little capitalist is taught from day one. You want to succeed, you've got to make more money out of your business than what you pay into it. And I can guarantee you that the only reason this man spent over three thousand dollars on this girl is that he expects to turn a profit. A really big profit. A girl that young, that pretty, and that naïve is going to earn her keep a dozen times over before he …"

"Cut it out." This time Caroline nearly shouted the words to make sure her husband heard. "Just stop." What had Calvin been thinking? Did he realize this wasn't just some nameless victim he was talking about? This was a girl Caroline knew. A girl who'd gone to Caroline's school. Walked the same hallways …

"I'll be back." Caroline jumped up from her seat, uncertain if she was more likely to break down into tears or throw up what little of her salad she'd picked at. All she knew was she had to get herself to the bathroom. Cursing her stupid heels, which made running impossible, she walked as fast as she dared without risking a broken ankle.

Safe inside the women's room, she sank into the plush couch lining one wall, thankful for the dim lights that could hide her face from anyone who might happen to pass by. She just had to catch her breath. That was all.

Her husband had always been like this. Curt. Calloused. Crass. He had to be. If he allowed himself to feel sorry for every single victim, if he allowed himself to feel even a fraction of their pain, he couldn't do his job.

Caroline understood that on a logical level. But she couldn't sit here in this fancy restaurant, watching other couples sip their fancy drinks and eat their fancy cuisine, and all the while listen while her husband talked about this little girl — a girl Caroline knew — with such gruesome candor. What would Mrs. Linklater think if she heard the way the lead detective in her daughter's case spoke about her situation?

Coming to Vegas had been a mistake. Why had she even bothered?

Calvin would never change. Nothing, not a hundred days of seminars or a hundred hours of prayers could soften his heart.

She wiped at her eyes, hoping she hadn't smudged her mascara too badly. Hoping there was some way to salvage this evening.

Hoping she could muster her courage so that in five, maybe ten, minutes, she could walk out there, sit down across from her husband, and pretend to enjoy her overpriced salad.

CHAPTER 23

Drisklay glanced at his watch and waved away the pesky, over-attentive waiter. The worst part about Las Vegas was how shamelessly everyone groveled around for a few extra bucks. All those tips added up, Drisklay supposed, but it was still degrading.

Where had his wife gone to? Probably to fix her makeup. She really took this idea of a formal dinner seriously. Maybe she was sitting in the bathroom pouting because he wasn't paying enough attention to her. Well, she knew he was working this case. And she of all people knew how all-absorbing this kind of investigation could be. What was he supposed to do? Just turn off his brain and ignore the fact that a young girl was missing?

He couldn't give up. He owed Mrs. Linklater that much, at least.

Closure. That's what the parents in cases like this needed. Sure, if they were reunited with their child, it was a nice added bonus. But what they needed even more than to hold their child again was to stop having to guess.

Whoever said that no news is better than bad news had never had to look a parent in the eye and say, "I'm sorry, but at this time we still don't have any new leads on your daughter's whereabouts."

Drisklay had thrown everything he had into this case. Clocked scores of hours searching the dark web for dating websites promising "barely legal" girls that matched the missing child's description.

It was disgusting. But it was his job. And who else besides him could get Becky Linklater home?

The girl was five foot one and a hundred pounds when she was sopping wet. She'd had experience as a figure skater, so she had some muscle and some endurance, but no training in self-defense. Nothing that could actually help her stand up to or run away from the brute she'd fallen in with.

Was she still with the same lowlife, or was Xavier just a middleman? Had he sold her to someone else the minute he got her away from home? Or was he with her now, holding her captive, watching his three-thousand-dollar investment mature?

Three thousand dollars. For a girl. Becky should have seen through the sham from the start. Drisklay had been married for over half his life, and in all that time hadn't spent even close to that much on gifts for his wife.

Three thousand dollars. But as far as traffickers like Xavier were concerned, it was simple economics. A human being was even more lucrative to sell than drugs or weapons because the same commodity could bring in money from dozens, hundreds, sometimes even thousands of customers.

Disgusting. The world was a sick and twisted place, but Drisklay knew better than to only blame men like Xavier. What about all the nameless johns — the attorneys, the teachers, the husbands, the pastors, the politicians — who bought girls like Becky day in and day out? It was simple supply and demand. And in a world where illicit photographs could be bought at the price of a fast-enough internet connection, was there any surprise that the demand for girls like Becky always outweighed the supply?

Xavier's job would always be lucrative.

Girls like Becky would always be exploited.

And why in the world was his wife taking so long in that stupid bathroom? Was she passing a kidney stone in there? He knew he'd regret coming to Las Vegas. What really griped him was how pouty Caroline got. Like when he told her he'd been on the phone with Alexi instead of at one of those stupid breakout sessions. And what good were these group meetings anyway? Chances for a bunch of grown men to sit around and cry because they weren't being the husbands their wives wanted them to be.

What had Caroline actually hoped to get out of this conference? What did she expect him to do? Jump on a plane back to Boston, grab her hand, stare her in the eyes and say, *Thanks dear, that was great, and now that we have the best marriage in the world, I'm ready to get back to work?*

That was the problem with events like these. Marriages whose problems could be patched up by listening to a couple hours' worth of lectures didn't need a conference in the first place. And marriages that actually were in trouble needed a whole lot more than a slideshow presentation and some overpriced meals.

Last summer, their marriage had been in trouble. Drisklay would be the first to admit it. He'd moved out, and neither of them expected that to change. But then he got into that accident last summer, and she was there to nurse him back to health. Things were better now. Most of that had to do with the fact that his wife stopped shoving Bible verses down his throat every blasted day of the week. Finally, he had the peace and quiet he'd always sought after in his own home.

Caroline still went to church, and sometimes she'd read her Bible at night before bed, but otherwise he had his old wife back. Either the excitement of her religious conversion was finally wearing off or she'd learned to tone it down whenever he was around. Whatever the case, he was glad he was no longer married to a woman whose life goal was to win his soul from hell and convert the rest of the planet alongside him.

There were enough freaks like that already.

He'd finished his steak and had to tell the waiter twice not to take his wife's salad away yet. He had no idea if she was done eating or not. What was taking her so long, anyway?

He'd been watching the entrance to the bathroom ever since Caroline went in. He hadn't seen anything suspicious, but what if someone he hadn't noticed entered before her? What if she'd been attacked?

No, other women had gone in and come back out. They would have seen or heard if there was a problem.

Which meant Caroline was ignoring him. Great. A night of silent treatment. But maybe that was all for the best. He had a lot of work to do. This case certainly had no intentions of solving itself, and time had ceased to be on his side months earlier.

Girls in Becky's situation could expect to survive four to seven years from the moment their life on the streets began.

The Linklater girl was most likely still alive, or had been a few weeks ago according to news from Alexi. But they still hadn't narrowed down her location. She was almost certainly out of the East Coast by now. Xavier had enough connections and street smarts to make sure to move her somewhere else. And unless Drisklay had a clue where he'd taken her, it was like hunting for one specific pair of cowboy boots in the entire state of Texas.

Still, until the case was solved or he got reassigned, Drisklay was going to keep working. He'd solved tougher mysteries in the past, relying on hunches and a gut instinct that almost never let him down. Except right now his gut was tired. And his strongest hunch was that Xavier's resources outmatched Drisklay's luck.

What he needed was a break. A single sighting. A geographic region. Somewhere he could narrow his focus.

He'd solved tougher cases before.

But never involving someone so young.

And never in time to save the victim's life.

CHAPTER 24

It was stupid for her to be crying. What had that speaker said in her session just today? *Men aren't wired to be as emotionally open as women are. Be patient with your husband if he comes across as cold or unfeeling. It might just be his personality, not any sign that he's angry with you or emotionally unhealthy.*

Caroline was pretty sure that she could Google the phrase *emotionally unhealthy* and spot a picture of Calvin, but she tried to remember what the speaker taught. She just had to be patient. Calvin might never be the confidant she wanted or needed him to be. That was why she had friends like Sandy, her pastor's wife. Friends she could pour her heart out to.

And that was why she had the Lord.

But still, couldn't Calvin see what he was doing to their marriage? Didn't he know that the longer he worked on cases like these, the more cynical he got? And he'd start talking to Caroline like he did tonight, as if she were one of the men at the station, used to thinking about victims in such a detached way.

But she couldn't.

Becky Linklater had been a student at Caroline's school. And now she was missing, her family was completely devastated, and all Calvin could talk about was profit. And on the night they were supposed to be going out on a nice, formal date.

She stared at her dress, despising the hot, clingy material that left no room to breathe or to stretch. Hating the fact that she'd spent so much energy earlier on her makeup only to have it smudged and smeared away by tears.

Not that Calvin noticed what she looked like. She could have been wearing leggings and an old t-shirt for all he cared. As long as he got his slab of meat, he was happy. Even better if he could eat it in peace without having to try to keep up anything even remotely resembling a meaningful conversation.

She was sick of it. Last summer, their marriage was at its lowest. He'd decided to move out, and she was prepared to count her losses. She really was. Calvin hadn't acted like a husband in years. And instead of trying to change him, she was going to accept the inevitable. Let him walk out of her life, no matter how painful it might be in the short term.

But she loved him. And by some inexplicable miracle, they continued to try to patch things up, in spite of all of Calvin's insults. His sulking attitude. His biting remarks about church. Now she didn't even mention it. Just drove herself to services every Sunday and came home without bothering to apologize or make excuses for where she'd been.

Calvin would never change. Tonight was a perfect reminder. If talking about a junior-high victim in such crude terms was his idea of romantic dinner conversation, was there any hope for her marriage at all?

But maybe it wasn't about the romance. Maybe it was more about being faithful. And if that was the case, she just had to grit her teeth, tell herself this was the man God had in her life for a reason, and do what she could to love him and pray for him. Calvin certainly couldn't stop her from that, hard as he might try.

It wasn't nearly as exciting as traveling the globe as a missionary or leading a whole classroom full of Sunday school kids to salvation, but at least for right now, it seemed like that was what God was calling her to do.

She wrote Sandy a quick text. *Can you pray for me? Had a difficult night.* Then she realized how late it was. Sandy was probably in bed by now. Caroline deleted her words without sending the message and took a deep breath.

She could do this.

She would do this.

Everything was going to be okay.

She glanced at herself quickly in the mirror. Maybe it was for the best that her husband never gave her more than a passing glance. Why hadn't she thought to get that nice waiter to snap a picture of her and Calvin when she actually looked presentable?

Well, it couldn't be helped now. She smoothed out her hair, patted a splash of cold water onto her face, and headed toward the exit.

She stopped when she heard a noise coming from one of the stalls.

Someone sniffing. Quiet, stifled sobs.

She glanced around. Nobody else was in here. She paused, waiting. The voice sounded young. Her heart beat faster.

"Hello?" She took a step toward the door of the stall. "Everything okay?" She glanced down at a pair of heels.

The crying stopped. The sniffing too. Caroline waited. "You all right?" she asked.

"Yeah." Whoever was on the other side of the door let out a little giggle. A very girlish giggle. "Just have some allergies. You know."

The girl cleared her throat, opened the door, and there she was.

She was dressed like she was heading to a club. Her face was covered in makeup, and her bangs had been teased like she was trying to bring eighties hair back into style.

But Caroline would know that head of blonde curls anywhere.

"Becky?" Caroline gasped. "What are you doing here?"

CHAPTER 25

Last summer

I am so mad right now. Like, I'm literally fuming. It's Friday, and I've been telling Xavier all week that once pay day comes around, I can find him some cash to help carry him over until his cousin gets his stupid act together and comes up with that money. All fine and good, and even though he's been super stressed, Xavier's still calling me every day. It's totally not the same as getting together, and I'm, like, physically hurting because I miss him so much, but I've just kept telling myself to make it until Friday and then everything will be fine.

So Mom came home after work today. I told her I'm bored and asked for twenty bucks to get a CharlieCard for the T. No big deal, right? Except she says that she can't because she's got the car insurance bill this week and she forgot to budget for it earlier. Okay, so just because she's irresponsible with her money, that means I don't get to go anywhere? What's up with that?

I haven't even told Xavier either, because I know he's been counting on me getting that CharlieCard so we can see each other. I even convinced him that I can walk the stupid three minutes to the bus stop and meet him at his place, and the plan was I'd just give him my CharlieCard after that so from then on he could come see me and not the other way around.

And we waited five stupid days for this stupid plan to work, and now Mom's all mad at me because I'm ungrateful and I'm spoiled and I have no idea how hard she works, blah, blah, blah. I'm so sick of it because all she does is complain. She complains about Dad never paying his bills, but then she can't even hand over a twenty so I can stop being a prisoner in my very own house? Doesn't she see how hypocritical she's being?

I'm starting to see why Dad left her, to be totally honest, because when she gets like this, she's super toxic. Like, I can't even be in the same room as her without starting to feel this rage boiling up inside me. I'm seriously wondering if I should ask Dad if I can live with him and Candy this summer. I really am. At least I'd have money to take the T.

Xavier just texted me, like, five or ten minutes ago and

wanted to make sure I got the cash from Mom, and he wants me to find a way to come over tonight or tomorrow at the latest. So now I've got the job of telling my boyfriend who I love more than anything that I can't see him this weekend either, because Mom is so stinking unreasonable, and she grounded me for not "being more thankful for everything." Blah, blah, blah. Can you imagine a more impossible woman?

I've already texted my dad to ask if I can spend the weekend at his place because he lives even closer to Xavier, and he wouldn't mind if I went out. Plus he's not totally uptight with his money.

Not like another parent I know.

Ugh. I'm so mad right now. Sometimes I wonder if I'm adopted. Seriously. I'd almost be relieved if I found out she wasn't my real mom. At least that would explain why she's absolutely impossible to get along with.

I just hope Xavier isn't too disappointed or angry when I tell him. Because he's literally worrying himself sick. He's got a sore throat and a stuffy nose, and he says he hasn't slept through the night in, like, a week. And I've basically wasted a week of my life too (thanks, Mom), but there's no way I'm waiting for her next paycheck just so I can ask for money for the stupid T. I'll grab her credit card and order one online if

I have to. Or tell Dad I need some money to buy books for my summer reading list. Maybe that's what I'll do.

I'll figure something out, Xavier, I promise. Because if I can't be with you, I'm going to end up sick too. I actually hurt thinking about how long it's been since we've been together. I'm so upset right now I'm about to cry. I mean it.

But I know life doesn't always have to be this hard, and I know one day God will work everything out for good, just like Woong's dad preached about last Sunday. It's all going to be okay. I just have to hold onto hope, and I have to pray that God will allow us to come together again.

Because I love you so much. And my life isn't going to be complete until you're back in it.

CHAPTER 26

Ugh, I still can't believe how immature Mom's acting. She's all like "If you can't appreciate the fact that I've got a full-time job and bills to pay, then you can earn your own money to take the bus."

So now, not only am I grounded but Mom's saying I don't get any spending money this summer except for what I'll earn watching old Mrs. What's-Her-Face's grouchy little girl. I have never seen a preschooler act so spoiled. I'll literally go insane if I have to babysit her all summer long.

And Xavier's mad at me and not answering my texts because I told him that by Friday I'd have some money for him, and now it's already Monday, and guess what? No money. Mom took all the cash out from all her usual places too. It's like she doesn't even trust me.

I'm dying of boredom here, and I would have told my dad on the weekend that I want to live with him and Candy over the summer, but he's out of town on some fancy cruise or something. Because that makes total sense. You can afford to take your wife on cruise, and in the meantime your daughter's grounded because she asked for twenty bucks so she could stop being a prisoner in her own home.

He's so entitled, it's disgusting.

And Megan's at that stupid horse camp. (I mean, seriously, are we back in elementary school?) And Carly's still not talking to me, so what am I supposed to do? I can't even text at night anymore because Mom threatened to take away my cell phone. I told her if she did that I'd run away and never speak to her again, and she was all like, "Fine with me. Maybe after a few weeks on your own you'd realize just how good you have it here."

Right. Because being trapped on house arrest is all fun and games. I mean, I'm so lucky. I should be ashamed for even thinking about asking to see the man I love at least once before the summer's over.

I'm just so sick of the drama. First it's Carly, then Mom … I wish Miss Sandy wasn't so uptight with Woong because he's literally, like, the only one of my friends I can text right now. But he's only allowed to check his messages after all his chores are done. Even though he's not homeschooled anymore, he basically has homework to do all summer long. Like, his mom seriously gives him workbooks and math assignments to do over the summer break. Can you believe it?

I don't know how people are supposed to live like this. Mom's treating me like I'm this little kid. Public service announcement: I'm not even in middle school anymore (thank God). I can guarantee you that if I went over and talked to Grandma, she'd tell me that Mom took the T by herself when she was my age. (If they even had the T back then.) But Grandma's at the nursing home now, and we hardly even see her anymore, so the whole thing is totally ridiculous. I have no clue how I'm going to survive today, let alone an entire summer like this.

So yeah, if anyone's reading this and you come home and my head's exploded and I'm on the floor bleeding to death, just know it was the boredom that killed me. I seriously hope it makes you happy, and I hope that twenty spare dollars you saved keeping me here a prisoner went an awful long way, because you're going to need it for therapy once you realize you killed your own flesh and blood by keeping her trapped in her own home.

CHAPTER 27

It's literally the worst thing in the world that could ever happen to me. I feel like I'm living in one of those horror novels where everything just gets worse and worse and worse and worse until finally the guy gets killed and everyone screams, and it's horrible and ugly and gross, then it's over.

That's, like, literally my life right now.

So what would you say if I told you that Mom took my phone? Notice I didn't say *her* phone. She doesn't even pay for the stupid thing. Dad does. But she said that as long as I'm in her house, she can take my stuff whenever she wants to.

Well, we'll just wait and see about that because Dad got me the phone so I could be in touch with him. And seriously, isn't this how, like, dictators start? They burn all the books and keep people from assembling and ban free speech. See, I really was paying attention when we studied the Constitution last year. I know my rights.

And I know you can't just take someone else's cell phone away from them because you claim they're acting spoiled and ungrateful.

Mom and I got into another fight this morning (big surprise there, right?) because I told her I literally can't go another week stuck in this house with no way to get around. And she was all like, doesn't Carly's brother have a car? Maybe he can pick you up. As if I even want to talk to Carly anymore.

Ugh.

Of course the laptop isn't working either, and even if it was that wouldn't do much good because Mom's so cheap the only wireless I get comes from my phone, and guess what?

She stole that from me.

It's not natural for your own mother to be so unreasonable. And guess what? She's at work all day today. With my phone.

I swear it's got to be illegal. I'd seriously call my senator or something, but hey, wouldn't you know? You've got to have a phone to do that.

I still can't believe I'm related to that woman.

It's only nine in the morning, and I'm already going out of my head. Literally out of my head. I asked Mom what I'm supposed to do all day and she was all like, "Read a book."

Seriously?

Does she even remember what it's like to be my age?

No, because it was forever ago in the dark ages, and cell phones weren't invented yet, so of course she doesn't understand. But she should. I mean, isn't it negligent to leave me here with no connection to the outside world? Like, what if someone broke into the house or there was a fire? How would I call 911? As soon as I get my phone back, I'm going to Google it because there's got to be some law about this, and I'm not even joking.

I can't stand that woman.

I mean, she could be a pain when Dad was around, but now that he's taken off on us, it's so much worse. Like, she doesn't even function. We don't talk anymore. About anything. As soon as Dad's home I'm calling him up and asking to stay with him for the rest of the summer. But wait. You need a *phone* to call your dad.

Someone kill me now. Seriously.

It's got to get better than this. Someone please tell me it's going to get better than this.

I mean, one day I'll be able to drive. That's going to change everything. If I had my license, I'd be out of here every day, and Xavier and I could go anywhere we wanted.

Just a few more years.

That's the problem with being so mature for my age. You're ready to handle way more responsibility except you're the only person in the world who knows it.

The worst part is I didn't get to tell Xavier why I can't talk with him today, so I know he's going to be freaking out.

Seriously, if I knew the summer was going to turn out this way, I would have gone to summer school or something. Anything would be better than this.

A prisoner in my own house. I can't believe it.

One thing I do know. When I have a daughter, I'm never taking her phone away. I'm going to respect her property and her rights and her privacy too. Now I've got nothing to do except for this entire list of chores Mom left for me ...

I really hope Xavier gets his car up and running soon.

I literally don't know how I'm going to stand this anymore.

CHAPTER 28

Well, we're into the second week of summer, and I guess things are starting to look up. I'm staying with Dad and Candy for now. Which basically means I've got the place to myself while they're at work.

Dad bought me a CharlieCard, so Xavier's been over every single day this week, and the other good news is he's getting his car fixed this weekend. See, I knew things would work themselves out in the end. They always do.

Candy has been pretty cool. She comes home about half an hour before Dad does, and the two of us cook dinner together. Or sometimes she drives me with her to choose some take-out. You have no idea how nice it is to be with people who eat real food for a change. No more canned food dumped into a microwave bowl and calling that dinner.

Last night we ate pad tai. When Candy comes home this evening, she's going to bring a premade crust so we can bake our own pizzas. I've got my phone back now too. Dad made sure of that. So yeah, all in all I'd say things are pretty good.

Way better than living at Mom's, that's for sure.

And the love of my life is getting his car fixed. Yay!

You know, this is a good example of how I just need to remind myself to stay positive. Last week was basically awful, but it's only the really good things that last forever. The rest of the stuff doesn't matter. What matters is that Xavier and I are able to spend each and every day together again. Plus I've got my phone, so even if we're apart, we can talk whenever we want to, and it's finally turning into the kind of summer the two of us dreamed of.

Just me and Xavier. It's funny. I haven't even seen Carly or Megan, and we hardly text anymore either. It's sad in a way because we used to be so close, but I'm way more mature than they are now, and when I do get free time to hang out with someone, I want it to be with Xavier. (Obviously.)

His cousin finally paid off that debt, so Xavier's taken me shopping like almost every day. You should see some of the presents he's gotten for me. Not the real cheap stuff either. I'm talking like real fancy things. A woman at one of the jewelry stores actually asked if we were getting engaged. Can you believe it? I laughed and was about to tell her how old I am, but Xavier put his arm around me and said, "That's the next step."

Holy cupcakes, you should have seen me blush. I mean,

I'm assuming that I blushed because I could feel how hot my face was, and my knees literally wanted to collapse under me right there. I swear he is the most romantic, sweet, and lovable person I've ever met in my entire life.

And he's all mine!

I still can't believe it. I mean, not many guys his age would pay attention to someone who's just getting ready to start their first year of high school. I still don't know how it happened really. It was just one day I was waiting for the bus, and the next day so was he, and then he's offering me rides home ... and now he's telling little old ladies at the jewelry store that we're one step away from being engaged.

I can't even!

Sometimes I get worried that I'm dreaming. That I'm making this all up because it's way too good to be true. Literally. I'd do that thing where you pinch yourself (except I never really understood that, because what if you just dream that your pinch hurts, right?). Anyway, whenever I get worried that I've made up everything because I'm living in this perfect fantasy world, all I have to do is look at my texts or all the gorgeous presents he's given me, and then I know.

This isn't a dream.

This is real life. This is real love.

And it's happening to me.

Me! Can you believe it? I mean, I never did anything in particular to deserve to be so blessed, but I guess it just goes to show that if you try hard to do the best you can with what you're given, and if you do your best to be a decent human being, good things come your way.

And if you're really lucky like in my case, *great* things come your way!

I've got to go now because Xavier's just texted, and he's heading over to pick me up. He has some friends he wants me to meet. I know I shouldn't be this nervous, but I totally am. I asked him what I should wear and told him I wanted to make a good impression on them, and he is so sweet. He said that if it's that important to me, he'll swing by this place he knows on the way to his friend's and he'll help me pick out something he's sure they'll like.

I mean, does it literally get any better than this?

You know how I said that every once in a while this feels too good to be true, and every once in a while I have to ask myself if there's a chance I'm just dreaming?

Well, all I know is that I am desperately, pathetically, and undeniably happy. And I'm undeniably in love. So even if this is a dream, I don't want to wake up.

Ever.

CHAPTER 29

So I met with Xavier and some of his friends today. It was ... well, it was all right. Not exactly like I was expecting. Maybe one of those things that I still have to think on for a little bit. But I got some cool pictures out of it. His friend's a Photoshop genius. And when I say genius, I mean that literally. So yeah, that part was super cool.

The rest, like I said, I just need a little more time to sort it all out. It's fine. Just not exactly what I was expecting.

But hey, that's what makes life interesting, right?

Of course right.

So anyway, now Xavier and I are even closer to being a real-life couple. I mean, we've been a couple for a while, but I have to admit it did feel kind of weird not hanging around with the same group. So now I know some of his friends. They're pretty cool.

Mostly, at least.

There was one guy there who gave me the creeps. I sort

of have this thing where I can tell if someone's legit or not. Like Carly's brother. Megan thinks he's absolutely amazing and wonderful, and she basically worships him, but every time I'm near him I can tell he's this major creep.

That's the same feeling I got with one of Xavier's friends, but the rest were all good. So that's not too bad. I mean, every group's got to have one bad egg or bad apple or whatever that cliché is, right?

I think if I'm worried about anything it's that Xavier is upset with me about something. He was just kind of quiet when he was driving me back to my dad's (did I mention he's got his car fixed now? Hooray!). I don't know. Maybe it's that we're used to only being together, just him and me, you know? But in the real world, couples can't just stay together with nobody on the outside ever coming into their space. So this is probably a good first step for us, hanging out with a group instead of just at my dad's place when nobody else is home.

I'll have to think some more and see if there was something I did that made him mad. Like I said, the afternoon didn't go exactly like I thought it would, but that's probably my fault. I mean, you can't really blame me because look at my friends. They're totally immature (sorry Megs and Carly!), and Xavier's friends are all in their twenties. So, you know, I just need to learn how to get along with a more mature crowd. It'll be good for me.

And in the meantime, I have to try not to worry so much about making Xavier angry. I mean, sometimes I get nervous around him, and that's just stupid. He's the love of my life.

He's like this big, giant teddy bear, and he's so sweet and he's so romantic and he gives me so many amazing presents, and I need to focus on things like that.

Not worry about what his friends thought of me.

So yeah. That was my day. Meeting some new people. Making some new memories.

And of course, being with the man I love.

You don't get much more perfect than that.

CHAPTER 30

Hey, just me again. Things are going all right, I guess. I say just all right because I've been hanging out with Xavier every day (which I LOVE), but we're spending all of our time with his friends now. The ones I met last week. And well, I guess I'm just being babyish about it all, but I really miss when it was just the two of us. I really wish we could go back to that.

Sigh. I'm probably just being immature and melodramatic, but it doesn't feel the same anymore. I mean, he's still my favorite person in the entire world, and I feel so thankful and blessed to have him in my life. But sometimes I wish we didn't have to spend so much time with his friends.

It's not that they're bad people. But they aren't Xavier. And when we're with them … I probably shouldn't say it. I know I sound like I'm whining and totally clinging and like some big attention hog, but when we're with them, I just don't feel like he pays that much attention to me. Which is funny in a way because he's always, like, super careful to tell me how I should dress before we get together. One of his friends is a photographer. I think I already mentioned that, but he's been taking a lot of pictures of me. They turned out really nice. But still ... nice as it is to get all the fancy clothes and everything else that comes with it, I kind of wish it were just Xavier and me again

There's some other stuff too. I probably shouldn't go into it. Like it's not a super huge deal or anything like that (nothing really bad, I should say). Just kind of threw me off. But only a little. It's probably because I haven't spent much time with guys Xavier's age. Sometimes they're just like that. And I need to remember what Mom always said, that boys mature a lot slower than girls do, but honestly, I thought by the time guys hit twenty they would have caught up. Might have been wrong.

Lesson learned.

So anyway, I just got back to Dad and Candy's. Xavier's friend, the one who's a photographer, said he's going to make me an Instasnap account. It's this new site where you can post pictures like that and sometimes you even get paid if you get enough clicks. So we agreed on a fifty-fifty split. He showed me this chart, and I guess there are some girls who aren't any older than me making, like, five hundred dollars or more. That's not even a month or a week or anything, that's for every single picture they post.

So I'm liking that side of things, and I figure it's probably totally worth it if it eventually means Xavier and I get to spend more time together. Because even though he got his car fixed, would you believe that cousin of his owes him a whole bunch more money? So I told Xavier to take my share from the Instasnap payment (I have no idea what you call that, royalties maybe?). I figure it's the least I can do with everything he's spending to buy me so many pretty things for these photo shoots, and honestly, there's not a whole lot I need money for right now anyway. That's what's so nice about spending the days at my dad's house.

Speaking of Dad, I better go because he and Candy will be getting home any time and I need to change. They think I'm spending my days over at Megan's, so it'd look a little suspicious if I got back wearing a new outfit every single day. Haha. Oh, and one more piece of good news. Candy's working late for the rest of the week, and Dad's going out of town for a few days, so that means even more time with me and Xavier. I'm going to ask him if he wants to do something just the two of us for a change.

Wish me luck!

CHAPTER 31

"I'm just so embarrassed." Margot pressed her fingers against her temples while her friend sipped her cup of tea.

"Don't feel bad," Sandy said. "I'm sure everyone involved understands."

That was the problem right there. They understood all too well. When Margot received Sandy's invitation to meet during her lunch break, she didn't want to accept. She'd be working late tonight. She hardly had time to take an hour off for lunch to begin with. Besides, Margo knew that if she got together with Sandy, she'd pour out her heart. Like always. But there were certain things she didn't want her pastor's wife to know. Like the fact that she'd been drunk last night. That not only had she called her ex-husband and harassed him, she'd also called the police station to tell them that Jack's new wife was involved in her daughter's disappearance.

The thought might be laughable if it weren't so humiliating.

"I sent Candy an email to apologize." Margot's words were mostly true. In fact, she had written Candy an email, but it was now at the bottom of her trash bin. Still, she felt better knowing that Sandy thought she'd done the right thing.

"I really don't know what got into me." She glanced up to see if Sandy believed her.

In reality, the two women were an unlikely pair as far as friendships went. Sandy was a conservative Christian married to the pastor of one of the largest churches in the Cambridge area. She and her husband were ridiculously and sickeningly in love and had raised dozens of children, including foster children and adoptees. Sandy was almost old enough to be Margot's mother, but her son Woong was in the same grade as Becky, and the two had been best friends for years.

"How's Woong doing?" Margot asked, hoping to move the conversation away from last night's faux pas.

Sandy smiled, but her eyes remained soft. Sad. As if she knew it would be inappropriate to show too much happiness when mentioning her child. The one who was home.

The one who was safe.

"He's doing all right. We're facing a little bit of spring fever, I think, having difficulties focusing on his assignments. It's so hard to believe the school year will be ending soon, but I dare say Woong's already decided he's done with his studies."

Margot wondered when, if ever, she could have a conversation that didn't remind her of all the months she'd spent without Becky. Margot and Sandy should be talking right now about the spring dance. Or fundraiser ideas for the booster club. Or how cute it would be when Becky was finally mature enough to realize that Woong had been head over heels in love with her since the moment they met.

Margot gave Sandy a smile. "That's got to be hard." She tried to sound sincere but wasn't sure if she succeeded or not.

Sandy reached out across the table and took her hand. "And what about you now? Any word on Becky's case?"

It was strange, the fact that Sandy used Becky's name. Everyone at the doctor's office stopped speaking it the day Margot returned to work. They'd ask things like *How's the investigation* or *Any word from that detective?* But they never spoke her daughter's name.

Not a single one of them.

Margot let out her breath. "Nothing new. The detective's out of the office. Taking a few vacation days, I think."

Sandy nodded as if she'd already known about Detective Drisklay's personal schedule.

Margot strained to fill the awkward silence. "I talked with his partner this morning. I mean, to let him know I wasn't thinking clearly last night when I accused ..." She let her voice trail off.

Sandy gave her hand a reassuring squeeze before letting it go. Funny, it had probably only been thirty seconds start to finish, but that was the longest physical contact Margot had with anyone in weeks.

"Do you and Jack still talk much?" Sandy asked.

Margot stared off past her friend's shoulder. "Well, after last night, I think I'll just lay low for a little."

Sandy didn't reply.

Margot cleared her throat, hating herself. She always felt guilty after getting together with Sandy, like their discussion could do nothing but make her friend as depressed as she was. But instead of alleviating her own sadness, it left Margot feeling just as heavy-hearted as before, maybe even more so because of the guilt she felt at dragging Sandy down.

"How are things at your husband's church?" she asked.

Sandy's eyes lit up. "Oh, things are going splendidly, praise the Lord. I told you about that issue he was having with that one particular elder who wanted him to resign. It was a ridiculous matter to begin with, but for a totally unrelated reason that man ended up moving to the West Coast. I'm sure it was the Lord who worked that out for us. We're going through a very peaceful time, which I've got to admit is a very welcome change for us."

Margot had never realized until she and Sandy started getting together that a church could be riddled with just as much politicking and backstabbing as any other job.

"I'm glad things are going better for you," she said honestly.

"Thank you." Sandy beamed again. "And I know you're tired by the time Sundays roll around, but of course you're more than welcome to join us for services."

Margot tried not to let her expression change. Tried to maintain her smile. It was like that one woman on the PTA who always found a way to mention the supplements she sold for a living. Sandy wasn't nearly that pushy, but each time she asked Margot to go to church, Margot felt more ashamed for not going.

Well, at least she had a decent excuse.

"I'll think about it. But it's still hard."

Becky and Woong had gone to church together for over a year before the disappearance. Margot loved that her daughter was receiving some kind of moral training, and she also appreciated one day to sleep in completely guilt-free. Every once in a while she'd join them, but she hadn't set foot in a church since Becky's disappearance. If she tried to now, she might turn into a crying, hysterical mess.

"I understand." Sandy's eyes were kind, her embrace

warm when the two women finally stood up to leave.

"Tell Woong hi for me," Margot said, forcing the words past the lump in her throat.

"I sure will." Sandy held onto her hand, giving it one last squeeze before reaching out for another hug. "I'm praying for you," she whispered.

Margot had a hard time finding words to express her thanks. She didn't necessarily believe everything Sandy and her husband taught at that church of theirs, but she did believe in God and figured that if he'd listen to anyone's prayers, it would be theirs. Since Margot had no idea how to pray on her own (not as if that kept her from trying), she was glad to hear that someone with a more direct line to God's ear was picking up the slack for her.

Don't pray for me. Pray for my little girl, she wanted to say, but Sandy was already gone.

CHAPTER 32

It was dark when Margot got off work that night. As she headed home, she promised herself that one day soon she'd tell Dr. Harris she just couldn't do any more overtime. Her body couldn't handle it, and the stress was going to give her a heart attack.

But what if she needed the money? What if Becky's kidnapper wrote and demanded ransom? What if Detective Drisklay decided the case had grown cold and gave up and Margot had no choice but to hire a private investigator?

What if ... what if ... what if ...?

And so she kept on working extra hours, earning money she had no idea what to do with. Set up a reward? Without a daughter to care for, without anyone else in her life, Margot wound up with money left over at the end of each month. For once since the divorce, she didn't have to pinch pennies. She still did, mostly because there was nothing she had the heart to buy, not while her Becky was still missing.

The real mystery was how a hundred-pound girl could

go through eight hundred dollars of groceries and spending money a month.

It didn't add up.

Sure, Becky liked to shop, but a lot of her clothes she bought on her own with the money she earned from her babysitting jobs. She needed money to get around town, but that was only an extra twenty here and there.

An extra twenty. Could this whole thing have been prevented if that stupid car insurance hadn't overdrafted Margot's account? Who raises prices like that without even giving warning? Of course, that had to happen the same week her mortgage payment was due *and* the day her daughter decided to throw herself the most melodramatic pity party in the history of teenage girls. All because she couldn't buy a CharlieCard. Of course, Becky had no idea that her mom was parking two blocks away from work and cruising her way through stop signs because the gas tank was dropping dangerously low and she still had to get herself to work.

So a girl has to stay home for a week or two out of the summer. Worse things have happened.

But Becky wouldn't hear of it.

"I'm gonna go live with Dad. I can't believe how selfish you are …"

And Margot had let the stress build up, taken it out on her daughter. It would have taken all of two minutes to explain the financial situation a little more clearly. Becky was a drama queen, but she could do basic arithmetic. If the money wasn't there, the money just wasn't there.

Margot should have explained. Should have been more patient. Should have taken just one extra shift and then she wouldn't have overdrafted. She would have been able to make a withdrawal from the ATM on her way home from work, meaning she could have given Becky money to take the T, and her daughter would have never had reason to move in with her dad.

It was under Jack's roof that pedophile had free reign to groom and brainwash her daughter. And just two weeks after Becky moved under his roof, she was gone.

It was Jack's fault Becky was missing.

Jack's fault, and Margot's stupid overdrafted account. That's what it all came down to. Another twenty dollars might have saved her daughter's life. What was twenty dollars? Two trips out together to get ice cream cones. Four fancy coffees.

Twenty dollars. If Becky came home now, Margot would shower her in twenties. After she finished hugging her, apologizing to her, and crying sweet tears of release.

That was what Margot would do if Becky came home.

If.

Such a small word, but so important.

If Becky came home.

Last summer, her thoughts had always been *when* Becky came home.

When had that one little conjunction changed?

It was perhaps one of the ugliest words in the English language.

If.

Margot pulled into the driveway. The dark driveway that led to a dark house where no smiling daughter waited to greet her. If Becky were home, what would they do? Go out to dinner, maybe? Stay in and watch a movie?

If Becky were home ...

She froze when she got out of the car. Was that a noise?

Just her imagination.

There was nothing here.

She stepped up to the porch.

There it was again.

She turned around. "Hello?"

Why was her heart racing so fast? Had she gotten used to coming home earlier and was scared of being outside alone in the dark? She was acting like she was five years old.

Time to go home. Go home and pour herself a nice drink. Just as long as she didn't go overboard on the vodka this time. She'd learned her lesson well enough last night.

She unlocked her house, turned on her porch light, and glanced around. Just like she'd known, nobody was there.

The thought should bring her a sense of relief.

But instead it just reminded her of the fact that she was terribly, tragically alone, and her daughter may as well have been light years away.

CHAPTER 33

Margot had just poured her second glass of wine when she jumped. The door. Someone was knocking on her door. *Becky.*

She ran to the entryway, stared out the peephole. *Like a trained dog*, she thought to herself. A trained dog rushing to greet his owner, except he doesn't realize that his owner's never coming home.

It wasn't Becky.

Or anybody else Margot was happy to see.

She held open the door, and her ex-husband's new wife stepped inside.

"Hello, Candy." Margot crossed her arms, trying to convince herself she was ready for this confrontation. The truth was, she wasn't.

"Hi." Candy shifted from one foot to the other. Good. Let the homewrecker feel a hint of the discomfort Margot had felt ever since she found out about the affair.

Margot glanced toward the porch before shutting the

front door. "You here alone?"

Candy nodded. "Yeah. Jack doesn't know I'm here." She glanced sideways at her. "I'd like to keep it that way."

Margot felt her curiosity pique. Good thing she'd had a few minutes to relax with that wine.

"Well, come in," she told Candy. "No use standing here in the entryway. Excuse the mess." Margot picked up a discarded bathrobe, rolled it into a wad, and flung it down the hall. She stood in front of the kitchen, wondering if she'd offer Candy a drink or not. Probably not. Unless it looked like this was going to take long.

Which she seriously hoped it wouldn't.

"What can I do for you?" Margot crossed her arms, trying to adopt the right pose. How are you supposed to appear when the woman who stole away your husband steps into your house unannounced? Especially when said woman is half your age and twice your bra size?

Candy took a step forward, a pleading look in her eye. "Can we sit down?" She shot a glance at the couch, still covered in laundry and junk mail.

Margot sighed. "Sure."

Candy let out a little squeak of surprise as the cushions gave way beneath her. Margot had forgotten to warn her how far the couch could sink down. Then again, Jack had sneaked

Candy into this home dozens of times before Margot finally wised up to his infidelity. Most likely, the woman had plenty of opportunities to get accustomed to this particular seat.

Margot remained standing by the kitchen.

"It's about Jack," Candy stammered.

Margot raised an eyebrow. "Yeah?"

Candy wiggled the ring on her right hand, staring as if mesmerized by the gaudy diamond. "There've been some things going on. Strange things." She glanced up quickly and then lowered her eyes again. Twisting her ring, she spoke into her lap. "At first I thought there might be another woman." Her voice was tentative. So full of uncertainly.

Margot's initial inclination was to laugh. Another woman? *Oh, you poor, pitiable baby.*

Her second inclination was to toss Candy out of her home. *Her* home. Not Jack's. Not anyone else's. She didn't have to invite this tramp into her house. Didn't have to sit here and listen while the woman who destroyed her marriage whined and complained.

What did Candy think? Who was the comedian who warned that when you marry your mistress, you create a vacancy? If Jack was willing to cheat on his wife of a decade and a half, didn't Candy worry that he might also cheat on his mistress of a few months?

It was almost comical.

Almost.

But not comical enough that Margot could get through this conversation without a little something to take the edge off. She reached for the bottle of wine and held it up. "Want a glass?"

A timid smile spread across Candy's face, accompanied by a look of both gratitude and relief. "Yes, please."

Margot was almost surprised she didn't call her *ma'am.*

Well, this could be interesting, she thought to herself as she poured out drinks for two.

CHAPTER 34

Margot's hands trembled as she clutched the phone against her ear. "Sandy, it's me."

"Margot? What's wrong? Are you okay?"

The minute she heard how tired Sandy sounded, Margot regretted dialing her number. She glanced at the clock. Why couldn't she have waited for a decent hour? "I'm so sorry to call. I know it's late." She stared at her mess of a living room, despising the fact that she was surrounded by such squalor but far too exhausted to try to do anything about it tonight.

"It's all right." Sandy's voice was full of gentle patience. "Did you hear any news of Becky?"

While Candy was there, Margot had done a magnificent job of holding herself together. A magnificent job until she heard her daughter's name. Half a second later, she was sobbing into her cell phone.

"You stay right there." Sandy's voice was laden with maternal authority. "Don't move a muscle. You just wait and I'll be there in half a second. I'm getting dressed right now."

Margot spent the next ten minutes telling herself she needed to get up and at least toss out the empty wine bottle before Sandy arrived, but when a quiet knock sounded at the door, she was still glued to her spot on the couch.

She jumped to her feet, dizzy and clumsy but finally upright. After tossing a lap quilt over a portion of the mess on the coffee table, she made her way to the door, although not nearly as quickly as she would have liked.

Sandy stepped in and immediately had Margot embraced in a strong hug that smelled like a strangely comforting combination of shampoo and tea.

"I would have brought you some brownies," Sandy began, stepping into the cluttered living room, "but Woong must have finished them off before bed. I declare, that boy has the metabolism of a racehorse to eat as much as he does and still be as tiny of a thing as he is. You know, I don't even think he's hit his real growth spurt yet. At one point the doctor wanted to check him for parasites, said that maybe he had a tapeworm or some nonsense like that. But look at me rambling on. Are you okay? You didn't sound too good on the phone. Did the detective call? Has he found anything out about Becky?"

Margot had promised herself that she wouldn't cry in front of Sandy. Not again. She gave her best attempt at a smile, apologized for the mess, and asked her friend to sit down.

She noticed Sandy eying the coffee table and stammered out an excuse. "I know your husband's a pastor and all," she began, her face flushed, "and I don't want you to think any less of me ..." She struggled to find the right words.

"What is it?" Sandy asked. "You know you can tell me anything." She leaned forward and took Margot's hand in hers.

"Well, I'm sure you must suspect it already, so before we have to make things awkward, I'll just come out and say it. I was drinking tonight. I was going to get the mess cleaned up before you got here, but ..." Here Margot's words gave out. What excuse did she have to offer? "Anyway, I just wanted to let you know. I'm not drunk. Not really. But I just didn't want you to think less of me."

Sandy hadn't let go of her hand. "That's fine. You know that you don't need to clean up for me. Not literally or figuratively, understand? I'm perfectly content just the way things are. I don't need to know about the drinking unless that's what you wanted to talk to me about. And if that's the case, I have a godly recovery program I can recommend. My daughter Blessing's been in and out of rehab in the past ..."

Margot shook her head before Sandy could dive into

sordid family details. "That's not it. I just wanted to get it out there at the beginning in case I make a fool of myself." She remembered the way she'd started blubbering on the phone, and her face grew hot again. "In case I make even more of a fool of myself, I guess I should say," she added with a half smile.

Sandy's eyes had locked onto Margot's and refused to let go. "Well, then, I want you to know that I've got all the time in the world. I told Carl I'll be out late, and he's going to wake Woong up to get ready for school in the morning. I'm ready to stay here and talk through the night if we need to. It's just you and me. I want you to know there's no rush. We can do whatever you'd like. We can talk about Becky or the PTA or whatever you like or not talk about anything. I just want to be here for you and be a good friend to you, because I think that's what Jesus wants us to do when those around us are hurting."

Margot bit her lip. If Sandy kept saying such kind things, it was going to make her start crying all over again.

Sandy gave her hand a squeeze. "Why don't you start by telling me about your evening? What's been going on since I saw you at lunch?"

"I didn't get out of the clinic until late," Margot began, finding it infinitely easier to talk about overtime and work schedules than what she really called Sandy to discuss. "When I came home, I thought I heard something on my porch when I was coming in. It was nothing," she added quickly when she saw the worried look overcome Sandy's soft features. "Just kind of set me on edge. Set me more on edge, I guess I should say." She tried to chuckle. "Well, I got home, and a few minutes later Candy came over. She's the one that …"

"Jack's wife, right?"

Margot couldn't look her friend in the eyes. "Yeah. That's her. She came over, and …"

"Was that awkward?" Sandy asked when Margot's voice trailed off.

"Oh, well, it was at first. Which probably explains why I offered her some wine, and …"

Sandy nodded in understanding.

"Anyway …" Margot didn't want to dwell on that facet of her evening. "Candy came over because she had some concerns. About Jack. She started by saying she thought he might be cheating on her." Any amusement Margot initially felt at the idea of her husband sleeping around had vanished when Candy gave her more details.

"And, well …" She hunted for the right words. "I asked her why she thought that about Jack, and her answers were um … Well, they were a little unsettling."

It was the least Margot could say.

"Upsetting about your husband?" Sandy pressed.

Margot winced at the words. "Yeah. About Jack."

Sandy was waiting. This was the perfect time for Margot to tell her everything, but she couldn't force her tongue and her brain to work in tandem. She wanted to deny it all. Pretend Candy was making it all up. But she'd brought evidence with her. Images Margot could never get out of her head.

She'd tried. After Candy left, Margot lost track of how much she'd had to drink before finally calling Sandy. Now, Margot wished she'd laid off the alcohol just a little. What she'd learned about her husband made her nauseated enough.

She stared at the floral pattern on the bottom hem of Sandy's skirt, unable to lift her eyes any further.

"Jack has a problem," she began. Man, she hoped she could get this next part out without crying. Or puking.

That would be nice.

"Jack has a problem." Repeating the words made them even more real in her mind. There was no way she could take them back now. No way to pretend them away.

No way to go but forward. She had to confess everything.

But could she? Could she actually form the words? Would speaking them out loud be the death of her? Would her heart stop beating the moment she brought the horrific truth to light?

"Talking to Candy got me really worried," she finally admitted. "And I know the detectives have looked at things from every angle, but they don't know about this. Not at all."

"Know what?" Sandy asked, her voice slow, her eyes gentle.

Margot sucked in her breath, certain that once she said the words, she'd be staring straight into the face of a truth that was too hideous to ignore. "I'm starting to wonder if he had something to do with Becky disappearing."

CHAPTER 35

Margot could only guess whether or not this conversation would be any easier to get through sober.

She was starting to doubt it.

After trying several times to fill Sandy in on the briefest details, she decided to back up and tell the story from the moment Candy walked into her home.

"She said she thought Jack was cheating on her." Margot didn't go on to explain how at first the confession brought a sense of smug relief. Poetic justice. If only the entire conversation could have been about something as commonplace as infidelity.

"She talked about Jack being on his computer all the time. Like real secret stuff." The thought of what she was about to say next made Margot feel even sicker than the alcohol did.

"Did he have a problem going to websites with objectionable material?" Sandy asked the question gently. Discreetly. As if she'd had this conversation with dozens of half-drunk women in the past.

Margot let out a little laugh. "I wish it were something as simple as a porn addiction. I really do." She would have never believed Candy if it weren't for the images she'd brought over, and now that she had seen them, she knew they'd be permanently branded into her memory.

Forever.

Branded.

She shook her head.

Sandy was still holding her hand. Giving it a slight reassuring squeeze. "You don't have to give me the details if you don't want to."

Margot let out another mirthless laugh. If only Sandy knew. This was no simple case of a man with a computer problem.

She could hardly get out the words. "It was her."

Sandy continued to squeeze her hand. "Who? His new wife?"

Margot squeezed her eyes shut as if she could blind herself to the photographs seared into her mind. "Becky." She nearly choked out her daughter's name. That single act had the effect of a dam breaking. "On his computer, he had pictures. Dozens of pictures. Of our little girl. Our Becky in all kinds of …"

Margot didn't care how many promises she'd made not to cry. It was either that or throw up on Sandy's lap.

Sandy sat rubbing her back. The confession was grotesque enough even Sandy had no idea what to say.

Grief and disgust crashed through Margot's body. A wail from the pit of her gut rose up to her throat. She tried to clench it shut. Silence its hideous cry.

She failed.

And Sandy just sat there massaging her shoulders.

Finally, her friend began to pray. "Father God, only you know what Margot's going through right now. But we ask you, Lord, to come and bring peace and healing. Bring peace and healing and comfort, Lord, because Margot is your beautiful creation and she is in so much need of your healing touch. We don't know what's going on in Jack's heart either, Lord, but we lift him up to you. Whatever his involvement might be, we pray that truth would be brought to light. And most of all, Father God, we ask that you bring Becky home. Wherever she is right now, Lord, show her how deeply she is loved. How special she is to you and to her mom and to everyone who knows her. Margot needs her daughter back, sweet Jesus, and my little Woong needs his best friend back, and this town needs to see Becky safely home where she belongs. We know this isn't too hard for you, Lord, but we also acknowledge that your ways are higher than ours, and so we pray not our will but yours be done. Because you are sovereign, and you are good, and you hold each one of us in the palm of your hand."

It was hard to remember when Sandy had let go of her hand to wrap her arms around Margot's neck, but by the time Sandy finished praying, her shoulder was drenched with Margot's snot and tears.

Margot wasn't sure if she was supposed to feel better or not. Sandy could talk to God all she wanted, but it didn't change the fact that her husband had dozens of images on his computer. Images of their daughter. Disgusting images grotesque enough they should land anyone who looked at a single one of them in jail.

Maybe it was the release that came after her cry. Maybe a burst of mental clarity fueled by adrenaline and disgust. Margot pulled away from her friend's embrace. "I need to call the detective." She stood up, feeling completely alert, and tried to remember where she'd left her phone. Maybe in the kitchen. She turned on the overhead light, imagining what kind of punishment could ever be severe enough to atone for Jack's sins.

"I'm gonna kill him," she muttered to herself. "I swear I'm gonna kill him." But not until after she called the cops.

Dragged Jack's name through the mud. Revealed to the entire world what a disgusting man he really was.

And this was the father of her sweet and innocent daughter?

She shoved dirty dishes away from her, sending a glass clattering to the floor. "Where is my stupid phone?" The question had been rhetorical of course, but Sandy called out from the living room, "This one, honey?"

Margot hurried back toward the couch, feeling sheepish. "Yeah. That one."

"You said you're calling the detective?"

Margot held Sandy's eye and nodded, never more certain about anything she was about to do. If Jack was lucky, the police would get to him before Margot did. Margot should have never let Candy out of her house. What if Candy went home and warned Jack away? He could be halfway to the airport by now. On his way out of the country with that laptop full of photographs …

She wouldn't let him. She snatched the phone out of Sandy's hand. Time to call Detective Drisklay. Where was his number? She knew she had it in here somewhere …

"Are you expecting company?" Sandy's voice was slightly on edge as Margot scanned her phone, searching for the detective's contact information.

Margot snapped up her head in time to see headlights shining on her living room wall. What time was it? Who would be coming here this late?

"Do you know who that might be?" Sandy asked, a hint of worry sounding so out of place in her usually calming voice.

Margot froze with her hand on the phone.

Footsteps up her porch.

Pounding on her front door.

"Margot, it's me, Jack. Let me in. We've got to talk."

Sandy's eyes locked with hers. Margot had never seen her friend frightened before.

"Margot!" More pounding.

"It's locked," Margot whispered, staring at the door. She dialed a 9. Just two more numbers and help would be on the way. Why was her hand frozen on the screen?

"Margot?"

She passed the phone to her friend. Sandy could handle situations like this. Sandy would know who to call. What to do. How to act.

A clicking sound from the doorway.

"Does Jack have a key to get in?" Sandy was whispering now, her finger poised over the phone just like Margot's had been. Why wasn't she calling the police?

The sound of a key.

The click of the lock sliding open.

And there was Jack. Becky's father. In her doorway.

Staring at her.

Had Sandy dialed 911? Margot's biggest regret was that she'd risked her friend's life just to have a good cry.

Jack was in her home, his face etched with determination. He took a step toward her. Margot stood frozen in place, wondering if he'd have the mercy to let Sandy leave first or if he was about to kill them both.

CHAPTER 36

Margot remembered the baseball bat she kept under her bed about two seconds after her ex-husband barged into her house.

"Margot, we have to talk."

She stepped instinctively between him and Sandy. Whatever was about to happen, he couldn't bring Sandy into it.

He held up his hand. "Listen, I know Candy was here. And it's not what you think."

More excuses? Margot was overcome with an overwhelming desire to throw up on Jack's polished work shoes.

He glanced behind her and addressed Sandy. "I'm sorry, could we have a minute?"

Sandy squared her shoulders and straightened out her flowered skirt. "Not until I know what's going on." Even though Sandy sounded bold, Margot thought she detected the slightest hint of a quiver in her usually calming voice.

Jack let out a chuckle. "Listen, ladies, I'm sorry if I scared you. But Candy said you'd been drinking and ..." He lowered his hands. "Listen, I just want to explain. Candy and I got into a fight and ..." He took a step forward. Margot kept her balance, ready to attack if he came too close.

"It's not what you think." Funny. Those were the exact same words he'd used when Margot confronted him about the steamy texts she'd found on his phone when they were still married. He was lying to her then, and he was sure as anything lying to her now.

"I don't want your excuses," she told him. Taking her cue from Sandy's display of courage, she straightened her body and met his gaze head on. "And I think you need to leave. Now."

He didn't move. "Not until you've heard what I have to say."

She balled her hands into fists. "I told you to leave. This isn't your house. Not anymore." The last word came out like a pitiful croak.

"There's a reason I had those pictures," he began. "I was trying to find her."

Margot narrowed her eyes. "You're disgusting. I can't believe I wasted my life with someone who ... with someone that ...."

Jack took one step closer. If he wanted to, he could reach out his arm and touch her cheek. "I was looking for Becky." His voice was pained. Pleading.

Margot's head was swimming. "And you found her?"

"Yes. I mean no. I mean, you don't understand. I hired a private detective."

A wave of dizziness swept over her. She reached out and held onto Sandy's shoulder to steady herself. "You did what?"

"Hired a private investigator. The police were putting all their resources into finding Becky. The trail was stone cold. So I hired someone. Top guy in the state. He did an image trace. He knows websites where girls are … he knows what he's looking for I guess is all I should say. And he came up with some of them. Sent them to me to confirm that they were really her."

Margot felt her body sinking into the couch as her legs decided they no longer wanted to support her weight. She shook her head. "How could you keep them? How could you hold onto them?"

"Because they're proof that our daughter is alive. The pictures were posted just a couple weeks ago. They're proof that Becky isn't some Jane Doe lying in a morgue."

Margot felt the bile rising up her throat and managed to

croak, "Water." Sandy sprang into action and raced to the kitchen.

A second later, Jack was sitting beside her, his leg brushed up against hers. "I know it's bad. I hate to think of what she's going through. But the pictures are new. It means we can find her. The PI I'm working with, he's looking at it from all angles. He's trying to nail down where the pictures were posted from. If that doesn't work, he's sent the images to this guy he knows who runs a database. It's got photos of hundreds of thousands of hotel room interiors. If he can find a match, we'll know where she is."

Margot was so stunned she didn't even realize that Sandy was holding out a glass of water until Jack took it in his hands and gently raised it to her lips.

She couldn't drink it without wincing in disgust. She didn't know which was worse. To fear her daughter could be dead or to know that she was alive and forced to endure … No. She couldn't even think about it.

She wouldn't.

"You should have told me." With shaking hands, she took the cup of water from her husband.

"I didn't want to upset you."

Upset? What was he thinking? "So you hired a private investigator without even telling me? Don't you think that's a piece of information I would have liked to know? And the fact that our daughter is alive? You knew she was ... You knew these pictures were ... I can't believe you kept this from me. Do the police even know about this?"

"Yes." Jack kept his voice calm, and Margot hated him even more for it. "I talked to the junior detective just this afternoon. I wasn't trying to keep anything from you, Margot. I just didn't know how to tell you."

She let out a mirthless guffaw. "Didn't know how to tell me? How about something like this? *Gee, Margot, I wanted to let you know there's a private investigator, the state's best, I've hired to help find our daughter. Have any information you might want to pass on to him? Feel like being involved in the case?* It's not that hard, is it? *Oh, and by the way, your daughter's* alive."

He lowered his eyes just for a second. "I didn't want to make things worse. You've been ..." He stopped himself, but Margot wasn't going to let him back down so easily.

"I've been what?" she snapped.

"Never mind." He was mumbling now. She hated it when he mumbled.

"I've been what?" she repeated, more demanding this time.

"This." He pointed at the wine bottles on the table, the

ones she thought she'd done a better job covering up before Sandy came over. "Calling me drunk in the middle of the night. Scaring Candy."

"I never scared that woman."

"She told me you kicked her out tonight."

Another laugh. "Oh, that's a good one. Listen, I don't know what issues the two of you are going through, but you seriously need help. She came to *me* because she thought you had something to do with Becky's disappearance."

He stared at her blankly. She had him now. "What?"

"You heard right. She was over here not one hour ago, crying and boo-hooing because she found your little stash of pictures and thought they were evidence against you."

"She thought ... I ...?" He didn't finish his sentence.

Margot held his gaze and refused to let go. "So you do have ears. Congratulations. For a minute there, I was starting to wonder."

It wasn't until Sandy cleared her throat gently that Margot remembered her friend was even there.

"I wonder if it wouldn't be best," Sandy began in her calm, maternal tone, "if we all got ready to call it a night. It seems like maybe there were some misunderstandings and miscommunications on both sides, and after a good night's rest ..."

Margot was in no mood to listen to diplomacy. And she wasn't about to let Jack walk out of here without some last words. "You know what, fine. I'm done with this conversation anyway. Thinking that you had this information and didn't tell me is making me literally sick to my stomach. And even if it wasn't what Candy thought it was, I still can't believe you held onto those photos."

"I held onto them because they give me hope."

Hope? Oh, that was grand. Whatever the man was on, it was a lot stronger than Margot's few glasses of wine. "Hope?" she roared. "Hope that what? Our daughter now has the privilege of …" She wasn't proud of what she said next and winced when she realized that not only her ex but also her friend Sandy was listening.

Jack took a step back toward the door as if to distance himself from her words. "Hope that Becky's alive," he answered softly, the rebuke in his voice just as strong as if he'd been shouting. "Hope that we're going to find her. Hope that we'll be a family again."

Margot didn't have the strength to answer.

"I guess I'll let myself out." Her ex-husband's voice was partially drowned by the roaring of her own pulse in her ears. She needed to lie down. She needed to puke. She needed a drink.

It was impossible to guess how much time passed. A minute? An hour? Margot was startled back to reality when Sandy squeezed her hand. "Would you like a little snack? Or maybe a cup of tea?"

Tea? No. Margot needed something stronger than tea.

A lot stronger.

Of course, she wouldn't admit that. Not in front of Sandy, Miss Mother of the Year. Miss Pastor's Wife. Miss Perfect Pollyanna Homemaker.

She forced herself to return the squeeze as enthusiastically as she could. "Actually, I think I just need to go to bed. Thanks again for coming over. I don't know how I could have handled this on my own." Margot's smile felt mechanical and fake, but she needed the house to herself. Like ten minutes ago.

"Thanks again." Margot hoped she sounded convincingly tired and exhausted. She hoped she sounded like a woman who needed to go to bed, not a woman who was planning to head straight to the bottle as soon as Sandy left.

"You sure? I'm fine staying here a little longer. We can pray ..."

"It's late." There was that same smile. The same forced squeeze. "Thanks again for coming over. You really are a saint. But it's late. We both should try to get some sleep."

Her thoughts turned to the half a bottle of vodka still in her cupboard. How long until her friend took the hint and left?

"Well, I'll be praying for you. Carl and I both will. Woong too, of course." Sandy stood up. Margot felt every ounce of energy drain out of her body as she did the same.

"Thanks for coming over," she said, counting down the seconds until she could open that bottle of vodka. Sandy couldn't leave soon enough.

Sandy was pecking around in her purse, muttering something about keys when Margot's cell phone beeped.

"Is that your phone, dear, or mine?" Sandy asked.

"Mine," Margot answered. "Jack probably forgot something." Mechanically, she picked up her cell and swiped the screen and read the text.

"What is it, sweetie?" Sandy looked concerned. Margot felt the blood drain from her face.

She held the screen out to her friend, unable to find her voice. Her hand trembled.

Sandy dropped her keys back into her purse. "Oh, dear. Let me call my husband. I'll tell him I'm staying over tonight."

CHAPTER 37

One day earlier

"Come on. Get dressed."

Becky kept her eyes on the floor when Xavier stomped over to her and tossed a black dress on the floor beside her. The hotel carpet was dirty and smelled like mold, but at least he had stopped kicking her.

"Get dressed," he growled again.

Becky didn't understand. Wasn't it too early to start seeing anybody? And she still hadn't eaten. It was one thing to keep her from food during the day, but at night while she was working, he always gave her something to keep up her energy.

My little business investment, he called her. But that was only when he was in a good mood. That was only when she brought home a pocket full of cash at the end of a long night. Lately, she'd had a harder time meeting quota. It wasn't her fault. Sometimes her dates refused to pay the agreed on amount. And then what was Becky supposed to do?

My little business investment. Sometimes he'd smile at her while he counted the wads of bills. Smile so warmly. So gently. Her heart would flip. It was him again. Her Xavier. Until he added something like, "I knew that necklace would pay itself back."

And that's how it had begun way back in Medford. All the way back to last summer. It started with gifts. Not just trinkets, but expensive jewelry. Gorgeous things Becky had never dreamed of even trying on before, let alone owning.

And now he owned her.

She thought about the last time she'd gone to church with Woong. That teacher in the new Sunday school class, Scott. The one who used to be a missionary. He'd told them a story about Jacob and Esau and how Esau was so hungry, he gave away his rights as the firstborn son just so he could eat a bowl of soup.

Is that what she had done? Traded in her soul for a few diamonds?

Not that Xavier let her wear the jewelry anymore, unless she was going out with a really important date. It had been like that at the beginning, high-paying clients who wanted her in pretty clothes and fancy jewels. Sadly, those were the best days she could remember after she and Xavier moved out here.

And then things changed. Slowly at first. Almost imperceptibly. Xavier had to work harder to book her dates. The men she saw stopped caring as much what she looked like.

And Xavier was worried about cash. Again.

The worst part wasn't the work itself. Becky had spent hundreds of hours as a little girl visualizing what it would be like to compete at the Olympics on the ice. All she had to do in this case was divert that same brain energy to imagining she was somewhere else.

That she was someone else.

When Xavier started calling her Ruby, that's who she became.

Those men with money could do whatever they wanted to Ruby. They were too drunk or hurried or desperate to realize that Ruby didn't even exist.

But Becky did. And she spent her nights dreaming of a world where she was safe. Where she never ran out of food to eat. Where her days weren't spent trying to sleep and her evenings spent trying to escape this horrific nightmare of her existence.

The nights, she quickly learned, would never last forever.

And when she was done with her dates, Xavier would

come. When they first moved out here, mornings were the best. He'd hold her. Hug her. Cuddle her. Tell her what a good job she'd done. Promise her that after another day, another week at most, he'd have his money from his cousin and buy them a proper place to live. She wouldn't have to work to support them anymore.

Becky lived for those mornings. Lived for Morning Xavier. Lived to feel him breathing beside her. To feel the rush of warmth when he leaned over and whispered in her ear, "You've done so much for me. How can I ever repay you?"

She hadn't realized his question was rhetorical, and one day she answered it. "Do you think I could call my mom?"

Immediately, she felt his body tense. "What?"

"Or write a letter. Just something. She must be so worried."

"You told me you never wanted to see that witch again." His voice had changed. This wasn't the Morning Xavier she looked forward to cuddling with at sunrise, the Xavier who promised to buy an apartment where they could live together and she'd never have to earn money like this again.

She rolled over. Tried to smile at him flirtatiously, but he wouldn't even look at her.

"I thought you hated her, and that's why you moved in with your dad in the first place."

"We got in a fight, that's all," Becky answered. "I just … you know, you're right. I guess I was just a little homesick." She said the words quickly, hoping they would make everything better. Hoping happy Xavier would return.

And he did.

But that night was the first night he beat her.

And then he beat her again a week later because she didn't bring him in enough money. He said he'd have to take back all that jewelry he bought her and sell it just so they didn't starve to death.

But things would get better soon. That money from his cousin … It had to be somewhere. And Xavier was the kind of guy who knew how to get what he wanted.

And as soon as he got paid back, Becky could stop working. They'd buy a nice little apartment, and everything would be okay.

Once Xavier was a little calmer, once he got paid from his cousin and money wasn't so tight, she'd find a way to write her mom a letter. Apologize for the things she said. Make sure to tell her not to worry.

I'm fine. I'm with Xavier. We're happy together.

Someday …

CHAPTER 38

"Put this on."

Becky stared when Xavier dropped the diamond necklace on her lap.

"I thought you sold that," she stammered.

"Haven't you ever heard of a pawn shop?" he snapped back. "Put it on."

She did what he said. The clasp was hard to manipulate in the back, and her wrist stung where he had twisted it earlier, but she finally managed.

How long had it been since she'd worn diamonds? That must mean a wealthy client tonight, right? A good sign. Because one high-paying date was infinitely better than a dozen low-paying ones.

A high-paying date might even mean a real meal at a real restaurant.

"Are we going out?" She hoped he didn't hear the way her stomach grumbled. Hoped he didn't see her mentally calculating how many granola bars Xavier could buy her if her date was a generous tipper.

"You're gonna have to fix your eye." Xavier scowled. Becky had been too busy fingering the diamonds around her neck to remember the bruises on her face.

She gave Xavier a smile. "Let me just get my makeup bag." She took a move toward the bathroom, but he grabbed her by the arm and yanked her back.

"I'll get it."

She knew better than to say anything. Nighttime Xavier was always in a worse mood than Morning Xavier. And if this rich date went as well as she hoped, Morning Xavier would be extra happy with her. Who could tell? Maybe this would be her last night on the job.

Ever.

Maybe she'd earn enough tonight to buy her and Xavier a dozen small apartments and fill every single cupboard with granola bars.

Wouldn't that make him happy?

She was generous with her makeup and moved quickly because Xavier still hadn't told her how much time she had to get ready. Butterflies flitted around in her empty stomach. She could almost pretend this was a real first date. A real first date with someone important. Someone important, powerful, and rich.

"How do I look?" She twirled in front of the mirror, glancing at Xavier to gauge his reaction.

He thrust a new leather coat into her arms. "Like a whore," he grumbled. "Put that on, and hurry up. We don't got all night."

CHAPTER 39

Becky was confused. This restaurant was one of the fanciest in town, but instead of dropping her off at the curb like she expected, Xavier got out and handed the valet the keys.

"You're coming too?" she asked.

"Of course I'm coming." He gripped her by the arm and hissed, "Just stop talking. You'll make yourself sound like an idiot, and I've got too much riding on tonight for you to mess it all up."

Becky didn't reply. She pictured how happy he'd be in the morning, counting out his bills. One day, she told herself, he'd understand. One day, he'd realize that while he'd been so obsessed and worried about money, she'd sacrificed herself for him. To make him happy. To bring him peace.

Because she loved him.

And he would love her back.

For real this time.

Xavier walked past the diners lined up to eat and

grumbled at the hostess, "I'm here to meet Donahue."

Donahue. Becky didn't know if that was a first or a last name. Either way, it was probably made up. The only men she dated who used their real names were the young ones who were nearly as nervous as she'd been starting out.

Xavier continued to grip her arm, but Becky smiled as they followed the hostess, wondering what any of the fancy diners who saw her right now might think.

Would they have any idea who she was?

Would they have any idea what she did?

Would they hate her if they knew?

She thought back to what life was like when she graduated from middle school and laughed at herself. Thinking she was all that, pretending she was smarter than the world. Acting as if she knew one stupid thing about life or men or love.

Well, she'd learned. Xavier had made sure of that.

Now there was hardly anything that could surprise her.

Except for the fact that Donahue was a woman.

Donahue stood when Xavier stepped up to her table, giving him a quick peck on both cheeks. She was tall, a full inch taller than Xavier.

Xavier shoved Becky forward. "This is the girl."

Donahue raised an eyebrow. "She's how old?"

"Old enough to know her place," he answered.

Donahue let out a grunt, and everyone sat. It was one of those fancy restaurants, where waiters wear tuxedos and the napkins look so clean you're afraid to wipe your hands on them.

Donahue reached out and touched Becky's curls. "These real?"

Becky glanced at Xavier, unsure if she was supposed to respond.

He leaned back in his seat and passed Becky a cup of water. "What you see is what you get."

Becky hadn't been on a date with another woman. Donahue was old. At least twice Becky's age. And big.

Becky sipped at her drink, kept her eyes on her boyfriend, and reminded herself that as soon as she made enough money, the only dates she'd ever go on would be with him.

Donahue signaled to the waiter, who gave her a nod. "I already ordered for us," she told Xavier. "Hope you don't mind."

And so Becky sat. And she waited. And she wondered what her friends were doing back in Massachusetts. Were Carly and Megan still on speaking terms, or had their friendship disintegrated when Becky was no longer the glue to hold them together?

How was Mom? It wasn't fair. First she'd lost her husband. Then her daughter.

Becky would make it up to her one day. When she and Xavier were rich, they'd send her money, checks every single month so she didn't have to work a minute of overtime ever again. Maybe Becky could convince Xavier to move her mom out here, and they could be next-door neighbors.

Life was going to get better.

It had to.

Daydreams filled Becky's stomach while she waited for their food to arrive. When it did, Xavier took an empty plate, grabbed a roll and few bits of salad, and shoved it in her direction.

Becky couldn't eat fast enough.

Donahue let out a chuckle. "You been starving the girl or something?"

Xavier continued to lean back in his seat. He gave Donahue a flirty smile, which made Becky wonder just how well the two knew each other, and then he shrugged. "She's watching her weight."

Another laugh. Shared this time.

By everyone but Becky.

Her food was gone. She watched Xavier twirl creamy

pasta onto his fork, and she felt dizzy.

"She much trouble?" Donahue asked.

"Nah." Xavier spoke with his mouth full. "Missed her mom at the beginning, but she's over that now."

Becky's eyes traveled from Xavier's pasta to Donahue's bowl of chunky clam chowder. While she watched Donahue chewing, Becky could almost taste the rich cream herself.

"No contact back home, I assume."

"Nah. Took care of that early on."

Becky glanced at her plate. Didn't they see it was empty? She took another sip of water.

"How's she work?"

Xavier set down his fork just inches away from Becky's plate. "Good. Hearty. No complaints." He punctuated each word like a chef chopping ingredients to a beat.

"Earns her keep?" Donahue continued to keep one eyebrow raised in a way that made her whole body seem slightly lopsided. Or maybe that was just because Becky still felt dizzy. Was there any salad left?

"Yup." Xavier took another bite of pasta, and the smell of the garlic would have been indescribably divine if it didn't make her feel so nauseated.

Donahue pouted. There was a bread crumb on her lip Becky couldn't help staring at. "You know her age could be a problem. I'm above board now. Mostly." She winked. Who was this woman, and why was she being so casual with Becky's man?

Xavier reached into his pocket and pulled out an envelope. "We've got papers for her. Ruby Molini, age 19."

Donahue glanced at the packet. "It's better than nothing. But you know I'm only doing this because we're friends."

Xavier leaned forward and kissed the woman on her cheek. "I knew I could count on you. You're an angel."

Becky thought she was about to throw up.

Donahue gave Xavier a concerned look and nodded. Becky felt her entire body swaying. She was so tired …

"Better take care of that," Donahue said dryly.

Xavier turned to Becky with a frown. "You look awful." He picked up her cup and held it close so she could drink more. He gave Donahue a knowing smile. "Kid insists on drinking nothing but Mountain Dew then acts surprised when she gets sick."

He shoved the glass closer, accidentally jabbing the straw against the roof of Becky's mouth. "Drink it up," he said. Becky heard the irritation in his voice. "More." He held the cup in place until there was hardly anything but ice left.

"Think that's enough?" he asked Donahue, holding the glass up for her to inspect.

"Likely." Donahue grabbed her purse. "I believe this is for you."

Becky tried focusing on the wad of bills the strange woman was shoving into Xavier's hands, but her eyes were having a hard time staying open.

"I think I'm going to throw up," she said before blackness and fog consumed her.

CHAPTER 40

The next day

Holy cupcakes, I think that woman drugged me. I seriously think that woman drugged me.

I was meeting someone. A woman. At a fancy restaurant. I was with Xavier. I thought it was going to be a date, but it was totally not, and now I'm in some strange room.

First things first, it's nice not to be chained to a bed. I can get used to this, even if the mattress stinks, but honestly with whatever that witch lady gave me, I probably could have slept through anything.

Xavier is going to be so mad.

I should have seen it coming. That woman had envy written all over her face. She wanted Xavier for herself. I should have known. A woman that age has absolutely no chance with someone like him, but I could tell she was desperate enough she'd still give it a try.

Is that why she dragged me to this dump? So she could

steal my boyfriend? Because she couldn't stand the fact that he loves me more than her?

The good news is I'm guessing this Donahue woman is loaded. Which means once Xavier finds out where I am, he can sue her. And then we'll be set up for life, because no one comes and drugs Xavier's girlfriend and tries to steal her away from him.

Seriously, who would even be that desperate?

I've just got to wait. Once Xavier comes to rescue me, we'll sue Donahue, have all the money we could ever need, and everything will finally work out for us.

We've been waiting so long. God must see. He must know how much we love each other, and I remember Woong's dad at church talking about how loving and forgiving God is. So he's not going to always be mad at me for the things I did because I never stopped loving Xavier and only Xavier, so all those other dates and things hardly even count.

But I'm afraid. I hate to admit it even to myself, but I'm scared.

Because what if this Donahue woman drugged me and took me to another city or another state? What if Xavier doesn't know where to look for me?

What if it takes him days or even a week to find me?

I don't know how I can handle being apart from him. I don't know what I'm going to do. I'm trying really hard not to panic, but I can't even tell where I am. How did Donahue get me here? Xavier would have fought her.

Oh, no. What if that's it? What if she killed him? What if she killed my boyfriend because she could tell that he was so in love with me? What if she murdered Xavier? Because he would have fought her. As soon as he realized what she was trying to do, he would have done anything to save me.

Except he didn't.

So does that mean he's dead?

Oh, my God. I don't mean it like a swear word either because Woong tells me that's a really bad sin, and I'm trying not to add any new ones to the ones I've already committed. So I'm not saying it in the bad way. I'm praying. I'm actually praying to God.

Do you hear me, God?

Can you tell Xavier I'm here?

Can you tell him how much I love him?

Oh, my God. You've got to get me out of here. I can't do this. I can't live without Xavier.

Oh, my God.

I need my boyfriend. I need my mom. I need to go home.

Oh, my God. Can you hear me at all?

I'm so sorry for the things I did. I know I don't have any reason to expect you to listen to me, but if you're anything at all like what Woong's parents say you're like, then you'll understand I didn't have any choice. I just loved him so much. And he needed the money, and …

Oh, my God. What if he's dead?

What if I did all those things just so that woman could kill him because she was jealous?

What am I supposed to do now?

What if she wants to kill me next?

What if I never see Xavier again?

Is he even alive, God? Can you at least tell me that much?

Miss Sandy told me once that you'll hear every single prayer we'll ever pray. She told me that even if we've sinned and done horrible things, all we have to do is confess that to you and you'll go ahead and forgive us and forget we ever did any of that.

I don't remember exactly what I'm supposed to ask, Jesus. I really don't. I just know that I've done these horrible, awful things, and … Oh, God, what if you were watching me that whole time? What if you saw it all?

I'm sorry. Can you forgive me? I know I'm gross and disgusting and every other bad thing. I know you think I'm the worst kind of person in the entire world to do the things that I've done, but will you please tell me that it's okay? Will you please tell me that you've forgiven me?

Will you please do that thing Miss Sandy says you do where you forget it all and act as if it never happened?

Because I'm in trouble, God. Xavier's gone. I don't know if he's dead or alive, but if he knew where I was, he wouldn't stop until he got me out of here. But here I am, so that means he must not have any idea.

And I don't know what this Donahue woman wants from me, but I didn't trust her the moment I laid eyes on her.

And I'm terrified. I'm so scared I can't even breathe. It's like I'm suffocating.

Oh, my God. What if she's put poison in the air? What if she's going to leave me here to die?

Please, God. Please get me out of here. I don't care how you do it, but Woong's dad says there isn't anything that's impossible for you. That's why you're God, right? So I'm going to close my eyes and count to three, and my prayer right now is that when I wake up, I'll be back home in Medford. And my Mom will be downstairs cooking bacon, and we never would have had that stupid fight about money. And I'll tell her I'm sorry. I promise you that. I'll tell her just how sorry I am. I'll even get on my knees and kiss her feet if that would make you happy and make up for even a fraction of the pain and worry I caused her.

Just please let me wake up in Medford. I'll do every single thing I'm supposed to do. I'll go to church with Woong. I'll tell Mom she has to come too. She'll believe. I promise you she'll believe.

And I'll tell Dad, too. I'll tell him and Candy how important it is to go to church too, and oh, my God. Is that footsteps?

Oh, my God. I'm still in a hotel room.

What about my prayers, Lord? Does that mean you're listening? Are you mad at me? Did I do too many wrong things? Is there some kind of limit? Oh, my God, she's unlocking the door.

How many chains does she have on that thing?

She's coming in here. Donahue. The woman who kidnapped me.

I don't know what she's going to do to me, but you've got to help me, God.

Please.

Can you hear me?

Are you there?

God?

Jesus?

Anybody?

CHAPTER 41

Becky couldn't catch her breath. Her body heaved, making the motions of sobbing, but instead of crying she was simply trying to suck even the smallest amount of air into her lungs.

"Come on," Donahue grumbled. "Enough of that. Straighten yourself up. You should be ashamed."

Sob. Suck. Breathe.

There was a sting in Becky's lungs, and with each failed inhale, a hole inside her chest cavity was ripped a little wider.

Sob. Suck. Breathe.

But there was no air to breathe.

"You really are green, aren't you?" Donahue lit up a cigarette and took a slow drag.

Sob. Suck. Choke. Cough.

Donahue glanced at Becky and raised an eyebrow. "You done now?" She gave a little sneer. "I hope you're well rested." She glanced at the bed. "Your shift starts in half an hour."

"My shift?"

Donahue was too busy focusing on her smoke to answer right away. Finally she said, "I'll send Precious in as soon as she's done getting ready herself. I don't know what kind of a schedule Xavier ran, but we've got a lot of girls, and to be completely frank, most of them are prettier than you. So any thoughts you had about being someone's little bright, shining star, you get them out of your head right now. I'm a patient woman, but one thing I don't tolerate is a diva. And if I even get a whiff of you that stinks of diva —" She leaned closer and sniffed loudly "—I find the nearest gutter and I dump you in it and will have forgotten that I ever saw you two seconds later. Understand me?"

Becky bit her lip and nodded.

"Good. Now, Xavier called you Ruby, but that's no good here. I get a lot of girls coming in who think that just because some man tattoos a nickname on your body that you've got the right to it for the rest of your life, but that's nonsense. You're working for me now, and I hate to break it to you, darling, you're no gem. You'll call yourself Sugar, and if I even hear a word from you about Xavier or about how things were easier when you were working for him, I know a tree trunk in the forest big enough to stuff your skinny body into. Get what I'm saying?"

Another nod.

"No divas," Donahue repeated. "No special treatment. You may have been Xavier's little pet, but here you're just another worker. Got that right? Nothing special. Let me hear you say it."

"I'm nothing special," Becky mumbled.

Donahue smiled. "Good. Xavier promised you wouldn't be any trouble." She stood to go. "Oh, and one more thing."

She paused.

Becky waited.

"You don't earn your keep, you don't eat. It's as simple as that. Any questions?"

Donahue didn't wait for an answer but shut the door. The sound of heavy locks clicking into place echoed in Becky's ears.

CHAPTER 42

Breathe. I've got to remember how to breathe, and then everything is going to be okay.

I can make this work out.

I always do.

I can do anything I set my mind to.

Including escape.

The problem is I don't know where I am. This doesn't look like the city anymore, but I really can't tell. And I feel like I was asleep for days. So did Donahue bring me somewhere else, or am I still in Las Vegas?

If I'm nearby, I can find Xavier. I just need to get out.

But how?

He's going to be looking for me. If he's still alive, he's going to be looking for me.

Come on. Think.

What would Xavier want me to do?

He'd want me to be safe. And to be brave. And to remember how much he loves me.

If I can manage that, I might be able to make it.

Yeah. That's it. Stay safe. Be brave.

It's going to be okay.

Remember when you were little and all you wanted was to skate in the Olympics? And you'd stay awake at night just visualizing it all. Picturing jumps you didn't even know how to make yet.

That's what you've got to do.

There's no reason to panic. Nobody's hurting you right now. Nobody's doing anything bad to you right now.

Right now, right at this exact moment, you're safe. You're not hungry. You just had a really long nap so you're not so exhausted.

It's all right.

You've got this.

But what if Xavier doesn't come? What if Donahue's killed him?

Then what am I supposed to do?

Just try not to worry. But how do I do that? What was that verse Miss Sandy had hanging up in her living room? *Do not worry about tomorrow, for tomorrow will worry about itself.*

That's good advice, Becky. Really good advice. Think about Miss Sandy. Remember how much she loves to bake for you and Woong? Remember how good her house always smells? Remember how happy you feel when you're over visiting and she comes and brings you milk and brownies for a snack, and you make Woong laugh so hard that milk shoots out his nose?

Remember that?

Remember why you always love going to Woong's house? It's not just that they're all so nice. It's the home itself. Remember how it feels to be in their living room? Like you're one of the family. Pastor Carl will come in and take off his tie after church on Sunday, and sometimes he'll fall asleep right there in his recliner while Miss Sandy gets lunch ready.

Remember the way you and Woong giggle every time his dad snores?

You remember, don't you?

You remember how to laugh.

And you're going to laugh again.

All those verses Miss Sandy told you and Pastor Carl preached about and you and Woong sat studying in Sunday school ... All those verses are true. Everything's going to turn out all right. Think about all the people in the Bible. Like that Samson guy. Remember him? He was in a world of trouble. They even plucked out his eyes, and when you get right down to it, everything that happened to him was totally his fault.

But God took care of him.

And he's taking care of you too.

Or who was that guy whose brothers sold him to be a slave? They even made a movie about him once. Remember watching it at Grandma's house when you were a kid? He could have been angry at his brothers. He could have hated God for everything he had to go through. And what about that woman who spread those lies about him?

He had it pretty bad. How many years does it say he was in that prison? I can't remember right now. But it was a long time, I think.

And in the end everything worked out all right for him too.

So that's what I've got to do. Keep waiting. Because everything always works out in the end.

And I already know that Xavier and I are destined to be together, and if there really is a God (which, of course there is), he's going to do everything he can to bring us back to each other. Maybe this is like one of those tests. And our relationship will be even stronger in the end. Maybe this will be enough to make Xavier actually scared of losing me for good so he won't take his stress out on me anymore.

Everything happens for a reason, Becky. That's just what you've got to keep on telling yourself. And when you get scared, just think about Woong shooting milk out his nose. See, you can laugh even here. As long as you're able to laugh, then you know you're going to be all right.

Just wait and see.

CHAPTER 43

"So, you're the new girl."

Becky stared at the young woman standing in the doorway of her room. "Yeah."

"I'm Precious." She took a step forward and stretched out her hand.

Becky wasn't used to shaking other people's hands. Especially not girls who only looked a year or two older than she was.

"What they call you?"

"Becky."

Precious shook her head of flowing jet-black hair. "No, I mean the name Donahue gave."

"Oh. I guess I'm Sugar."

Precious pouted her full lips, crossed her arms, and tilted her head to the side while she looked Becky up and down. "You don't look like no Sugar to me."

Becky didn't know what to say.

"Where you from, Sugar?" Precious plopped onto the

side of the bed.

Precious had left the door slightly ajar. Becky tried to see what was on the other side, hunting for clues that could tell her where she was.

Precious turned around. "If you're thinking about running, don't." She gave a casual toss of her hair. "Donahue's got cameras all over this place. Cameras and dogs."

"Dogs?"

"Yeah. You know, not the cute little fluffy kind. The kind she's got to keep chained up or they'll turn even on her."

"Oh."

Precious reached into her handbag and pulled out some makeup. "So, I'm supposed to get you ready tonight. You worked the Strip before?"

The Strip? That meant she was still in Vegas. Thank God. Everything was going to be just fine. She nodded her head. "Yeah, I know the Strip fairly well."

Precious gave a little snort. "Where you say you're from?"

"Vegas," she answered defensively but felt her resolve melting under Precious's intense scrutiny. "But originally Massachusetts."

"Massachusetts?" Precious repeated with disdain. "Let me guess. Suburb baby. Got in a fight with your mom, ran away from home, and then some man promised to take care of you, and you ended up here?"

Becky shook her head. That wasn't how it happened. "I moved out here with my boyfriend."

Precious snorted again. "Whatever you want to believe."

Becky was ready to talk about something else. "So, are you from Las Vegas?"

"Born and raised." Precious sat up a little bit straighter. "Been working for Donahue about five years now."

Becky squinted her eyes while Precious applied her foundation. "How old are you?" she asked.

Precious paused as if she wasn't certain at first if she wanted to answer. Finally, she replied, "Nineteen."

"That's young."

Another snort. "Not here. But I've been around the longest, which has its perks. My quota's about half of what you other girls have to make."

"How much are we supposed to make?" Becky asked.

When Precious told her the answer, Becky thought she must be joking. "That's way more than what I was doing for my boyfriend."

Precious held a few different tubes of lip liner up toward

Becky's mouth. "Well, hate to break it to you, but your boyfriend was an amateur. How many girls he got working for him?"

Becky was repulsed by the question. "None. It was just the two of us."

Precious snorted. "Sure it was."

"No, we weren't like … It wasn't like that." Becky searched for the words to make Precious understand. "Things were different."

Precious puckered up her lips while she ran the liner several times around Becky's mouth. "Course they were."

Becky was too tired to argue. It was time to change the subject again.

"So, do the clients come here?" She was still looking at that inch-wide gap in the doorway. Still wondering how fast you'd have to race to outrun a snarling guard dog. And Precious said they were usually kept on chains …

Precious laughed. "Here to this dump? What're you talking about? We go on calls. And we only work the Strip. You've seen the driving billboards, right?"

Becky had never quite gotten used to seeing the images plastered to the sides of trucks, advertising 24-7 escort services. And Donahue expected her to act like one of those women?

This was a horrible misunderstanding.

"But I'm not ..." Becky leaned her head back to try to get Precious to stop fidgeting with her lips long enough for her to get a full sentence out. "I don't ... I'm not a ..."

Precious's eyes widened. "You're not a what?"

"I'm not ..." Becky sucked in her breath. "I'm not like that."

"Sure." Precious took the lid off a tube of lipstick and frowned as she held the color up against Becky's skin. "Whatever you gotta tell yourself."

"I'm really not," Becky protested. "We ... I ..." She stopped. How could she explain it? Sure, she'd done a few things when Xavier needed the money, but that was totally different. She wasn't a call girl. Wasn't an escort. She'd only done it part time. Only temporarily. Only for Xavier.

She wasn't ...

She couldn't ...

Precious furrowed her brow. "Hey, if you're gonna cry, do it now before I do your eye makeup, all right? Because I've got ten other girls besides you I've got to get ready." She let out her breath and frowned at Becky. "Listen, you seem like a nice, sweet girl, and I'm sure you came from a nice, sweet home back wherever you're from, but you're here now. All right? You're one of Donahue's girls. That's not gonna change any time soon. Your best shot at getting through this? You do what I tell you when I tell you and how I tell you. We've got loyal clients. Mostly locals. Which is way better than you can expect from most of the other joints around here.

"You get a couple guys who like you, who'll request you by name, you've got it made. All right? Donahue's a good businesswoman. She doesn't put up with the kind who rough us up. So you stick with her, you stick with me, and everything's gonna be good. I've met too many young girls like you, all sad and pathetic and still in love with whoever sold you here. No, don't argue with me. I'm still talking to you. You love him, but that doesn't change the fact that he sold you. Don't argue with me. I get it. I understand. I was your age once. But you listen to me. No, don't turn away. I'm not through."

She cupped Becky's chin with her hand. Her touch was firm and gentle at the same time. How could that be? And did Precious feel the way Becky's jaw was shaking?

"Get that boy out of your head." Precious held her gaze and refused to let it go. "He's not coming back for you. He's forgotten all about you. And the whole time he was with you, I can tell you this … The whole time he was with you, he was working a dozen other girls. Don't go all wide eyes on me. Trust me. I know what I'm talking about, and the girls who survive in this business are the girls who keep their dignity, keep their sense of humor, and don't go crying over no guy. You get me?"

Becky sniffed and gave a little nod.

"Good." Precious stopped pinching her face. "Now don't forget what I've told you. And just because I've told you what's up, don't think that I won't come down hard on you if I've got to. You ever seen a horse race?"

Becky shook her head.

"Well, let me tell you how it works. Say a racer buys himself a horse. Spends a lot of money to get the best breed. Well, he's not going to waste all that money, so he's going to feed it, give it food and good shelter. But when it's time to work, he's gonna take out his whip, and that horse is gonna realize soon enough it's only alive for one purpose and one purpose only, and that's to earn money. You get what I'm saying?"

Becky didn't.

"So you just remember them horses, got that? And when things get hard, you ask yourself what someone'll do if his horse stops earning his keep. What'll happen to the animal then? You think on that, and you keep on Donahue's good side if you know what's best for you. Got me?"

"Yeah." Becky swallowed. "Thanks."

Precious rolled her eyes. "Well, don't thank me yet. You've got a long night ahead of you. But the sun always comes up. Just keep telling yourself that. Sun always comes up. Then you'll come back here, you'll take a shower, you'll go to sleep. If you need it, Donahue'll have some pills. Help take the edge off. And you'll sleep until it's time to wake up and get ready and do it all over again. That's life now, all right? And you remember what I said about them horses, and you remember what I said about that boyfriend of yours. Get him out of your mind and think about what's going on right now. Right here. And then one day, maybe in five years down the road, you'll be in my shoes, getting someone else ready for her first night, and she's all nervous, but all the while you're laughing on the inside because you've already done your time and now you get to sit back and relax. Trust me, it don't come easy, but it's worth it. You hear me?"

Precious stood and tossed a dress onto the bed. "If that don't fit, there's more clothes down the hall. And if one of the older girls tells you she wants this one, you just take it off and find something else. That's the way we do things around here. You're on the bottom for now, but new girls'll be coming in before you know it. Time moves double speed around here. Enough to make your head spin at first, but you'll get used to it. Any questions, you ask one of the older ones."

Precious walked out the door, and in another second, it was closed behind her. Becky didn't even wait to hear the locks click into place before she fell on her bed and sobbed into her pillow.

CHAPTER 44

You know what I really hate? When people get so jealous and are so unhappy with their own lives, they feel like the only course of action to take is to try to ruin someone else's day. I just met this real gem of a girl named Precious (that's sarcasm right there), and holy cupcakes. She's like the most unhappy, toxic girl I've ever met. Like Precious on her good days would make Carly on her worst days look like a saint. That's how bad she is.

I just spent like fifteen minutes listening to her pretend to know what kind of guy Xavier is. As if she's even met him. And there's only one reason for someone to be that nasty and negative, and that's if she's jealous. She has no idea what Xavier and I have. Or maybe she does, and she knows she'll never have anything even as close to as genuine as what we've got, and so she's out to poison me against him.

I am so sick of toxic people. I've been doing some serious thinking, and even if I were back home, I don't think I'd hang out too much with Carly anymore. Because she's like that too, totally negative. It's just that I couldn't see it as clearly until now.

So hey, that's another good thing about this test I'm going through. I'm learning some good lessons!

Always look for the positive, right? That's what's going to help me get through this and back to Xavier. And any time I worry about the things Precious said to me, any time the seeds of doubt she planted start to spring up in my heart (hello, metaphor!), I'll just remember that the happiest I've ever been in my entire life is with Xavier. And that counts for everything.

People can say what they want. They can put on an act and try to fool you.

But they can't change the way you feel.

And the way I feel about Xavier now is exactly the way I felt the day we left home to start a new life together, except now I'm even more in love with him. So yeah, so much for sweet little Precious trying to steal away my joy.

Because you know what? I'm tough. And I'm strong. And I'm just going to hold onto hope that everything works together for a reason, and if I start to feel worried, I'm just going to remember that Bible verse Woong's mom has hanging on her wall. *Do not worry about tomorrow, for tomorrow will worry about itself.* I might not be getting the quote exactly right, but I know that's basically what it's saying.

So I'm going to remember that all things really do work together for a reason. And I'm going to keep on hoping that one day, somewhere, somehow, this will all be a bad dream behind me. Because I know that worse things have happened to other people around the world. I mean, hello, I read Anne Frank in Mr. Daly's class. And worse things have happened in history. Way worse. And I'm not going to stay here forever. God wouldn't let that happen.

So I won't stop believing (hey, isn't that one of those really old songs you hear at bowling alleys on Karaoke night?). And one day, I'm going to be free. And I'm making myself a promise right now that when I'm out of here, I'm going to do everything in my power — and I literally mean *everything* — to make sure that other girls don't have to go through things like this ever again.

Who knows, maybe Xavier and I will open up one of those homes for runaways or something. So they don't have to walk the streets or worry about getting robbed or taken advantage of or anything like that.

I wish I remembered who that guy was in the Bible, the one whose brothers sent him to prison. Because even in prison he did a lot of good things. And then when he got out, didn't he, like, save the entire country from starving or something like that? I wish I had paid attention to more of the details. Maybe I'll ask Precious if there are any Bibles around. May as well study up now, right?

But seriously, I'm starting to wonder if the reason God brought me here is so I could see how easily a runaway could fall into a really bad situation. And I know God's not going to let me stay here very long, which means he must be planning on using me to teach other girls and make sure they won't have to go through things like this.

So now that I know my life's mission (haha), maybe God can just go ahead and tell Xavier where I am so he can rescue me. Or maybe one of my dates tonight is going to be like one of those undercover guys who's out looking for people like me so he can help. And I'll tell him where Donahue keeps all her girls and warn him about the dogs, and we might all be free by this time tomorrow!

So yeah, when you put it that way, I kind of have a busy night ahead of me. Good thing Donahue slipped me those sleeping pills or whatever it was. I probably needed a really good nap (haha).

CHAPTER 45

Two hours later

Caroline stared blinking at the young girl in the bathroom, trying to decide if her eyes were playing tricks on her or not. A second earlier she'd been so certain …

"Becky?" she asked tentatively. "Is that you?"

With a burn of shame, Caroline realized she was wrong. The hair had thrown her off, those blonde curls. What had she been thinking?

"Sorry." Caroline took a step back. "I just …"

And there it was. The flash. The spark of recognition.

Familiarity.

Caroline saw it in the girls' eyes.

"Becky?" Instinctively, she lowered her voice to a whisper. "What are you doing here?"

A heavyset woman barged out of a stall and came up behind the girl. "Is there a problem?" She stood a head taller than Caroline and probably outweighed her by a hundred pounds. Her expression was angry.

She glared at Caroline, who resisted the urge to turn around and run away. She stared at the girl's eyes. Any sense of familiarity or recognition was gone. It couldn't really be Becky. Caroline had been mistaken.

Hadn't she?

"Is this your mother?" Caroline asked.

The curly blonde nodded emphatically.

"Of course I'm her mother," huffed the heavyset woman. "And if I see you trying to molest my daughter again, I'll call security."

Caroline cleared her throat. Imagined herself standing another foot taller and having about an extra hundred pounds of courage. "It's just that your daughter looks quite a bit like someone I know."

The woman gave a snarl and a sneer at the same time. "I'll bet she does."

Caroline didn't know what that meant, but she couldn't back down. Not now. "Please." She reached out her hand hesitantly and froze with her fingers just inches away from those springy blonde curls.

"Please," she repeated, "I think that … I'm just trying to make sure that …"

The woman let out an impatient huff. "Do you want to

see my ID? Maybe run a credit report? Should I give you my social security number?"

Caroline lowered her hand. "No. No, it's nothing like that. I'm sorry. It's just that she looked so familiar."

The woman situated herself between Caroline and the girl. "Whatever." She turned to go.

"Wait." Caroline was desperate. Her heart was beating high in her chest. She knew it was impossible. Knew this girl couldn't really be Becky Linklater. Knew she was acting absurd. But something about the child tugged at her soul.

"I'm sorry," she stammered. "But I heard her crying. I was worried for her. It would mean a lot to me if I could just hear it firsthand from her that she's okay."

The woman scoffed and gave the girl a tiny shove. "Go ahead. Tell this woman what she wants to hear."

The girl kept her eyes to the floor.

"Come on. You ever seen this woman before?"

The child shook her head.

"You want to tell her why you were crying in the bathroom and making a scene?"

Another shaking of the head.

The woman held Caroline's gaze. "She was crying because her boyfriend just broke up with her. I tried to tell her what a lowlife he was to begin with, but kids these days insist on learning everything the hard way. You satisfied?"

Caroline nodded and stepped away to let the two pass. Her face burned with shame. Her heart still raced with adrenaline.

What had gotten into her? Confronting some complete stranger because her daughter reminded her of a missing kid from the East Coast. The mother certainly hadn't been the most charming woman in the world, but that was hardly an excuse for Caroline to meddle like that.

What would Calvin say?

Oh, no. Calvin. How long had she left him waiting out there?

This was not going to go over well. She resisted the urge to glance once more in the mirror to see how bad she looked and hurried back into the restaurant. She rehearsed her apology for taking so long while she rushed to their table.

But when she got there, her husband was gone.

CHAPTER 46

The good part about her husband's absence was that it gave Caroline time to think.

The bad part about her husband's absence was that it gave Caroline time to think.

Time to think and time to change her mind. Dozens of times.

It couldn't be her. It makes absolutely no sense morphed seamlessly into *That girl was Becky Linklater, and I've got to notify security.*

It only took a few minutes to finally decide. Keeping one eye on the bathroom door in case the girl came out, she flagged down a waiter.

"Excuse me. I know this sounds silly, but is there a security guard I can speak to?"

She felt ashamed even saying the words, but the waiter didn't change his expression at all. "Of course," he replied. "Right away."

Caroline soon realized that when he said *right away*, he truly meant it. Thirty seconds didn't pass before she was staring at a burly, broad-chested man in a black uniform.

"You needed security?" he asked.

She nodded, thankful that he as well as the waiter didn't seem surprised by her request. She nodded toward the bathroom. She had kept her eye on the door the entire time, and neither the curly-haired girl or the woman she was with had come out. "I saw a girl in there. A teen. She was crying. Um …" She struggled with her words, realizing this was the part that was most likely to make her sound like a crazy woman, but if she didn't at least pursue the issue, she'd never be able to forgive herself.

"I'm from the Boston area. I'm a teacher there. And there was a girl who disappeared from our school last summer. And the child …" She glanced at the closed door one more time.

"You think the girl in that bathroom is the same girl missing from your school?" So far, the security officer hadn't laughed at her, questioned her sobriety, or complained that she was wasting his time.

A good sign.

She nodded. "Yeah. I mean, I couldn't say so for certain. I couldn't swear it in court or anything. She was with an older woman. Said she was the girl's mother, but the entire interaction was a bit strange ..."

"I'll go check it out." He straightened up, and Caroline realized just how tall he was. "In this one?" He pointed toward the woman's room. What was he going to do? Barge right in?

Caroline nodded, still trying not to feel guilty. What if that woman really was the girl's mother? Well, if so, what was the worst that could happen? They'd lose a few minutes out of their evening, and by the sounds of it they weren't having the most fabulous night out anyway.

And maybe, just maybe, the security guard would realize something was wrong. That the girl really didn't belong to that woman.

And maybe, just maybe ...

The security officer muttered something into a radio. A few seconds later, a female in a similar uniform appeared beside him and entered the bathroom.

Caroline let out her breath. Good. Probably she'd been overreacting. But she wouldn't be able to sleep tonight if she hadn't pursued it. At least the security officer had taken her seriously. She doubted restaurants in many other parts of the country had their own security personnel who'd react the same way.

She took a sip of water to try to calm her nerves. So much for a peaceful and relaxing date night with her husband. And while he was probably on some phone call about the case, she was conjuring up pictures of his missing victim in random bathroom stalls.

Apparently even in Las Vegas, they couldn't escape his work. Not either of them.

Well, this is what she signed up for when she married a cop. If she had known then how things would turn out … Well, she wouldn't think about that now.

She took another sip of water and saw her husband walking toward her. On his phone. Of course.

Well, this time she couldn't complain that he was the only one distracted by the case. She finished off her cup of water, tried to smile as Calvin sat down, and hoped that one day maybe the two of them would learn to date like a normal couple.

CHAPTER 47

"All right. Yup, thanks." Drisklay sat back down in his seat and ended the call. He'd been hoping that he could finish up the conversation and get back to their table before Caroline returned, but of course he hadn't been so lucky.

Caroline was sitting at their table, her salad still untouched. Great. She was mad at him for ruining her perfect little date night. Well, the Linklater case wasn't just going to put itself on indefinite hold just because his wife wanted to pretend they were a happy couple.

He shoved his phone into his pocket, ready for whatever words of accusation she threw at him. How dare he take a work call in the middle of their night out, he was such a rude and inconsiderate husband, her pastor would never step out if he were having dinner with his wife. The same complaints ad nauseum.

But Caroline didn't say any of those things. She just looked at him quizzically when he sat down across from her.

"You okay?" he finally asked.

She shook her head. "No." She stared past his shoulder. What was she looking at?

"What's going on?" It wasn't normal for Drisklay to initiate a conversation to get his wife talking. This couldn't be a good sign.

She forced a little smile. "Well, there was a girl in the bathroom. Looked a lot like Becky." She lowered her eyes, looking almost embarrassed. "I ended up telling security just because I couldn't be sure if it was her or not."

Drisklay scowled. It was bad enough he had to take calls from a frantic Margot Linklater, raving about some photographs she found on her husband's laptop. Drisklay had already seen the images and just that afternoon had talked with the private investigator working the case. Even on vacation, he couldn't escape this investigation.

Apparently, his wife couldn't either. Wasn't this the same woman who always complained that he couldn't leave his work at home? "What'd security say?" he asked.

She sighed. "They sent a female officer in there. Nobody's come out yet. I've just been waiting."

Now Drikslay was staring at the bathroom door just like Caroline. "Did you get a good look at her?"

"Who, the girl, do you mean?"

Who else would he mean? Drisklay left the thought

unspoken.

The bathroom door opened. A security officer came out first, followed by a broad-shouldered woman accompanied by a teen. Caroline was right about one thing. Those blonde curls alone were enough to bear a striking resemblance to Becky Linklater if nothing else.

The woman smiled at the security officer, put her hand behind the blond girl's back, and they headed off. For the briefest second, the girl turned her face, and Drisklay saw her features clearly.

"What do you think?" Caroline asked.

Drisklay hadn't taken his eyes off the pair.

"What do you think?" his wife repeated. "Think that might be her?"

Drisklay didn't answer. He was already out of his chair.

"Be back in a minute," he muttered to his wife and jumped away from the table.

CHAPTER 48

Caroline had never spent a longer five minutes. Twice the waiter came and asked if he should clear Calvin's plate, but Caroline had no idea if her husband was finished eating or not. So far on their formal date, they'd spent more time away from each other than together.

Not that Caroline would complain.

Before Calvin ran off, she convinced herself the girl in the bathroom couldn't have been Becky. It would be too much of a coincidence. Tens of thousands of teens had blond curls like that. It didn't make every single one of their mothers a kidnapping suspect.

But then she remembered the way Calvin had stared at the girl as she exited the bathroom. How quickly he jumped out of his seat and took off to follow her. What was he going to do? It wasn't like he had any jurisdiction out here. And even though he traveled with his handgun, Caroline knew for a fact it was tucked away in their hotel room safe.

So what was he doing?

She wasn't sure which scared her more — the fact that her husband was out tracking down what might be a dangerous kidnapper or the fact that the girl from the bathroom really might be Becky Linklater.

And Caroline had almost talked herself out of notifying security.

It was a perfect time to pray — for her husband's safety, for Becky, wherever she might be. But Caroline's entire body was surging with adrenaline. It took all her mental acuity just to stay in her seat instead of running after Calvin.

What was he doing?

She hadn't realized she'd been holding her breath until she saw him rounding a corner, making his way through the crowded restaurant. Her heart was still racing, but at least she could breathe a little easier now.

"What happened?" she asked as he nonchalantly pulled out his chair and sat down. "Where did you go?"

"I wanted to get a photo." He pulled out his phone and nodded at the waiter who hurried toward the table, eager to clear his plate. This time, Caroline didn't complain about her husband working through what was supposed to be their fancy dinner. She watched while Calvin sent a text and then waited for him to fill her in on what was going on.

"I just sent the picture to the mom," he finally explained.

"So you really think it might be her?" Caroline leaned forward in her seat.

Calvin shrugged. "The resemblance is striking, to say the least. And we got other photographic evidence just this afternoon that places her in the Vegas area."

Caroline thought about how angry she'd been at her husband for spending so much time on his phone today and was suddenly ashamed.

"Don't get your hopes up too high," he said, "but it's possible you just located our missing person."

CHAPTER 49

Drisklay was on the elevator heading back up to his room when the text from Becky Linklater's mother popped up on his cell.

Yes, that's her. I'm sure of it.

Drisklay couldn't have said it was an actual surprise, but he was still a little taken aback. The photograph itself was from an awkward angle. It caught the girl in profile. The most he'd expected was a response like *That looks like it could be her but I'm really not sure.*

Yes, Mrs. Linklater was a pain to work with. Yes, she called him at ungodly hours to ask about the case or share senseless information that did absolutely nothing to help with the investigation. She was emotionally unstable enough that Drisklay understood why her ex-husband decided not to let her know about the PI he hired.

But she was a mother.

And if Drisklay knew anything about investigations like this one, it was to trust a mother's instinct.

If Margot Linklater said the girl downstairs in that hotel restaurant was his missing person, Drisklay wasn't going to argue.

As soon as the text came in, Drisklay punched the button to have the elevator take him back down to the lobby.

"Where are we going?" Caroline asked.

"You're going back to the room," he answered. The last thing he needed was for his wife to tag along while he tracked down a kidnapping victim. "I'm going to talk with security."

Caroline clutched his arm. "So that's her? Did you hear back from her mom? That really was Becky? Why didn't you get her when we saw her then?"

Caroline didn't understand the procedure behind operations like this. And there was no way he was going to get her any more involved than she already was.

"Once you get to the room," he told her as the elevator opened to the third floor, "just lock yourself in. I'll call you when I'm ready for you to open it up. I'll call," he repeated, "not text. Just stay in there with the deadbolt fastened."

Her eyes widened. "Are you going to be in danger?"

He tried not to roll his eyes. "I'm going to talk to security. You go wait in the room. You know how to get to my gun in the safe if you need it?"

"You think I'll need the gun?"

"No. But do you know how to get into the safe?"

She nodded tentatively.

Drisklay didn't feel very convinced, but there wasn't time to waste. "See you soon," he called to his wife and waited for the elevator to take him back down to the lobby.

Time to talk with security.

CHAPTER 50

Caroline's hands were trembling when she put her key card into the lock and opened the door to her hotel room. Before shutting herself in, she turned on the lights and peeked into the bathroom and the walk-in closet, half expecting to see Becky's abductor lurking in the shadows, ready to pounce.

It was ridiculous. Caroline was just overreacting. Her husband was always like that, always so paranoid. When they first checked into the hotel, he asked to get a room by the stairs so he'd be near the emergency exits. That was the kind of man he was. Caroline wouldn't allow his cautious personality to get her so worked up.

At least not about her own safety. She was perfectly fine. It was Becky who needed her prayers.

God, she pleaded, *please watch over her. Keep her safe. Help Calvin and the security officers find some way to help.*

She pictured Becky's mom back home, terrified for her daughter. *And please help Margot,* Caroline added. *Give her peace and comfort, and help her not to be too worried.*

It was one of those silly prayers, the spiritual equivalent of putting a single Band-Aid on an open jugular. But it was all she could think of to say. For a moment, she thought about calling Sandy, but it was too late on the East Coast. She'd just have to wait.

Caroline undressed, feeling silly for getting so gussied up earlier, for worrying like she had about whether or not her makeup was exactly perfect. First of all, Calvin wouldn't have noticed if she'd come down to dinner in yoga pants and flannel. Second of all, who cared what she looked like if Becky Linklater was here in this very hotel?

Caroline wouldn't allow herself to think about how much a child like that must have endured. And to be so far from home …

She still couldn't understand how their paths could have crossed after all these months. The only thing she could come up with was that God had led her and her husband to this exact place. The thought brought at least some sense of solace. Maybe this conference wasn't about her and Calvin fixing the problems in their marriage. Maybe it was about getting Becky back home to her family where she belonged.

Thinking about how much Becky and her mom must have suffered these past months, Caroline felt ashamed of all the mental and spiritual energy she'd squandered whining about her husband.

So Calvin didn't like to go to church. At least he wasn't kidnapping underaged girls and transporting them across the country.

Sure, Calvin was hard and cynical, but he was on the right side of the law. His entire life was spent protecting poor victims like Becky. And all Caroline did was complain.

I'm sorry, Lord. She wished she could say more, but she'd never been all that eloquent with her prayers.

I'm sorry, Lord, she repeated, then sat down on the hotel bed and stared at the clock.

It was going to be a long night.

CHAPTER 51

Margot set down her cell phone and stared at her friend. "I'd know my baby anywhere," she told Sandy. "They've found her."

She felt strange saying the words. Empty. There was no textbook to tell her how mothers should react in this sort of situation. Was she supposed to feel ecstatic and grateful? Her daughter was alive. By a bizarre string of events, the detective working on her case had actually laid eyes on her in a Las Vegas hotel.

But what horrors had her precious baby girl endured? What torments had she suffered? Margot recognized her daughter right away from the detective's photo. Even though he warned her the image wasn't ideal, Margot had no doubt. The child in that gaudy dress was her Becky.

In all the extra makeup, she looked quite a bit older, but the sad and painful expression in her eyes, even when viewed from profile, reminded Margot that her baby was just a child.

A child who'd endured terror and torment even Margot at her age couldn't fathom.

How do you reconcile that? How are you supposed to function? And yes, she was thankful her daughter was alive, but that meant Becky had been suffering each and every moment for the past nine months. While Margot ate and drank and went to work and slept in her nice, safe bed, what was her baby girl forced to endure?

Dozens of times a day, Margot imagined how she'd react if Detective Drisklay called her and told her they'd found Becky's body. There would be tears. A torrent of grief. Her friends would rally alongside her, offering joyful congratulations.

But now ... Becky was alive. Margot should be overwhelmed with gratitude. So why did she feel so lost? Why did she feel so scared?

Sandy was still at her house even though it was after one in the morning. She'd called her husband briefly so he wouldn't worry and made plans to spend the night at Margot's.

"No mother should go through something like this alone," Sandy said.

But that was exactly how Margot felt. Alone.

Sandy's family wasn't perfect. She and her husband had

taken in multiple foster kids and adoptees. Some of them were doing great. Others battled daily with addictions and crime and abuse. But through it all, Sandy kept her hope in God. She had her husband and her husband's church, a community of faith that were always ready to show the family their love and support.

Who did Margot have?

"Can I get you another glass of water?" Sandy asked gently.

Margot shook her head.

Sandy rubbed her back. "You just tell me when you get hungry or thirsty and I'll fix you something up real quick."

How could Sandy even talk about food at a time like this? How could she talk about anything? The only thing Margot's mind could focus on was her daughter's scared, sad eyes in that photograph.

Her Becky.

Her precious baby girl.

Margot couldn't find the words to say. Thankfully, she knew Sandy understood. Sandy was a true friend, one who didn't expect Margot to keep up ridiculous chitchat at a time like this.

Margot didn't have to say a single word. And so she prayed. She'd been praying ever since her daughter disappeared, but tonight her pleas were far more heartfelt. Far more frantic.

She promised God anything. Did he hear her? Anything as long as she got her daughter back safe and sound.

And when she was done praying, she started right in all over again. Just in case he hadn't been paying attention the first time.

And she waited.

Waited to hear back from Detective Drisklay.

Waited to learn they'd saved her daughter.

Waited for God to finally answer.

CHAPTER 52

Margot had lost track of how many times Sandy had paused their conversation to pray for Becky's safety. While her friend talked to God, Margot kept her eye on the clock. When was the detective going to call back with more news?

Becky was in Las Vegas. Margot texted Jack to let him know, but she still hadn't heard back. Figured.

Las Vegas. How could her little girl have ended up so far away from home?

Please let her be safe. Sandy's prayers were long and eloquent, flowing with trust and hope and beautiful phrases that sounded as if they could have been taken directly from the Bible. Margot's prayers by contrast were short and succinct.

Bring her home.

That was the only thing that mattered.

Sandy gave her hand a squeeze. "Are you doing okay?" she asked.

No, Margot wasn't doing okay. Not even close. But at

least with Sandy she didn't feel like she had to pretend.

"It's just impossible sitting still, wondering what's happening over there."

"I know," Sandy crooned. "I know. But we'll trust God's timing on this. He's at work in this situation. I just know it. He wouldn't have led that detective all the way to Nevada just to let Becky slip through his fingers. At least I really don't think so."

"I know," Margot whispered. She'd been holding onto the same feeble hope for the past hour and was thankful to hear it voiced by someone as rational and calm as Sandy. She gave her friend a smile. "I'm really glad you came over. Thank you."

Sandy beamed. "It's my pleasure. You know, I've been praying for you and for Becky every single day since she went missing, and I don't even pretend to know what kind of good God might be bringing out of this situation, but I know he's at work. I just know it."

"Thanks." A rush of gratitude surged through Margot's body. Through her spirit. She'd felt this way before when she got together with Sandy. This peace. This calm. She shook her head. "I really don't know how you do it. You'll have to tell me your secret."

"What secret?" Sandy cocked her head to the side and

eyed her quizzically.

"How you always know exactly what to say. How you're so encouraging. An hour ago, I probably could have strangled Jack with my bare hands, but now we're here together, and I just feel ... I feel peace. I'm scared to death for my daughter. I could throw up I'm so nervous. But I still feel this bizarre sense of calm. Like I know that everything's going to work itself out in the end."

Sandy smiled at her. "That's the Holy Spirit, darling. He's right here comforting you."

"Yeah," Margot answered dismissively. "I know God's everywhere, but I really only feel this way when I'm with you."

Sandy smiled again. "It's not me. That part you've got to remember. It's the Lord working through me. I'm just along for the ride." She let out a pleasant chuckle. "Now, tell me. I know we've talked some about the Lord, but where are you at in your spiritual walk? How is your prayer life?"

"I've been praying every day. It seems like ever since Becky went missing, I've done nothing but pray."

"That's good."

Margot let out her breath. "Maybe. But the only time I get the sense he's even listening is when I'm with you." She let out a laugh. "Probably because you're so much of a better

Christian than I am."

She was surprised that Sandy didn't chuckle at her joke.

"I'm sorry," Margot said. "I just meant that ... Oh, I don't know. Your husband's a pastor. You've got your life in order. You're at church almost every day. You pray and read your Bible. You're like this super-saint. And I'm just me. I guess that's what I mean. God's going to listen a lot more to you than he is to someone like me."

Sandy was frowning at her. "It isn't what we do that earns us favor with the Lord."

Margot waved her hand in the air. "Oh, I know. I was just joking really."

Sandy shook her head. "No, this is something I wanted to talk to you about anyway, and I'm glad God's led the conversation around to this. I'm so happy to hear that you've spent time praying. If I had to go through half of what you have, I'd go crazy if it weren't for the Lord's strength holding me together. But the Christian life isn't just about praying or reading the Bible or being what you call a super-saint. In fact, it's not really about that at all."

Margot wasn't entirely sure she appreciated the conversational turn, but at least Sandy's words were giving her something to focus on while she waited for the detective to call.

"The Bible says that all of us are sinners," Sandy continued. "That we all are equally guilty before the Lord for the terrible things we've done. That means I'm no better than you, and you're no better than me."

"How do you always seem to be so close to the Lord then?" Margot asked.

"Because I've asked him to forgive my sins," Sandy answered. "Because I have his Holy Spirit living inside me. You know, darling, it's not enough for us to just say we believe in God or we have faith that the Bible is true. It's so much more than just head knowledge. A relationship with Jesus starts when we admit that on our own we're entirely unworthy of God's love and forgiveness."

"Oh, I already know I'm unworthy of that." Margot wasn't sure why she felt so compelled to interrupt. Thankfully, Sandy didn't seem put off or annoyed.

"The only thing that makes me different from some others," Sandy continued, "is that I've put my trust in Jesus to forgive my sins. I've recognized that on my own I can't be nearly good enough, nearly godly enough to earn the Lord's favor. But I've put my trust in Jesus and the death he died on the cross when he hung there from those nails to take the punishment for my sins. Have you ever trusted him in that way?" She leveled her eyes to look straight at Margot.

"I'm not really sure," she had to admit.

The intensity in Sandy's eyes never diminished, and Margot couldn't look away as her friend kept talking.

"Jesus loves you," Sandy said. "He wants a close, intimate relationship with you. But the Bible says that our sins separate us from God. Your sins, my sins, all sins are equally heinous in the sight of a holy God. That's why he sent Jesus, his Son, to take the punishment for our sins on the cross. Jesus suffered so we wouldn't have to. He died so we wouldn't spend an eternity separated from God's love in hell. He gave up his life so that our souls could be saved."

Margot tried to remember if she'd heard this before. It sounded just like the kind of thing Sandy's husband preached, but it somehow felt as if she was learning these things for the first time.

"The Bible says that God loved us so much he sent his Son to take the punishment for our sins." Sandy's voice was radiant with hope and conviction. Her slight southern drawl had become even more pronounced than normal. "He died so we could have a relationship with him. And to start that relationship, all you have to do is ask him to forgive your sins. Tell him you believe that it's his death, not your own good works, that can make you acceptable in his sight. When you do that, the Bible says even the angels in heaven rejoice.

God says he'll put a new heart in you and give you a new spirit, a spirit not of fear but of power and love and self-control. It's a wonderful gift and a wonderful responsibility. Is that a step you'd like to take?"

Margot blinked at her friend. She didn't understand everything. Couldn't figure out logically how Jesus dying on the cross could save her from an eternity in hell. It didn't make sense that Sandy would call herself a sinner just as desperately in need of salvation as a murderer or kidnapper or child abuser.

There were plenty of things Margot didn't know or understand. But she was convinced of one truth. She wanted the peace and joy and radiance that Sandy possessed. She wanted to close her eyes and pray as if she were talking to a friend she met with every single day.

She wanted to experience this kind of peace all the time, not just when Sandy was nearby.

And so she found herself nodding her head. She scarcely noticed the hot tears streaking down her cheeks as she stared at her hand in her lap.

"Yes," she answered. "Yes, I want to take that next step."

CHAPTER 53

Margot was still wrapped up in Sandy's arms when her phone rang. She'd gotten so caught up in praying with her friend that she'd almost forgotten about the detective.

Almost.

"Yes? This is Margot." Her voice was breathless as she answered her cell.

"Drisklay," he answered curtly.

The air gushed out of her lungs as soon as she heard his voice. "Do you know where Becky is? Did you get her yet?"

"Security cameras were able to track her from here to a second motel. We believe that's where she's being held."

"Held? But she's okay, right? You're going in there to get her?"

"The Las Vegas Police Department is working on it right now. I just wanted to let you know we're getting closer."

"And you know she's in there?" Margot insisted. "You're sure their cameras have the right place?"

"As sure as we can be."

She didn't know if she liked his cryptic response but figured it was better than not knowing anything.

"Is there anything else you need from me?" she asked. "Anything I can do?"

"Just sit tight," he answered. "I'll call you when I have more information."

In all her interactions with Drisklay in the past, she couldn't have said she particularly liked the detective, but right now she felt like kissing his feet or cleaning his toilets … Something. Anything to show him how thankful she was.

Becky wasn't a missing person anymore. The Las Vegas police knew right where she was and were going to rescue her from whatever demon had stolen her away. They would see the culprit brought to justice, and Margot would have her daughter home again. Suddenly, all her worries about Becky returning to her sad or broken or traumatized or anything but the perfect girl she was seemed ridiculous and foolish.

She hung up the phone and smiled at her friend. Tonight would be a night Margot could never forget. Not only had she finally taken that one step to draw closer to God, that one step to begin an actual relationship with the Lord, but she was getting her daughter back.

And nothing, not any fear or uncertainty or doubt, could ever steal away her joy.

CHAPTER 54

Becky was surprised to realize that Donahue could hit just as hard as Xavier. Maybe even harder.

"You making eyes at that woman in the bathroom? Is that why she thought she knew you?" Donahue's breath smelled like burnt cigarettes. Becky's arm hadn't stopped stinging since Donahue dragged her out of the car and back into the motel where she'd gotten ready tonight.

"You looking at her?" She gave Becky a shake.

"No," Becky stammered. "I didn't say anything."

Another slap. Where was Xavier? Why hadn't he come to find her yet?

"I didn't ask if you said anything. I asked if you looked at her."

Becky shook her head. "I swear I didn't."

Donahue didn't appear convinced. "You know that woman?"

Another shake of the head. "I've never seen her before. I promise."

"You listed as a runaway or something? You one of those rich, spoiled princesses with your picture hanging up in Walmarts and junk like that?"

"No, I'm not. I'm nobody."

"Xavier didn't tell me you had people looking for you. You sure you don't know who that woman was?"

"I'm sure." Becky hoped she sounded convincing. Hoped it was enough to placate Donahue. At least for now.

"I don't have to tell you not to raise your eyes, do I? Xavier said you were smart. Said you already knew the life."

"I do." Becky nodded her head. "I know. I don't look at anyone. Swear it."

Donahue let out her breath. "He said you weren't going to be a problem."

Becky continued to nod so fast she gave herself a headache. "I'm not. I'm not a problem. Promise."

Donahue loosened her grip. "You better be telling me the truth. You better learn real quick to lay low and just do what you're told because that's how I run things. Got it?"

"Yes." Becky nodded once more. Tried to make herself sound confident as she swallowed away the lump in the back of her throat. "Yeah," she croaked. "I got it."

"Clean yourself up," Donahue ordered. "I'll find Precious to get you a dye job. I'm not sending you out where you're going to be noticed again. You've got a lot of work to make up for tonight, and we've already lost almost a full hour, understand?"

Becky nodded her head.

CHAPTER 55

Holy cupcakes, I just totally ran into a teacher from back home. Donahue brought me to one of the hotels on the Strip, said that's where my first clients were tonight. I wasn't feeling well and had to use the bathroom, and there's where I ran into Mrs. Drisklay. She was one of my teachers back at Medford Academy. I mean, okay, she wasn't ever one of my teachers, but Woong had her for some of his classes, and I recognized her right away. I'm not even kidding. I knew it was her. I even recognized her voice because she was the one who always did the announcements over the loudspeakers.

I couldn't let her know it was me, obviously, or she and I both would have been in huge trouble. Donahue was right there, but Mrs. Drisklay even sent in a security guard to check on me.

Right there in the bathroom.

"Excuse me," she said, talking as nice and polite as Miss Sandy back home. "Someone asked me to check in here. Said this girl looks like a runaway from out East?"

And Donahue started to giggle, said it's not the first time someone's questioned whether or not we're related, mentioned something about my fair skin and blond hair. Then she showed the officer some pictures on her phone of these so-called "family vacations." I don't even know how she got them or if they were Photoshopped or just pictures of someone who looks like me, but they must have been convincing.

The officer apologized for the fuss and let us leave. That's when Donahue decided to bring me back to the motel and dye my hair before I go back out to work. Donahue's definitely not the kind of woman you can just go against. She's tough.

But I'm tougher.

And smarter.

And I've got more to lose.

I have no idea what Xavier was thinking, leaving me here, but if he had any idea what kind of a monster she was, he would have never let me stay with her. I've put enough together to know Donahue doesn't plan on letting me go back to him either. But I've got it all figured out.

At least I hope I do.

Mrs. Drisklay's in Vegas for some marriage thing. After I went out of the bathroom, I saw where she was sitting in the restaurant, and there was a sign with the name of the group. I'm guessing that means she's staying at the same hotel. I don't know the room number, but hopefully that won't be too hard to figure out.

If Xavier knew how Donahue was treating me, he'd want me to run away and find him. And I know just how I'm going to do it.

I need to wait for the right time. It's got to happen soon because I've got to get to Mrs. Drisklay before she heads back home. And now that I think about it, I remember Woong telling me that her husband's a cop. I think his mom's friends with Mrs. Drisklay outside of school (which isn't a surprise because Woong's mom is literally friends with everybody she meets).

So after Precious comes and fixes my hair and Donahue sends me back out to the Strip, I'll find my way to that same hotel. Donahue said I'll be working in a different one the rest of the evening, but I'll figure out how to get to Mrs. Drisklay. I'll tell her husband that Donahue is trying to kidnap me, and I'm back with Xavier before the night's over.

At least I hope so.

I'm so nervous I almost feel like I'm about to throw up. Donahue said she has a lot of dates lined up for me, and I've got to figure out the best way to get out of here. Maybe I'll find a really nice old grandpa type. I've dated guys like that before, and when they're done, it's like they start to feel sorry for you and tell you that you should be back in school and blah, blah, blah. But maybe if I can convince one of them to give me a ride to Mrs. Drisklay's hotel ...

Okay, God. I know you're listening. And I know you want me back with Xavier just as much as I do. So please help me. Help me find a date who's willing to give me a lift without Donahue finding out. And please help me to find Mrs. Drisklay's room without too much trouble, and help her husband to know what to do to get me back to Xavier.

And God? Please help me get through the next few hours. Miss Sandy said that your heart breaks when bad things happen to your children, and you know the kinds of things I sometimes have to put up with on nights like this. I don't want to do it anymore. I never wanted to do it.

If you help me get out of here, if you help me just find Xavier, I promise to change. I'll tell him I don't want to do anymore dates. I'll find some other way to earn us the money. I've got the fake ID. I could probably even become a waitress or something. I'll scrub toilets. I'm serious. Anything is better than this.

I know I probably don't deserve your help after all that I've done, but that's why I'm promising to change. I just want you to help me get out of here.

That's all I'm asking.

CHAPTER 56

Okay, so I kind of lost track of time, but I'm starting to wonder if maybe Donahue and Precious forgot about me. If I wasn't so worried about what's going to happen next, I might even be able to fall asleep before too long. I wish Xavier was here. He was always really nice about letting me borrow some of his sleeping pills if I was having a hard time getting to bed. I miss him so much it literally hurts.

I've basically haven't stopped thinking about him since Donahue brought me back here. The other thing I've been thinking a lot about tonight is my mom. I feel kind of bad for how things turned out. I mean, I never meant to make her so worried. When we left Massachusetts, Xavier told me I could call home as soon as we figured out where we were going. Then when we got here, any time I brought it up, he'd say, "Why do you want to call her? She doesn't understand us. She'll just try to talk you into coming home."

And I believed him. Mostly because he was right. Mom wouldn't understand. But I still wish I had found a way to let her know I was safe. Even a letter would be better than nothing.

I wonder if Mrs. Drisklay believed the security guard and decided I'm really someone else. I wonder what Mom's doing right now. Is she awake? I wonder if she and Dad still fight all the time, or maybe they're so worried about me they've learned to put some of their differences aside. Hey, that's another good thing God might have worked out from all this, right?

And speaking of God, I really think that this time away from Xavier is in the end going to be one of those mixed blessings kind of things. Because I remember once going to youth group with Woong, and the teacher there was talking about how we shouldn't put anything in front of our love for God, and anything we love more than God is basically an idol. And I hate to put it like this because it sounds like I'm actually worshipping him, but I can see how in some cases maybe I've treated Xavier that way. Like an idol.

I mean, I know he's not perfect. But he's so good to me. And now that we have this little bit of time apart, I think it's helping me focus more on my relationship with God. Which is another reason maybe tonight and Donahue getting so mad at me and bringing me back here might be another mixed blessing. Because let's be totally honest. I know most

Christians really aren't supposed to be doing the kind of stuff Xavier's had me do. And I told God that if he got me back to Xavier, I'd stop going on dates. Because in spite of all these things I've done, I really do still believe in the Bible, and I'm mature enough to know right from wrong (even if I haven't always made the best choices). So what I'm thinking is maybe God heard my prayer. Maybe he heard me tell him I didn't want to date around anymore, and me being stuck here is his way of answering that.

So yeah. Another blessing.

It's funny how you can find them just about anywhere once you learn how to look.

Well, I'm getting pretty tired. Another answer to prayer, I guess. Maybe I'll try to lie down and go to sleep ...

Wait. Is that someone at the door? Is Donahue coming back to beat me up some more? Or maybe it's Precious, finally coming to dye my hair so I can go back out tonight. I wish she wouldn't. I just want to sleep.

Am I still going to be in trouble?

Okay, God. You know me. You know I need a little extra help right now. You know how much I want to try to stay positive, right? I don't know who it is who's unlocking the door right now. I just pray that whoever it is won't try to hurt me or make me do things you don't want me doing anymore.

All right?

Okay, thanks.

I'm ready now. You can let them come in.

CHAPTER 57

Back in her hotel room, Caroline pulled out the pocket Bible she'd packed in the bottom of her carry-on. In general, she tried not to read it when Calvin was around. It wasn't that she was ashamed of God's Word. She just knew that if she did it where he could see her, she was opening herself up to all kinds of ridicule.

Tonight, she was reading through the Psalms. Reading words that felt like they were written for her at this exact time and this exact place.

He who dwells in the shelter of the Most High will rest in the shadow of the Almighty.

There were so many people on her heart to pray for. For her husband's safety as he passed information onto the Vegas police. Becky, who'd seen far too much for a girl her age. Becky's mother, who must be frantic with worry back home.

Caroline prayed for them all. She couldn't be by her husband's side. Calvin wouldn't hear of her joining him in his work, and the truth was Caroline would only get in his way. But that couldn't stop her from praying.

She turned to the next verse of the passage.

I will say of the LORD, "He is my refuge and my fortress, my God, in whom I trust."

One day, she believed, even Calvin would recognize that it was God who'd been guiding him. It was God who led them to this particular hotel. It was God who led him to Becky Linklater. God who was using him to ensure her safety.

One day, she believed, her husband would acknowledge Jesus as the Son of God, and they would worship him together.

She didn't know when, and she didn't know how, but she believed with all her heart that the day was coming.

Surely he will save you from the fowler's snare and from the deadly pestilence.

Strange that she didn't feel scared at all. Usually, when she knew Calvin was working a particularly dangerous case, she was nothing but nerves and anxiety. But right now, she felt indescribable peace. God wouldn't have led her and her husband to the exact same city where Becky Linklater was held captive, wouldn't have led Caroline to the exact bathroom in the exact same hotel just so they could go home and let the trail go cold again.

Something was going to happen tonight.

Something big.

Something that she and Calvin and Becky and everyone else involved would never forget.

God was at work. She'd never felt so certain of anything before. Like a sailor who instinctively knows when a storm's brewing or a baker who can sense without checking the oven the exact moment the bread's ready to come out.

That's how certain Caroline was that God was at work. That he was going to protect her husband. Protect Becky Linklater.

And bring this entire saga of an investigation to a happy ending in the way that only he could do.

She just had to keep praying. Praying and waiting to see what he was going to do.

He will cover you with his feathers, and under his wings you will find refuge; his faithfulness will be your shield and rampart.

Yes, God was faithful. Faithful to Caroline and to Calvin, faithful to Becky Linklater and her family. He was faithful to fulfill every single promise he ever made in all of Scripture.

You will not fear the terror of night, nor the arrow that

flies by day.

"Yes, Lord." Caroline was speaking out loud now, unable to contain the intensity of her zeal. "Yes, Lord. You are the one who delivers us from danger, from the pestilence that stalks in the darkness, from the plague that destroys at midday. You are the one who keeps my husband safe, who protects helpless children like Becky. You keep us safe and free us from fear. You are so good, Lord."

Tears raced down her cheeks. Tears of love and gratitude. Had she ever felt as close to God as she did at this exact moment?

Love swelled up in her heart. Love for the Lord who could reach out in a Las Vegas hotel room to send down so much comfort and peace to her. Love for her husband who worked tirelessly and put his own safety on the line to protect the vulnerable. Love for Becky, a girl who she prayed would be rescued from a life of terror and fear and brought back home to the family that loved her.

As she finished reading through the Psalm as her body relaxed more than it had in weeks. Maybe months.

If you make the Most High your dwelling — even the LORD, who is my refuge — then no harm will befall you, no disaster will come near your tent. For he will command his angels concerning you to guard you in all your ways; they will lift you up in their hands, so that you will not strike your foot against a stone.

She pictured Becky Linklater, surrounded by God's holy angels who were sworn to protect and shield her from all harm. She pictured Calvin, brave and remarkably strong as he told the Las Vegas police department what they needed to know. That was her husband. The man she married. The man she loved.

As she read the last verse, it was as if God was speaking to her directly about Calvin.

He will call upon me, and I will answer him; I will be with him in trouble, I will deliver him and honor him. With long life will I satisfy him and show him my salvation.

There was nothing left for Caroline to say but amen.

CHAPTER 58

Holy cupcakes, it's him. It's really him! I can't believe God answered my prayers so quickly. If I ever in my entire life start to doubt Xavier at all, I'm going to remember what he did for me. Coming all this way to get me out of this prison.

I still don't know how he found me, but I don't care. I'm just so happy to see him. I wish I had a phone. I want to text Woong. Want to tell him how happy I am and let him know that prayer works!

Thank you, God. I don't want to be like those men in the Bible who forgot to come back and thank you for healing them. Because I'm so grateful, Lord. You seriously rock.

I'm so happy I could literally burst right about now.

I'll have to find Mrs. Drisklay's email or something and find a way to tell her I'm all right. She's probably still worried. Poor thing. She probably wonders if that really was me or if she just accosted some innocent girl and her mom in a Vegas bathroom. Either way, you've got to feel sorry for her, right?

She's a good woman. I hope she's having a good time at that conference. I hope she's not spending too much time worrying about me.

And did she get in touch with Mom, I wonder? I'll have to let Xavier know that when we get to wherever we're going after here, I'm going to call my mom. I'm putting my foot down this time. It's not right to leave her so scared and worried. And if Mrs. Drisklay calls her and says she thinks she saw me at some Las Vegas casino, Mom's immediately going to think the worst, and I've got to put her mind at ease.

Everything's working out, just like God promised it would, and I literally couldn't be happier. This has turned from the absolute worst to one of the best days of my whole life. Seeing Xavier here in this hotel room where I've been trapped, it's like day one of the next stage in my life. A new chapter. Not even a new chapter, like a whole new sequel. And this one's going to have an even happier ending. Can you tell I'm pretty excited? I could seriously laugh out loud right now. Haha. I just did.

Xavier doesn't seem to know what I'm giggling about. He looks kind of upset, but that's probably just because he's been so worried about me. Give me all of two seconds to explain, then he'll understand. He's literally the best thing that ever happened to me, and I'm never going to stop thanking God for bringing us together.

CHAPTER 59

Margot let out a deep and weary sigh. "Well, thank you, Alexi. If you hear from Detective Drisklay, please ask him to call me right away."

"Of course," Alexi answered. Margot had met him a handful of times before, and even though he was infinitely kinder and more humane, she still wasn't convinced he was nearly as competent as his partner.

She glanced at the time. It had been nearly an hour since Detective Drisklay had given her an update, and even that update hadn't contained anything new. The FBI was on the case, getting together everything they needed for an extraction. They knew exactly where her daughter was. Now they just had to get her out.

The FBI. Margot was glad that everyone was taking her daughter's situation seriously, which felt like a welcome change from the cooling case it was turning into, but she couldn't rid her mind of images of men in black bullet-proof vests and riot gear throwing tear gas and dodging bullets to whisk her daughter to safety.

If that's what it took to bring her daughter home …

Sandy was still awake, bustling around, making coffee, toasting bread, urging Margot to eat and drink and keep up her energy.

"I've got a real good feeling about this," her friend had stated several times that night.

If only Margot could be so convinced.

After she prayed, after she took that step to actually confess her desire to be a Christian, a peace had washed over Margot. It was miraculous. Healing. Unforgettable.

But where had it gone?

Margot was glad Sandy was here. Glad to have that moral support. But it would also be infinitely easier to face the uncertainty of tonight with a few more glasses of wine. Margot wondered if now that she was saved she should rid her house of alcohol. She hadn't asked Sandy about it yet because she was afraid to hear the answer.

And she figured that the Lord understood there were more pressing matters for her to worry about at this exact moment.

Time ticked by with torturous regularity, the second hand of the kitchen clock marching relentlessly forward. Yet the minutes stretched on and on. Her phone battery was already half dead just from all the times she'd swiped the screen to see if there were any calls or messages she'd missed.

Becky. Her Becky. Her little girl.

She was going to be rescued.

She was going to be safe

She was going to come home.

Wasn't she?

CHAPTER 60

Becky was so happy to see Xavier that it took her several moments to longer than it should have to realize he didn't return her smile. He stood in the hotel hallway, glaring at her. Behind him, she thought she heard one of Donahue's guard dogs snarling.

"Xavier?" She said his name quietly, as if she didn't quite believe that she was seeing him here. "Xavier?" she repeated, this time with a little more confidence. A little more joy.

She rushed toward him.

And then stopped.

"What's wrong?" She felt the blood drain from her head when she saw the ferocity in his eyes. "Xavier?" This time her voice was no stronger than a pitiful squeak.

He stepped in and slammed the door shut. She winced automatically, frozen in place as he clasped the inside lock.

"I'm glad to see you," she started to stammer but stopped when his eyes landed on hers.

Eyes full of hate and rage.

What had she done? Why was he so mad?

Instinctively, she made herself smaller, cowering. What was it? Was he angry that she'd gone to work for Donahue? Didn't he realize she had no choice?

He raised his hand, but she was too stunned to react before he slapped her across the cheek. Hard.

She staggered backward.

Another slap. Or was this one his fist? She couldn't tell.

"Baby, what's wrong?" When she opened her mouth, she tasted the blood. Was it from her nose or her mouth? What was he doing? Why was he acting like this?

"Stop," she pleaded as his next punch landed her on the floor. As his feet came toward her, she curled herself into a ball, wrapping her arms protectively around her head. "Don't." She couldn't get the words out. Couldn't even catch her breath.

"Never once have I gotten a single complaint from Donahue about one of my girls." He was panting while he spoke, his words punctuated by his kicks. "Not until you. After everything I did …" Another kick. "After all those gifts I bought you." Kick. "All that money I wasted."

He slammed his shoe into her rib, and she cried out. "Please!" she wailed when she caught her voice. "Don't. I'm sorry. I won't do it again. I'm sorry."

"I'm the one who's sorry." He was straddling her now, his weight against her throat. Collapsing her airway. "Sorry I didn't get rid of you sooner."

She clawed at his forearms, struggling to throw his weight off her.

"I'm sorry I wasted my time on you." Punch. "Sorry I even thought you might be a good investment." Punch. "Sorry I ever met you."

She was drenched. Drenched in blood and sweat. Probably tears, too.

He eased up for a moment, and breath rushed back into her lungs. "I'm sorry," she sobbed, like a chant that could ward off an evil attack. "I'm sorry. I'm sorry. I'm so sorry."

The punching stopped. She blinked her eyes open.

Was it over?

The door swung open. "What's going on in there?"

Becky didn't know whose voice it was. She didn't care. She reached out and grabbed hold of an electric cord, yanking down until a lamp fell on top of Xavier. It gave her just enough of a distraction to roll out from under him. She lunged toward the door, every muscle in her body aching, but Xavier grabbed her by the ankle and slammed her body back to the ground.

She couldn't see. Couldn't move. For several seconds, she couldn't even breathe.

"Get your hands off her." The voice was familiar. That woman who helped her do her makeup earlier. Becky forced her eyes to focus. Precious. What was she doing here? Didn't she realize it wasn't safe?

Xavier wasn't safe.

"You stay out of this." Xavier growled.

Precious's voice was strong. "You take your hands off her and leave right now or I'm going to ..."

Xavier punched Precious in the gut. Becky didn't have time to warn her. All she could do was let out a little squeak that came far too late.

"Don't tell me what I can or can't do," Xavier snarled. "This girl is mine. Do you hear me? She belongs to me."

Becky had to do something. She'd never seen her boyfriend hurt anyone else before.

"Xavier, stop." The words seemed to catch in her throat. She wasn't entirely sure she'd said them at all.

A distraction. An intervention. She had to do something. Precious was on the floor now, and by the crazed look in Xavier's eyes, it was clear he didn't plan on tiring out any time soon.

"Get off her!" Becky leapt on his back. Clawing.

Pounding. Kicking.

He threw her off with a roar.

"Sugar, get out of here."

It took Becky a moment to realize Precious was talking to her.

"Get out of here," Precious repeated. She shielded her face with her forearms as Xavier kicked her head. "Go!" she shouted.

Blinded by tears and sheer terror, Becky blinked once at Xavier. At the man she'd loved so deeply. The man she'd sacrificed so much for.

The man she'd hoped to grow old with. Kind, gentle Xavier. Doting and spoiling and charming.

One more blink, and the phantom was gone, and Becky was running down the hall, fleeing from the demons of her past.

CHAPTER 61

Oh my God. And I'm not using it as the swear word, Lord, I promise. But seriously.

Oh my God.

I don't know where I'm going. I don't know what to do. And what about Precious? I can't just leave her in there, can I? I need to go back. Need to do something. Xavier's going to kill her. He's literally going to kill her.

God, I'm so sorry. So sorry I didn't do a better job loving him. I should have known he was getting so stressed. And I shouldn't have made Donahue mad tonight in the bathroom. It's all my fault. I'm so sorry. Please don't blame me for what he does to Precious. I couldn't help it. I didn't know how to stop him.

God, I don't know where to go. I can't go back. I literally can't go back. He's going to be coming after me. I know he is. There's nowhere I can go where I'll be safe. He found me at Donahue's. He would have killed me. Oh my God, I seriously think my boyfriend was about to kill me.

Why didn't I realize how stressed out he'd gotten? I've been so foolish and selfish. I should have been a better girlfriend. Should have worked harder. Lord, I'm so sorry. Please tell Precious I'm so sorry. This isn't her fault. It's mine. And now she might be dead.

Oh my God, what if Xavier kills her?

He's insane. He's literally and entirely insane. And I love him so much, God. I love him so much I can't stand to think about him hurting so much. Being so angry. If he kills Precious, they're going to find him and he's going to go to jail, and it'll be my fault. My fault ...

Lord, I'm so sorry for everything I've done. I know Miss Sandy says you only have to ask for forgiveness once, and I don't want to argue with her, but seriously I doubt she's ever been in as much trouble as I am. And I know for a fact she hasn't sinned as much in her entire life as I have in this past year. I'm so sorry. Please tell me what I need to do to get back on your good side. Tell me what I need to do to be right again. I never meant for anything of this to happen, God. I promise.

I don't know what to do now, Lord. I don't know where to go. You got me out of Donahue's, Lord, and I know I'm supposed to be thankful. But now I'm out here in the wide open. My dress is torn. My face is all bloody. I'm a huge mess. I'm so terrified I can barely see where I'm going, but my legs refuse to slow down.

I'm lost. I'm cold. I'm exhausted.

And, God, I don't want to admit this now, but I'm really, really scared.

CHAPTER 62

Becky had lost track of how long she'd been running. She'd never been in this part of the city before, but she figured that if she went along with the heaviest traffic, she'd eventually end up at the Strip.

How did everything turn out this way? Xavier had come back for her. He'd come back to take her away from Donahue's. Except that wasn't what happened.

What went wrong? How could she have let him get so angry like that? How could she have run away when Precious was in so much danger? And what about the dogs? What if the guards thought Xavier really was a bad guy and put the dogs on him?

Becky's stomach was swirling with fear, guilt, and adrenaline. It was hard to guess the hour. It was evening when she ran into Mrs. Drisklay in the bathroom, but that felt like it might have happened weeks ago. She hadn't slept since then, but it was still impossible to guess if this was still the same day and not several lifetimes later.

Where was Xavier? Was he all right? Would he come looking for her? She had no idea you could be so terrified of someone and love him so much all at the same time. Was this how Mom felt after Dad left? So hurt she couldn't stand the sight of him, but still so much in love the idea of being apart was enough to kill her?

Mom …

Where was she now? Had Mrs. Drisklay called her?

Mrs. Drisklay …

For the first time since she escaped Donahue's, she stopped running. Her calves and shins throbbed. Her bare feet smarted with cold. Her body still thought it was supposed to lurch forward, and the momentum nearly knocked her onto her face. She doubled over, panting loudly, her lungs stinging from both her sobs and her exertion.

Should she go back to Donahue's? Xavier never stayed angry for long. And if he was in trouble, he'd need her. If the police got involved, she could tell them it was all a mistake. He hadn't meant to hurt anybody. He was trying to help. She could tell them she'd been kidnapped. That Xavier was only trying to save her and was acting in self-defense when he attacked Precious.

He'd calm down. He'd hold her. Tell her that he loved her. And then …

And then what?

Buy her that apartment he'd always promised, tell her she could stop working, and settle down so they could live happily ever after?

Precious's words still echoed in Becky's mind. *The whole time he was with you, he was working a dozen other girls.* It couldn't be true, could it?

Becky thought about the past several months. Xavier always coming home later and later, always with some excuse. Some days he'd leave her chained to the bed the entire day. She'd been so ready to accept his lies about where he'd been. Deep in her heart, had she really known?

No, what was she thinking? This was Xavier she was talking about. *Her* Xavier. He would never do anything like that. Would he?

You love him, but that doesn't change the fact that he sold you. No. Precious had been lying. Xavier wasn't like that. Maybe some real sick men did disgusting things like that, but Xavier was different.

Wasn't he?

She should go back to him. The bottom of her foot was bloody, and she was shivering now with cold. Funny, she hadn't realized you could be sweating and freezing at the exact same time. Life with Xavier wasn't always easy, but you weren't supposed to give up on somebody the second things got hard. That's what Dad had done to Mom, and Becky wasn't going to be anything like that.

Her mind was made up. She was going back to Donahue's.

Going back to Xavier.

It was the right thing to do.

So why did her legs refuse to move?

CHAPTER 63

Margot's hand trembled as she clutched her phone against her ear. "I'm not sure I understand."

"Mrs. Linklater, your daughter wasn't in the motel by the time the men arrived." Detective Drisklay's voice held a hint of compassion. Margot wondered if in her shock her mind had simply made it up.

"But you said you had surveillance. You said that's where she'd been held." Her head was swimming. It felt as if she were in some sort of *déjà vu* loop where she kept asking the same questions and the detective kept repeating the same answers, and still she couldn't understand.

The detective sounded uncharacteristically patient. "We found a girl on the scene. She was pretty injured. They're taking her to the hospital now. She helped Becky run away. She got your daughter away from the people holding her captive."

In the back of her mind, Margot thought that the words were supposed to bring joy and relief. "But why didn't the

FBI see her then when she ran away?"

"There was another exit," Detective Drisklay explained. "She got out through a nightclub the next door over. At the time, the men in the extraction team didn't know the buildings were connected."

"I don't understand." Margot lost track of how many times she'd said the same words. From the kitchen, Sandy stood over a teapot, watching her sympathetically.

Detective Drisklay let out a sigh. "The good news is that your daughter has escaped immediate danger. Based on the injuries of the girl who helped her out, you should be thankful Becky's even alive."

Margot's breath caught at the words. "But you're telling me you still don't know where she is?" It didn't make sense. How could a girl as young and helpless as her daughter simply disappear?

"The LVPD has men out looking for her now. And they've put out alerts to all the nearby hospitals as well."

Margot didn't fight the tears of fear and confusion that cascaded down her cheeks. "Is she hurt?"

"She might be. That's why we put out the alert. Your daughter's a smart girl. She just needs to get herself to a hospital or to a phone to call 911, and emergency responders will be ready to take it from there. She'll be in good hands,

Mrs. Linklater."

Margot had never heard Detective Drisklay speak to her this gently, and she tried desperately to believe him. She tried to croak out her thanks, but only a tiny sob escaped.

"Are you still working on your flight plans to Las Vegas?" he asked.

Margot was grateful for his question. Grateful to have something else to focus her attention on besides the fact that her daughter was abused, beaten, and now missing. "Yes. I'm expecting a call from my husband any minute with the details." As much as Margot wanted to be in Las Vegas to meet Becky the moment she was found, she was terrified of the time in the air where she'd be unavailable to receive any updates.

"Well, you keep me posted on your travel plans," Detective Drisklay concluded, "and I'll let you know when they've found your daughter."

Somehow Margot found the strength to thank the detective and ended the call. As soon as she put the phone down, Sandy was at her side, urging her to take a sip of tea.

"Have they found Becky?" Sandy asked gently.

Margot shook her head.

She stared at the mug. It wasn't the glass of wine her brain and body were desperately convinced she needed, but it was a sign of love and comfort.

She offered Sandy a weak smile. "I'm really glad you're here."

Sandy reached out her arms and wrapped her up in a comforting hug. "That's what friends are for, my love. That's what friends are for."

CHAPTER 64

Caroline had never felt a connection like this to the Holy Spirit. There were no words to describe the energy she felt giving fuel to her prayers as she sat alone in the hotel room. It was as if God himself had taken a hold of her soul and was praying directly through her.

Lord, I ask that wherever Becky is, whatever she's doing right now at this exact moment, that you would be the one to protect her and shield her. I ask that she would feel the strong and powerful arms of her heavenly Father surrounding her, keeping her from fear and pain.

We pray for her deliverance, Lord, from the physical bondage that's held her captive as well as from whatever emotional trauma she's had to endure. God, no girl should have to go through the amount of suffering that she has, I know it's only by your tender mercy and grace that she can ever hope to find healing, but that's what I pray for, dear Lord. Full and complete and perfect healing, that whatever scars and wounds have inflicted poor Becky would be healed perfectly in the powerful name of Jesus. Build her up. Teach her that she is your precious, beautiful child. Free her from whatever lies she's grown to believe after all the terrible things she's been forced to endure. Free her from terror, from trauma, and from any other danger.

Silent tears flowed down Caroline's cheeks as she prayed. The air grew so thick with the presence and glory of God she sank to her knees by her hotel bedside.

It's not only her I pray for, Father. I pray also for any other girl and boy who's been trapped in a life like this. I pray that you would give them perfect healing, perfect deliverance, and perfect freedom. Even though they might right now live in fear and helplessness, I speak victory and strength over them today. I speak freedom and declare that they will no longer live as slaves.

Caroline had never prayed so boldly before, had never done anything besides ask God to hear her petitions and hope that he was inclined to listen. But now it was as if she herself were singlehandedly writing the life narrative of any child caught in the clutches of abuse, setting them free instantaneously by the power behind her words.

I speak life over these victims, Lord, and declare that they will no longer be held captive. I speak to the evil men and women holding them in bondage, and not only to them but to the powers of darkness and the principalities of this world who are keeping your precious children enslaved in such horrific ways. In Jesus' name, I break the power of slavery, of addiction, of captivity that's impacted your sons and daughters for so long.

You are the Father to the fatherless, Lord, so rise up and defend these poor and helpless creatures. Set them free from their physical bondage and heal them from their emotional trauma. You are the only one strong enough to tear down these strongholds that have held them captive for so long. And I believe you are going to do this and even more.

Her head was raised heavenward, her tears streaming down her cheeks. Her eyes didn't even process the hotel room ceiling above her head. It was as if the entire array of God's throne-room was stretched out before her. If she could just find a fraction more focus, she'd see it clearly for what it was.

Glorious.

Her hands trembled when she let out her breath. The sense of intense divine presence lifted, but the air was still filled with a sweet, comforting peace. She felt both exhausted and euphoric. For a minute, she remained kneeling, wondering what it was she was supposed to pray for next. Finally, she realized that her work was done, and she crawled into bed, perfectly content, perfectly convinced that she'd accomplished more to advance God's kingdom tonight than she had in all her years as a Christian put together.

CHAPTER 65

Drisklay got off the phone with Mrs. Linklater. She'd made arrangements to fly out to Vegas and was just a few minutes away from boarding the plane. He promised to send her an email if anything new developed, and he looked forward to the fact that he wouldn't have to answer any more of her frantic calls for the next several hours while she was in the air.

He'd already called Alexi, filling his partner in. Everything was in the hands of the FBI and the Vegas police now, even though from the looks of it they'd let his victim slip right through their fingers. Well, Becky Linklater was out there somewhere. Just like he'd told her mother, if Becky was smart, she'd call 911 or get herself to an emergency room, and then this whole nightmare would be behind her.

He figured Caroline would still be awake but opened the door to their hotel room as quietly as he could just in case. Shining the light from his cell toward her, he was surprised at how relaxed she looked while she slept. There was a peacefulness to her expression that almost made her face glow. Her face was radiant, her skin surprisingly soft and smooth.

He reached out his hand. So close.

He stepped back when she blinked her eyes open. "You're back?" Her voice was both groggy and childlike.

"Shh. Try to go back to sleep." He set down his phone and glanced at her once again to see if her features had changed.

Caroline sat up in bed. "What happened? Did they get Becky?"

Drisklay loosened the top few buttons of his shirt. He wasn't ready to get undressed yet, but he could at least make himself a little more comfortable. "No, not yet."

She clutched at her blankets as if they might save her from drowning. "She's still trapped at that motel?"

He shook his head. "No. She ran off. They don't know where she is."

"Have you talked to her mother yet?"

Irritation and impatience replaced whatever sense of tenderness he'd felt looking at his wife sleeping just a minute earlier. "Of course I talked to her mother."

Caroling let out her breath. "That poor woman has been through so much."

There was nothing Drisklay could say to disagree.

Caroline reached over and touched his sleeve. "How are you? I bet you're exhausted."

He shrugged. "That's life."

She scooted over in bed. "Come and get some rest. Even if it's just for a few minutes."

He paused for a moment and considered. The bed did look inviting.

"Come on," Caroline urged. "I'll wake you up if your phone rings. Shut your eyes. Tomorrow's probably going to be another long day for you. Just for a few minutes."

Drisklay shrugged and kicked off his shoes. "Guess it wouldn't hurt to sleep off that last pot of coffee."

CHAPTER 66

"Would you like a drink?"

Margot stared at the flight attendant, then at the wine bottle near the back of her little push cart.

She licked her lips. "Just some cranberry juice, please."

She glanced at the time. Two more hours before the plane landed in Vegas. She could do this. She could hold it together just a little while longer.

Margot clutched the Bible Sandy had given to her when she dropped her off at Logan Airport.

"Start in Isaiah 40," Sandy had told her, "and just keep working your way through until God brings you the comfort and healing you need."

Margot was still hunting for that comfort and healing after her first three chapters. Frustrated and desperate, she turned the page. A highlighted passage caught her eye.

When you pass through the waters, I will be with you. She wasn't exactly sure what it meant to pass through the waters, but something about the words slowed her racing heart.

Lord, she prayed, *it's not me I need you to be with. I need you to be with my daughter. I need you to be with my Becky.*

She opened her eyes and kept on reading. *When you pass through the rivers, they will not sweep over you.* How much pain and terror had her little girl already suffered? How much more pain and terror would she endure before she was back in Margot's arms again?

Lord, I'm so sorry. I'm sorry for everything. I'm sorry for not being a better mom. I'm sorry for being so bitter with Jack. I'm sorry for not loving my family as I should. I'm sorry for everything, God, and I promise I'll make it all up to you and a hundred times more if you just bring my daughter home safe and sound.

She flipped open her phone and checked her email. The thirty dollars she spent for in-flight wi-fi access was the only tether she felt to the real world. Her connection to Detective Drisklay and to news about her daughter.

But other than an encouraging prayer from Sandy, her inbox was empty.

She turned her phone off and tried to focus more on her reading.

When you walk through the fire, you will not be burned; the flames will not set you ablaze. Walking through the fire.

That was something Margot could picture. What else would you call these past months of hell, uncertainty, and waiting? And what had it been like for Becky? Alone. Scared. Abused. Thinking about what her daughter must have been through sent shards of torture splintering through her soul. Margot wondered if she'd make it to Las Vegas or if the stress and strain would kill her before the plane ever landed.

With shaking hands, she picked up her phone again. Still no word from the detective, but she took the time to re-read Sandy's prayer.

God, I thank you so much for taking such good care of my strong and beautiful friend Margot. I thank you for the love and grace you poured out on her tonight as you granted her your sweet gift of salvation. I thank you that not even a sparrow falls to the ground apart from your will and that all the days you've ordained for Margot and her sweet daughter Becky were written in your book before one of them came to be.

Margot inhaled deeply, trying to steady her breathing. She took a sip of cranberry juice and read on.

Be with Margot while she's on that plane. Give her comfort. Give her grace. Give her peace.

Margot licked her lips. So far, she'd made it through take-off and the first leg of the journey without crying, but if she kept on reading Sandy's kind and faith-filled words, she'd start sobbing and never be able to stop.

She closed the email, refreshed her inbox, and waited. Still no news from the detective. She squeezed her eyes shut, fighting off the start of an unbearable tension headache. She had no idea how she'd survive the rest of this flight, but she needed to be put together when she landed in Vegas.

Her daughter was counting on her.

CHAPTER 67

Caroline had only been asleep for ten or fifteen minutes before Calvin returned to their hotel room, but now she felt as if she'd slept for ten or twelve hours. Was this what it felt like to pray your hardest and know with certainty that God heard you? Is this why her friend Sandy always came across as so calm and rested?

Caroline glanced at her husband, who was snoring slightly and drooling on the hotel pillow. Calvin could fall asleep in ten seconds flat. In the carefree days of their early marriage, she'd even timed him. Ten seconds flat, even with his veins pulsating with caffeine from all that cold coffee he drank and his mind swarming with details of all the cases he'd been working.

Caroline was surprised she didn't feel more anxious. It was as if every single fear for Becky and her safety had been poured out to God in her prayer, and he took those fears and tossed them into his sea of forgetfulness, never to be seen or heard of again.

It was nothing short of miraculous.

At first, the feeling left Caroline confused. Becky hadn't been rescued yet. If anybody knew where she was, they would have called her husband by now. Since this was still an open case, shouldn't Caroline keep praying?

Several times, she started to talk to God, but each and every time she was overcome with a strange and inexplicable sense of finality, as if everything she needed to pray had already been spoken. Now she just had to wait.

In a way, it was nice to think that God had already solved this mystery. Already brought Becky to safety.

But what was Caroline supposed to do in the meantime?

She watched her husband in bed. Their schedules had been so hectic lately, she'd forgotten how relaxed he looked in his sleep. Such a change from his appearance when he was awake.

God, she prayed, *I want him to know this same peace I do. I want him to feel the same love and power you showed me tonight.*

Again, she felt like there was more she was supposed to say, but her spirit remained quiet. Calm. Assured that God heard. Calvin belonged to God. She sensed it just as profoundly, as powerfully as she'd sensed God's presence in this hotel room earlier tonight.

Calvin belonged to God. It wasn't her job to nag or plead or beg. Maybe the timing wouldn't come as quickly as she hoped, but one day God would show himself to her husband. One day, Calvin would know the indescribable love of his heavenly Father. One day, Calvin would call on the name of the Lord and worship the one true God with joy and passion.

Until then she would wait. Calm and serene, just like her husband, who was snoring beside her.

She would wait and trust that God was constantly at work even when she couldn't see him. Even when she couldn't sense him.

Even when her husband drove her crazy.

She smiled, thinking about God's grace, his mercy, how she didn't deserve any of the love or peace he'd poured into her spirit.

For the first time in months, maybe even in years, she felt an unbridled, overwhelming love for her husband. She leaned down to kiss him. Her lips brushed the scruff on his cheek, and she tried to recall how long it had been since their last intimate connection.

He didn't stir. She pictured herself leaning over and kissing him again when a ringing noise startled her out of bed.

Someone was calling the hotel room phone.

CHAPTER 68

Becky couldn't believe it actually worked. The whole time while she was talking to the front desk, she'd been terrified they were going to realize she was lying, that they were going to call the cops on her and make her go back to Donahue's. But it worked!

If Becky ever found herself doubting in God again, she'd just remember everything he'd done for her tonight. Like the cab that just happened to pass after she made up her mind where she needed to go. She still felt bad she couldn't pay the driver, but he must have realized she was in some sort of trouble because he only gave her a little bit of a hard time about it.

Convincing the front desk to call Mrs. Drisklay's room wasn't as hard as she expected either. She'd taken a small risk assuming that Mrs. Drisklay was checked into the same hotel where she'd seen her eating earlier, but in the end all she had to do was cry a few tears (not even fake ones), tell the man behind the desk she was in trouble and needed to see her aunt, and he called up to Mrs. Drisklay's room.

Now she was standing in the lobby trying not to shiver and sob while she waited for Mrs. Drisklay to meet her. The first thing Becky noticed when the elevator doors opened were the rings around Mrs. Drisklay's eyes, but the sadness in her expression vanished almost immediately.

"Becky." Mrs. Drisklay hurried up to her, wrapping her in a warm hug. The comforting physical touch was enough to set off Becky's tears again, but this time she wasn't alone. Mrs. Drisklay was crying too.

"Thank God you're safe," she breathed. "Thank God you're okay. Calvin, she's okay." Mrs. Drisklay pulled away just enough so that Becky could see the sour-faced man standing behind her and repeated, "She's okay."

Mr. Drisklay didn't say anything, but his wife kept repeating, "Your mom's on the way. She's on a plane right now."

Becky's head was spinning. It was hard to focus on Mrs. Drisklay's words. Everything was overwhelming. The love she felt pouring out from this teacher. The rush of comfort and relief at the sight of a familiar face. The mention of her mom was enough to nearly choke her.

"Come on, Calvin," Mrs. Drisklay said to her husband. "Let's get her upstairs." She draped her arm protectively around Becky's shivering frame while the elevator doors shut the three of them in. "We're going to get you cleaned up and dressed and warmed up and you're going to be just fine."

"She needs to see the forensics team first." It was the first time Becky heard Mr. Drisklay speak, and she was surprised by how emotionless his tone was.

Mrs. Drisklay wrapped Becky in her arms. "You do whatever you need to do," she told her husband, "but I'm not leaving this poor thing here all cold and torn up like this. She's coming up to our room and we're calming her down and we're letting her talk to her mother."

Becky's legs nearly collapsed. Thankfully, Mrs. Drisklay was right there to lend her support. Becky's mind was in a haze, and her body finally registered how broken, tired, and battered she was. But she somehow managed to allow herself to breathe, and as the ground raised beneath her, she realized for the first time in nine whole months that she was safe.

CHAPTER 69

Holy cupcakes, my body hasn't stopped shivering. And the weird thing is I don't feel scared. Not right now at least. And I'm not cold, either. Mr. Drisklay doesn't want me to take a shower. He's a cop. I guess he's the one who's been working on my case back home. How's that for irony, right? Anyway, once Mom gets here and can give consent, he wants me to go to the hospital and do one of those tests. You know. So they can prove that ... well, I'm not going to think about it right now.

He hasn't let me change my clothes, but Mrs. Drisklay turned up the heat so high in the hotel room I'm starting to sweat. But I guess my body doesn't know I'm warm yet because it still keeps shaking.

I'm glad Mrs. Drisklay is the kind, motherly type. She's taking care of me and even sent her husband out to bring me a sandwich from downstairs. What I really want is a huge, greasy slice of pizza. But a sandwich is a good place to start.

My mom's flying all the way to Vegas to meet me.

Funny, I can't think of a single time that she's been on a plane. I think we all went to Disney World as a family when I was real little, but I don't even remember that. If she comes straight from the airport to the hotel, it'll take about two more hours.

Two hours and I'll see my mom! Can you believe it? So I'm pretty excited about that.

Mrs. Drisklay's even called the airlines. Wants to see if there's a way we can talk by phone since it's been so long.

It's weird to think of everything that's happened since I left. But I guess I'll have time to sort all that out later. One day at a time, Becky. You're smart enough to take things one day at a time.

Mr. Drisklay's back with that sandwich now. I guess I didn't realize how hungry I am! Hope my hands stop shaking or I'll make myself an even bigger mess.

Speaking of mess, we're back to that old argument. Am I going to the hospital when Mom comes so they can do one of those tests on me or not. Well, actually it's Mrs. Drisklay and her husband having the fight. I'm just sitting here eating my foodz

"It's too much trauma," Mrs. Drisklay says.

"Can't be worse than what she's been through." To be totally honest, I have to agree with her husband on that one.

They're talking in the bathroom. I think it's adorable. They don't realize I can still hear every word they say. But like I said, I'm just so happy to have something to eat.

"It's her choice, Calvin." Hmm. Calvin. That's not a name you hear very often. Woong's dad likes Calvin and Hobbes comic books. Once Woong and I were crazy bored so we read, like, five of them in a row. I prefer Peanuts, actually. That was always Grandma's favorite. But Calvin and Hobbes isn't bad either. Still, it's not the kind of name you hear every day, know what I mean? Then again, Drisklay isn't all that common either, so there's that.

Mrs. Drisklay's phone rings, and she and her husband end their conversation really fast. I think it's the airlines because she's either been on hold with them or waiting on a call back for a while.

Mrs. Drisklay's smiling now, holding out the phone. "Someone wants to talk to you," she tells me. She makes her voice all high like I'm three years old, but I don't mind. It's been quite a while since anyone's thought to baby me.

She passes me her cell, and then she says, "Say hi to your mom."

CHAPTER 70

No matter how hard she tried, Margot couldn't stop her hands from trembling. For a moment, she was afraid she was going to drop the receiver.

"Becky? Can you hear me?" Standing in the back of the plane, she stepped to the side to let the flight attendant with his pot of freshly-brewed coffee pass then gripped the receiver even more tightly. "Becky? Are you there?"

"It might have a short delay," a second flight attendant explained, addressing Margot with large, sympathetic eyes.

"Mom?"

At the sound of her daughter's voice, Margot felt like her legs would give out. "Baby, are you all right? Can you hear me? I'm here, baby. I'm flying to you. I'm going to be there so soon. Are you okay? Are they taking care of you?"

The flight attendant signaled to her partner, and they both slipped away quietly. "Becky?" If the call disconnected before she heard that magical voice again, Margot would die.

"I'm here, Mom."

It was her. She'd been so stupid to worry. When the flight attendant told her that her daughter was on the line and wanted to talk to her, Margot had been too afraid to believe it. What if it was another trafficked girl with the same blonde, curly hair?

What if Becky had been so traumatized by what she went through she forgot her past entirely?

What if she was still angry about that blasted CharlieCard?

"Mom?" Becky's voice was laden with tears, and it took all of Margot's strength to force air in and out of her lungs.

"I'm so sorry." Becky was sobbing now. Her Becky, her poor, injured baby. She was sobbing, and Margot wasn't there to wrap her up in her arms. The ache in her chest grew ever more poignant until she felt almost certain it would consume the entire plane.

"Baby, I'm on my way." She realized that she was shouting, but she had to make sure her daughter heard her. "I'm almost there. It's all going to be okay."

"Mom, I'm sorry." Becky was still crying. Margot was afraid her soul might implode with the ache of not being with her little girl.

"Shh. Don't say that. I love you. I love you so much. You're my perfect, precious little angel." She choked on her words. Once she caught her breath again, she could only whisper into the phone, "I'm coming, baby. I'm almost there."

A flight attendant seemed to appear out of nowhere, her eyes still full of compassion. She gave Margot a soft smile, squeezed her arm gently, and waited for the call to end.

After a heart-wrenching goodbye, Margot went back to her seat, wondering if her heart was strong enough to withstand the rest of this flight. How much longer until she landed? She stared at the time. She could do this. She could make it.

She would see her Becky soon.

CHAPTER 71

It was Xavier. Becky knew it. He was here. He'd found her.

She tried to roll over, but she was stuck. Had he chained her to the bed again? Where was she?

The whole time he was with you, he was working a dozen other girls.

Who was the woman with the taunting voice? Why did she sound so familiar? That's right. Precious.

Precious ...

Something happened to Precious ...

Becky was running, her bare feet slapping the cold, ungiving pavement. And Xavier was chasing her with a gun.

She had to get away ...

Becky was drenched in sweat when she woke up. While her heart raced, she looked around, trying to remember where she was.

"Your mom just texted."

Becky blinked up at the kind-faced woman staring down

at her. Mrs. Drisklay.

"Her plane just landed. She'll be here soon."

Becky sat up in bed, her mind now completely alert. Her mom was coming? She wasn't ready. She had to change. She had to bathe. She had to …

"What is it?" Mrs. Drisklay looked at her worriedly. "What's wrong?" She was probably trying to understand, but what did she know about everything Becky had lived through?

But that was the point. Becky *had* lived through it. She had survived. How many times had Xavier threatened to kill her? How many times did Becky think the shame, the pain, the horror of her surroundings would one day completely annihilate her?

But she was alive. Nobody had killed her. Not Xavier. Not Donahue. Not any of the hundreds of nameless clients.

She was here. She was alive.

Mom was already in Vegas. Mrs. Drisklay had said so herself. Mom was here and had come to take her home.

Becky was a survivor. And the nightmare was finally over.

CHAPTER 72

Margot grabbed the first cab waiting in line at the airport curb and practically yelled the name of Becky's hotel in the driver's ear.

Nine whole months. Nine months without her sunshine, her life, her precious little daughter. Nine months of torture, of pain, of uncertainty.

And now it was all coming to an end.

Her heart was racing, her palms sweaty. She was glad the cab driver didn't try to make any small talk or she would have blabbered Becky's entire life story to him. Why couldn't he drive any faster? Didn't he know what a rush she was in?

Margot called Becky's father the moment the plane landed. Jack had been so overcome with emotion he couldn't even respond. Candy finally took the phone, told Margot how happy she was that Becky was safe. And for the first time, Margot was able to listen to Jack's new wife without wanting to throw up or commit murder. It had to be progress, right?

She wanted to text Sandy but knew her friend had to catch up on all the sleep she'd missed in the excitement of last night. As for Margot, she hadn't managed to sleep at all on the plane. How could she? Becky was alive. She was safe. Another few minutes, and Margot would hold her daughter in her arms.

The sun was just starting to rise when the cab pulled up in front of the hotel. Margot felt weak as she scurried through the front doors, scanning for Detective Drisklay, who was going to meet her in the lobby. The stench of stale cigarette smoke made her even more lightheaded, but that didn't matter. She was going to find her daughter. They were going to be reunited.

It was time to bring Becky home.

CHAPTER 73

Drisklay tossed his Styrofoam cup into the nearest trash and made his way toward Mrs. Linklater. When he saw the look on her face, he worried she was going to faint. He stepped toward her, ready to steady her if she turned out to be as weak-legged as she appeared. "Mrs. Linklater," he greeted.

"Where's my daughter?" Her voice was breathy. Desperate.

Drisklay took her by the elbow and led her toward the elevators, flashing his room key at the security guard on station. "She's sleeping now. There's a child protective agent on their way here, and my wife is with her now. Mrs. Linklater ..." He cleared his throat then waited until they were enclosed within the small elevator before proceeding. "Your daughter has been the victim of terrible crimes. As soon as we can, I hope you see how important it is to get her to the police station and then a hospital to be checked out."

Mrs. Linklater's eyes widened. "Is she sick? Is she hurt?

Oh, dear Jesus, what if she's pregnant? Does she have a disease? Is that what it is?"

Drisklay reached out his hand once again to steady her. "The police need to interview her, then a forensic nurse will want to …"

He didn't have time to finish before the elevator doors opened. Mrs. Linklater raced out. "Which way?"

Drisklay led her down the hall, glad his wife was there to help deal with the overwhelming emotion that was sure to accompany such a reunion. He got to his hotel door and knocked gently. "It's me," he called to his wife, trying to keep his voice low to avoid waking up any of their hotel neighbors lucky enough to be asleep at this ungodly hour.

The door cracked open. Mrs. Linklater brushed past him and dropped to her knees by the side of Becky's bed. "Thank you, God. Oh, my sweet baby. It's okay, sweetie. It's okay. It's all over. You don't have to cry now."

"Mommy?" Becky croaked.

Mrs. Linklater wrapped her arms around her daughter. "That's right. Mommy's here. Nobody's going to hurt you anymore, I promise. Everything is all right now."

Since he was apparently the only one with any sense of privacy, Drisklay quietly shut the door behind him and pulled the latch shut. His wife was standing back, tears streaming down her cheeks. Caroline stepped up to him and wrapped one arm around his waist.

"Thank you," she whispered.

Drisklay cleared his throat, wondering why it felt so scratchy and dry.

Probably he just needed more coffee.

CHAPTER 74

Holy cupcakes, I can't believe she's actually here. My own flesh-and-blood mommy. Like, I literally can't believe it. I'm so scared I'm going to wake up and realize this was all a dream and cry my eyes out.

Not that I'm not crying now. You should see me. I mean, we're talking ugly tears here. Me and Mom both. Oh, my goodness, I never knew you could be so happy and so sad at the same time. Like, my heart literally feels like it's going to break. I thought if I ever saw Mom again, I'd just be glad and thankful and relieved. But it wasn't until she came in here and I saw how old she looks and thought about how scared she must have been these past nine months…

I literally might die of heartache. I can't stop thinking about what I put her through. Oh, Mom, what did I do to you?

She keeps telling me it's okay. Keeps telling me there's nothing for me to apologize for, but she doesn't know the half of it. What has Mrs. Drisklay's husband told her, I wonder? Does she know what I've done? Does she know who I became for Xavier? Is she going to hate me when she finds out? So I keep apologizing in advance.

"Baby," she says, "nothing you could do will make me love you any less. None of it was your fault. None of it at all."

I wish I could believe her. I wish to heaven I could believe her. She keeps saying the same thing over and over, and that's what makes me doubt that Mr. Drisklay told her everything.

Holy cupcakes, what if she's going to have to hear it from me?

"It's all over now," Mom's sobbing into my shoulder. My arms hurt just from clinging to her. "It's all over," she says again.

But somehow, I know it's not.

"There's someone from the police station on their way," I tell her.

"I know, baby. I know."

Funny, I used to hate being called her baby, but now I can't soak in the word enough.

"They want me to go to the hospital," I explain. "They want me to tell the police what happened."

"You don't worry about that right now." Mom straightens up just a little. She's still leaning over and holding me, but I can sense the tension now in her body. She doesn't like what I'm saying. "We'll worry about that another time."

Mom's crying harder now, which of course makes me feel worse. I've really hurt her. I haven't just messed up my own life. I've messed up hers.

Mom's rubbing my back. "All I want you to know is that you're safe and that I'm here for you and that I've never, ever, ever stopped loving you."

I shut my eyes, trying to keep all these emotions inside my body or I literally might explode. I didn't even realize how much I've been shaking until Mom asks, "Are you cold, baby?"

Am I cold? I have no idea. She wraps me in the hotel blanket, but I honestly couldn't tell you if that makes me feel better or worse. She's touching my face. I think I'm pretty bruised. It's obvious it hurts her to see me like this. I wish I hadn't made her suffer so much already …

Mr. Drisklay clears his throat and steps toward us. His wife's trying to hold him back. I can tell he's stubborn. And I know what he's about to say.

"The social worker's downstairs waiting in the lobby.

Your mom can stay with you while you talk to the police, and then you need to decide about undergoing a forensics test."

Mom's body tenses again, but this time I answer before she can.

"I'll do it." Seeing how much sobbing I've just been doing, I'm surprised my voice doesn't squeak or crack.

"I'll do it," I repeat.

Because nobody should have to go through what I have.

And if I can do anything to keep other girls from suffering in that same way, then that's exactly what I plan to do.

CHAPTER 75

Three months later

So you know how people tell you that life goes back to normal after something bad happens? Well, I have something to say about that.

They're liars.

I've been home for a couple months now. Miss Sandy helped homeschool me over the summer so I'll be ready to start tenth grade with the rest of my class. Even though staying home and studying with Miss Sandy might sound like torture, I have to admit I love it.

Mom's doing well. She doesn't want to leave me home alone anymore while she's at work (big surprise after all the ways I messed things up), so I hang out at Woong's with him and Miss Sandy. I can think of worse things. (Smiley face.)

Carly and Megs have basically turned their backs on me. I don't think it's entirely their fault either. Carly's jealous that I'm the one getting all the attention (as if this were the kind of attention anyone wants!). Megan tried. She really did. She even invited me up to her cabin for the weekend but totally understood when I said no thanks. Don't tell anyone, but I sleep in Mom's bed every night. Dad paid to get us a fancy new security system in place too, but even with that I still sleep with the lights on.

Things with Dad are going okay. He honestly has no idea what to say when we're around, but Candy is absolutely fantastic. I guess when she was in high school, she was raped the night of her senior prom. She never told anyone about it until just a few years ago either. But it's kind of nice because she knows the kind of things to say and not to say, and it doesn't feel as awkward with Dad when she's around.

Miss Sandy is amazing (of course) even if she does make me do way too many worksheets. I know I said it before, but I honestly love spending my days with Woong. He's never once asked me about what I went through, but it's not the way Megan does where she acts all scared like I might break if she says the wrong thing. I just literally don't think it's on his mind at all. To him, I'm just the same old Becky I was before I left.

If only that were the case.

I'm seeing a counselor now, actually two of them. Mom leaves work early every Thursday to take me to a trauma specialist who works with teens. And Miss Sandy has a friend from church who's a Christian therapist, and I talk to her every Monday and Wednesday. The best thing is after those meetings, Miss Sandy takes Woong and me to the ice staking rink. Woong's even learning how to go backwards on the ice.

I have to admit I'm a little nervous about starting school again in a few weeks. Everyone in Medford knows what happened to me, and I literally mean everyone. Miss Sandy offered to homeschool me through the school year too, but it would honestly be really strange being at her home all day while Woong's away. My therapist says she thinks the routine will be good for me. Dad said if school doesn't work, he'll hire me a private tutor and I can do my school stuff at his house. Candy is around during the days now that her work schedule's changed, so I wouldn't be alone. It's actually really nice to have choices.

Oh, speaking of choices, that reminds me. I mean, I totally guessed that when I came home I'd have nightmares (which I did) and flashbacks (which I still do). But I had no idea how hard it would be to just make a simple decision. Like, the first morning I spent home, Mom asked me what I wanted for breakfast, and I literally started sobbing in the kitchen because I didn't know how to answer. My therapist says it's just because I spent so long having someone else making all my decisions for me, but I didn't know it at the time, and I was really weirded out.

Mom's good about those kind of things, though, and truth be told, she cries just as easily as I do now. I never would have thought about how people's actions can hurt their families just as much as the victims themselves.

Which brings me to Xavier.

Yeah. Him.

The police in Vegas and Boston both wanted me to testify against him, but I couldn't make myself do it. My therapist says the choice is totally up to me, and even though sometimes I wish I were braver, I just couldn't sit there in a court and face him again.

I guess they're still trying to charge him, though. Once I went missing, they took all our texts from our phones. Plus they have some evidence from the forensics test and pictures from after he beat me up in Vegas. Mom says she hopes they give him the electric chair. Now that she's a Christian, I'm a little surprised to hear her talk that way. And when I'm being totally, totally honest with myself, I don't want anything bad to happen to him.

My counselor and I talk about him a lot. She says he was grooming me from the beginning, how even that first day he pulled up to the bus stop he was just looking for a victim. I wish I could believe that. In fact, I wish I could hate him as much as Mom does.

But then I think about the good times we had together. I think about Morning Xavier, the sweet words, all the pretty gifts he gave me, the plans we made for the future. I'm not stupid enough I'd ever try to get together with him again (at least I hope I'm not that stupid), but I'm still trying to sort through all my feelings about him.

It's complicated, as you can imagine.

Woong's dad has been meeting with my mom. It's funny to think that she became a Christian while I was away. I sometimes wonder if that's what God knew it would take for her to be saved, but then it doesn't really sound all that fair. I can't believe that God would have *wanted* me to go through all that, so I try not to think about it from that standpoint and just focus on how glad I am she's a Christian now too. We're going to church every week, and Miss Sandy gave us this family devotions Bible we read together at bedtime.

Oh, and speaking of church, did I mention that we're getting baptized next week? Mom and me both. Usually, when people get baptized at Woong's church, they do it in front of everybody during one of the services. They stand up there with a microphone and tell everyone why they want to be baptized. And Mom and I both agreed we didn't want to do that. Pastor Carl's church is pretty big too, and they were even worried that the newspeople would come if they found out I'd be giving a speech. Mom's been really clear that I'm not giving any kind of public talks or anything like that. It sounds a little silly, but she's actually made it a rule. No interviews until I'm at least eighteen, and then I'll be an adult, so I can make that choice if I want.

Know what I say to that? Fine by me.

So instead of doing a baptism during the church service itself, Pastor Carl's going to open up the sanctuary on Saturday afternoon. It'll just be a few of us. Me and Mom (of course) and Woong's family. Dad and Candy are coming too, at least they will be if Dad can reschedule one of his lunch meetings that day. But even if he can't, Candy says she wouldn't miss it for the world. We also invited Mr. and Mrs. Drisklay, which I think will be kind of special because of the way God used both of them to help get me home.

I'm a little nervous about it. I've never really liked being the center of attention. Mom said she'll go first, and I'm glad because that'll give me time to really get myself prepared. Sometimes I wish I'd gotten baptized as soon as I got home. I kind of wonder if going under the water will finally make me feel clean again.

That would be nice.

So, just a few more days and I'll be officially a Christian. Haha. Miss Sandy says I'm already a Christian because I believe Jesus died for my sins and forgave me so I can go to heaven. But still, this feels like a really big step, and I'm glad all these important people in my life are going to be there for my big day.

Mom's and my big day, I should say (although I have to admit I have no idea if my grammar's right or not on that one. Sorry, Mr. Daly).

CHAPTER 76

Margot was glad Pastor Carl had agreed to open up the sanctuary on a Saturday. If she got this nervous speaking in front of just a few people she knew well, imagine how much more difficult it would be to share her testimony in front of the entire church.

She'd already decided she didn't want to talk about Becky's kidnapping. As much as she could, she was trying to put all that behind her. It made sharing her salvation story a little tricky, but she managed.

While she talked, Sandy sat in the front row, beaming at her proudly. Margot still couldn't express how thankful she was to her friend for all the ways she'd supported and helped her during the past year.

Jack had come too, bringing Candy along with him. They were really only there for Becky, but Margot knew it meant a lot to her daughter to see them both.

Becky sat in the front row, with Woong on one side and Caroline Drisklay on the other. Margot smiled once at her daughter before reading the testimony she'd written out for the service.

"You all know what our family was going through when I became a Christian, so I won't go into all those details here. I do want to thank Sandy and Carl for encouraging me during such a difficult time. Sandy sacrificed countless hours of sleep to be there when I needed her, and Pastor Carl, you've been an amazing source of knowledge and inspiration whenever I have questions about what it means to live out my new Christian walk.

"I used to think that churches were full of mean-spirited people, but you and your family have taken us in, given us love, and really healed us in ways I can never describe. Woong, I want to thank you too for being such a great friend to my daughter. She tells me that it's the Bible stories she learned at your church that helped get her through some of the scary things she went through."

Margot's throat threatened to clench shut, and she was glad she was nearing the end. "This time last year, I assumed I was going to heaven because I grew up going to church and I hadn't committed any major crimes. Now I know that it's only the grace of Jesus that forgives any of us, and I'm so thankful that you came here today to join me while I make this step of faith."

She glanced up at Pastor Carl, who was standing behind her, smiling. "You ready?" he whispered.

There was only one way to find out. Margot stepped into the baptistry. The water was warmer than she'd expected.

"Margot Linklater." Pastor Carl's voice was resonant and deep. "Because of your personal declaration of faith and your testimony of salvation, it is my delightful privilege to baptize you in the name of the Father and of the Son and of the Holy Spirit."

CHAPTER 77

Caroline had never been to a private baptism before and wasn't sure if she was supposed to clap when Margot came out of the water or not. Thankfully, Sandy began the applause, and Caroline was happy to join in.

The day was perfect. A bright, sunny August Saturday that felt more like the start of spring than the end of summer. In two weeks, Caroline would be back to work, ready to welcome in another class of students.

While Margot stepped out of the baptistry, Caroline glanced at the time. Her husband hadn't made it. She'd tried telling herself it didn't matter, but the truth was it did. He knew how much today meant to her, didn't he? Calvin still refused to come to church with her on Sundays, but this was different. He knew how much she wanted him to be here.

Of course, Calvin was already neck-deep in several other cases. At the same time, he kept gathering evidence so the man responsible for luring Becky away from her home and selling her into a life of slavery got the justice he deserved.

Caroline was proud of her husband. Proud that he'd saved Becky. Proud that once Xavier was behind bars even more girls would be spared such unthinkable suffering.

But that still didn't excuse him from missing today.

Becky stepped up to the microphone, looking youthful and glowing in her simple white gown. A tiny, gold butterfly necklace hung around her neck. Margot was relieved to see her looking so healthy. Her mom said she'd gained back weight she lost while held captive, and the nightmares weren't as bad anymore either. Thank God for that.

After seeing Becky and her mother safely reunited, Caroline hadn't spent all that much time with the Linklaters. Even though they attended the same church now, Caroline usually went to the early service. Every so often, she'd see Becky and her mother coming into the sanctuary in passing, but it was hard to know what to say to either of them.

And so she prayed.

Sitting here watching both Becky and her mother get baptized felt like the answer to all her prayers.

So why couldn't Calvin have made more of a point to be here? She knew his work was keeping him busy, but still…

"Becky?" Pastor Carl said. "Would you like to tell everyone here why you've decided to become baptized?"

Caroline had just resolved to pull herself out of her

resentful funk and focus on the baptism when the back door opened. She turned around, and there was her husband. He looked especially handsome today in his uniform. He gave her a curt, slightly apologetic nod as he tossed his Styrofoam cup into the trash can at the back of the sanctuary.

He slipped into the seat beside Caroline with a whispered, "Sorry," and silenced his cell right as Becky began her speech.

"I told my mom I didn't think I'd need to write out everything I wanted to say," she began with a shy smile, "but now I kind of wish I had."

Caroline's heart went out toward her. The poor girl's hands were shaking as she spoke.

"But anyway, my mom said it really well when she was up here earlier. We went through a hard time last year, and I know it was God who got us through. Even at the worst, I could feel the Lord with me and knew he was answering my prayers. I still don't know why everything happened the way it did. But like Miss Sandy said, we might not know why he allows bad things to happen to us, but we can trust that he'll make good things come of it. And I can think of a whole lot of good things already. Like Mom becoming a Christian. And me deciding to be baptized."

She took in a choppy breath. "I think before everything

happened, I was just kind of your normal girl, you know? And I cared about a lot of things that right now I realize weren't all that important. After going through what I went through, you learn a little bit. Like who your real friends are." She smiled in the direction of Woong and his mother sitting proudly in the front row. "And how important family really is. So I guess I just want to say that even though I don't understand why I went through what I did, I trust that God is good. And I'm really thankful for the way he watched over me and Mom. And Dad and Candy too," she added with an embarrassed smile, almost like an afterthought.

"And I guess the reason I want to be baptized today is because I've spent enough time focusing on stuff that doesn't matter, like what other kids at school think of me. And I want God to know that he's the most important thing in my life. I made God a promise to use my story and the things that happened to me to help other girls in the future. I don't know how it's going to work out or even where I'm going to start, but I know baptism's all about new beginnings. And just like I'm starting new in my walk with Jesus, I just wanted to share that side of things too. So I guess that's what I wanted to say."

She glanced sheepishly at Pastor Carl, who gave her a fatherly smile.

Caroline was surprised to feel her husband's leg brush against hers, and she glanced over to see him watching her. Tentatively, she took his hand, and she gave it a squeeze.

God certainly had carried Becky and the entire Linklater family through the valley of the shadow of death. And he had been silently at work in her marriage too.

Calvin was still far from the Lord. He still poked fun at her religion and accused her of being brainwashed.

But he was here. And as he watched Pastor Carl lower Becky beneath the water, she sensed a kind of quiet reverence from her husband where before she would have expected only cynicism.

Everyone clapped when Becky came up out of the water, and Woong gave a congratulatory holler, jumping out of his seat to present her with a Darth Vader towel. Caroline glanced out of the corner of her eye, startled to see the slightest hint of a smile on her husband's face.

She gave his hand another squeeze, let the joy of the Linklaters' celebration wash over her, and thought about all the miracles she'd witnessed in the past year. Becky's safe return. Her mother's salvation. Even the legal work falling in place to get Xavier the sentence he deserved.

Seeing Becky Linklater smiling on the stage, hugging Woong and drenching his Avengers T-shirt, Margot realized she was witnessing another miracle right now. Not only was Becky safe, she was in the process of finding true healing. Caroline had no doubt that Becky would fulfill the promise she'd made to help other girls in the future.

After the service, Calvin stood up to shake Carl's hand.

"So glad you could make it, brother." Carl's voice was welcoming and strong.

Calvin gave him a genuine smile. "I wouldn't have missed it for the world."

Caroline put her arm around her husband, thankful when she didn't feel him tense or pull away.

Today, she was celebrating the Linklaters' miracles, but one day she believed her husband would make a declaration of faith just like Becky and her mom had earlier. It might not happen this year. It might not happen in her lifetime, but she believed with all her heart it would come true.

God was a God of miracles, and Caroline was certain he wasn't finished with her — or her husband — yet.

From Alana:

If enjoyed this fast-paced Christian thriller, you'll love

Forget Me Now, another Christian suspense novel full of twists, turns, and nail-biting excitement. *Forget Me Now* features several of the characters you've met in *SAVE ME ONCE* and is basically guaranteed to keep you up *way* past your bedtime devouring chapter after chapter. *Forget Me Now* is the story of a girl who wakes up with no memory and will keep you reading ... and guessing ... late into the midnight hours. If you like intense psychological dramas, surprising twists and turns, and a powerful message of faith, then you'll love this next riveting thriller.

Buy *Forget Me Now* today, or keep scrolling for a special sneak peek.

CHAPTER 1

Springtime. I've always loved the spring. And today's going to be perfect. It's the senior trip today. Time to get myself up and out of bed.

Ow.

Wait. Why does my head hurt this much?

A knock on my door. Mom? No, she doesn't knock that way. Who is it then?

The door cracks open. "Dad?" I squint at him. Maybe it's

because I don't have my contacts in yet. Is that what's wrong? He looks different.

"Dad?" I say the word again because I'm not sure it came out right last time.

"Hiya, Mimi." He's smiling at me. That cheesy grin. I try to remember the last time he came to my room in the morning. Why isn't he at work already?

"Hi," I answer tentatively. My head is swirling with questions, but it's also swirling with pain. Pain and fog and confusion. I think I'm scared, but it's hard to remember.

Remember ...

Dad sits on the corner of my bed. He looks smaller. Maybe it's because he hasn't done this since I was a little girl, coming into my room like this. There's something in his eyes. Like he's embarrassed to tell me something. No, not embarrassed. That's not quite right. So what is it?

Oh, no. Has something happened to Chris? Is that what he came in here to tell me? What if Mr. Gomez finally got arrested? Or even worse, what if his dad beat him up? I know I promised Chris I wouldn't tell about his family, but I didn't know what to do. I had to let somebody know. Did Chris's dad find out and get so mad at him that he ...

"How you feeling?" Dad asks me, and I honestly have no idea how to answer.

He takes a deep breath, and I prepare myself. It's Chris. I know it is. I promised when we started dating that I wouldn't tell anybody about his dad. What could I do? He was crying on my shoulder, just like a terrified little child. And he was blubbering, begging me not to share his secret. So I assured him I wouldn't. I made him a promise.

And now something terrible has happened.

I should never have told …

But why does my head hurt so much?

Dad clears his throat. "So, baby, do you know what today is?"

What kind of a question is that? Of course I know what today is. It's the last Friday in May. It's senior skip day. Chris and I were planning to …

I glance at the clock. The time is right. Same time Mom wakes me up every morning. That part hasn't changed, except it's Dad here and not Mom. But there's something else not quite right.

Dad's got his hand on top of my blanket, holding down my leg. Does he think I'm about to jump up and sprint out the door? Mom couldn't be having second thoughts about senior skip day, could she? She's been as excited about our camping trip as I have …

So it is Chris. I knew it. Something happened. Something

terrible. I shiver a little. Dread? Uncertainty?

"Mia." As soon as Dad says the word, my stomach drops. *Mia.* Not Princess or Mimi or any of those other pet names that he always uses.

Mia.

I try to sit up, but I'm so dizzy. He takes his other hand to keep me down on the bed. Something's glistening in the corner of his eye. I refuse to admit it might be a tear. When's the last time I saw Dad cry? Come to think of it, have I ever seen Dad cry? It must be something else. The bright light shining in from the window, blinding him, making him squint.

Except there's no bright light shining in from the window. Just that early morning gray.

My brain feels like it's trying to tell me something. Trying to wake up or recover some missing piece. But I have no idea what I've forgotten. No idea why Dad's looking at me with a tear in the corner of his eye. No idea why he's the one waking me up instead of Mom.

"Mia, I want you to listen to me very carefully," he says. I stare into his eyes, looking for comfort or strength. Instead, that tear. That one single sparkling tear.

It must be worse than I thought. What if Chris is dead? What if his dad …

"You've been out of it for a little while," Dad says. I want to laugh. You have no idea how much I want to laugh. It's the kind of thing Mom might do. A joke. Like the time she changed my clock then ran into my room and told me I missed my AP psychology test when instead she just wanted to wake me up early so we could go get donuts before she dropped me off at school.

But Dad never jokes. Not like this. And he never gives surprises.

"What do you mean?" I croak.

Dad sighs, and there's something vaguely familiar about that sigh, like I've heard it before. It's like studying for a calculus exam only to walk into the wrong classroom where the teacher hands you a test in French. The problem is you don't know French because you've been studying Spanish since sixth grade so you can become a doctor and set up a free health clinic along the Mexican border.

In other words, I have no idea what Dad's saying.

"There was an accident," he begins, wincing when he gets out the word. "A terrible accident."

There's something in the way he says it. Something in his voice, his expression. I'm not entirely convinced this is all about Chris anymore. Because if my boyfriend got into an accident and died, Mom would be the one to tell me, and she'd be crying for real, not just sitting here with one single tear in the corner of her eye. Mom adores Chris. Dad not so much. So if there was some kind of accident, if something happened to my boyfriend, Dad wouldn't be the one to come in here and tell me about it. Which can only mean ...

I sit up in bed, ignoring the pain in the back of my skull, shaking off the dizziness as best I can. "Where's Mom?" I demand.

Dad's holding my shoulders, trying to pin me down. I think I'm crying, but I'm not sure. My throat feels sore, like it wants to let out a sob. "Where's Mom?" I repeat. "I want to talk to Mom."

And a strange flash, a sort of *deja-vu* flits through my head, but only for a fraction of a second. A fraction of a second that throws me totally off balance, makes me stop struggling so hard. Because I've got this sense I've done this before.

Dad opens his mouth.

"Mom can't be here right now, Mimi. We have to have a talk."

CHAPTER 2

Dad hands me a cup of coffee in one of his masculine travel mugs. Coffee in bed? Is this my dad or has he been taken over by space aliens?

I glance around for my phone on my nightstand. It's reflex, really. Wake up. Sit up in bed. Check for text messages. Because I'm certain that sometime between now and last night when Chris and I got off the phone, my boyfriend texted me. He always does.

"Don't worry about your cell right now," Dad says. Apparently he's become a mind reader all of a sudden. "Drink your coffee," he tells me, and his voice sounds more like him. Controlled. In charge.

I obey but wince. Dad always makes my coffee too sweet. Probably because he's so used to drinking his black. Except I only drink coffee on special occasions, and he's never once brought me a drink in bed.

"Too much sugar?" he asks, glancing slightly away.

"It's perfect." I give him a smile. At least I try to, but it makes my head hurt even more, and now Dad's the one to wince.

"Had enough?" he asks. He takes the mug and places it on my end table, picking up a hot-pink zebra print binder I've never seen before. "Do you know what this is?"

I shake my head. It looks like something I would have begged Mom for when I was back in second grade. The folder is so over-the-top frilly I'm surprised it doesn't have unicorns and glitter.

Dad opens up to the first page and shows me a photograph taped to the inside cover. "Do you know who this is?"

I roll my eyes. At least I start to, but a splintering headache makes me stop.

"That's Chris," I tell him. What in the world is going on?

Dad nods then turns the page.

"And this?"

"It's last Christmas," I answer mechanically. "Mom wanted us to finally get a picture with all four of us in it, except she couldn't figure out how to use that selfie stick you got her." It's a funny memory… except I'm not laughing.

Neither is my dad.

He points to another photo. "Do you know her?"

I blink at the girl with bouncy brown curls. Then blink

again. Dad's pointer finger is covering the bottom corner of the picture. I reach out for my glasses, the pair I keep on the end table, but they only make my headache worse.

"Do you know her?" he asks again.

And again I blink. "Kelsie?" I hear the uncertainty in my own voice. It isn't because I've forgotten my best friend. Kelsie and I have been inseparable since middle school. We do everything together, but that still doesn't explain this picture. Still doesn't explain why I'm lying in a strange bed wearing a flowery hospital gown, taking a selfie with Kelsie.

A selfie I don't remember.

What's going on?

Dad leans in a little closer. "Do you know when this picture was taken?"

"No," I whisper. For a minute I wonder if this is some strange photoshop joke. But then I remember that my dad never jokes. Never does anything unexpected.

If this were Mom, she'd be busting a gut laughing by now. Telling me how she paid some graphic design student a few bucks to interpose me and Kelsie into someone else's hospital photo just to see how confused I'd get. Then she'd tell me breakfast was ready, and she'd laugh about it some more while we ate.

But this isn't Mom. This is Dad, and Dad never laughs.

He lets out a cough and turns the page. "Do you recognize any of the other people in this picture?" He's leaning closer to me now. So intent. I feel like I did a few weeks ago when he watched me open my acceptance letter to NYU, his alma mater. I was nervous, not because I have my heart set on going to NYU, but because I knew how disappointed Dad would be if I didn't get that scholarship I applied for.

"It's my friends from school," I answer. And there we are. Me and Kelsie. About a dozen others, some holding balloons, get-well posters, all of us posing for the camera. We're in the same hospital room. I'm wearing that same ugly gown, trying to smile.

"Do you remember taking this picture?"

There's an answer Dad's expecting from me, except I can't give it to him. I shake my head.

"No," I tell him, realizing without understanding why that I'm letting him down. But I can't lie. Not about something like this. My heart is racing faster than normal. Just how strong was that coffee?

"Are you sure?" There's a squeeze in Dad's voice, a tension. Which again makes me wonder what all this means or how it is that my answer is hurting him so deeply.

I stare again at the picture. I know these faces. Happy,

smiling teens. My friends for years.

But why are we in a hospital room? And why am I dressed in that hideous gown?

Something isn't right. The lump in my throat, the racing of my pulse, they're all telling me the same thing. It's like this is the most important test I've ever taken, and I'm failing miserably. But I can't make up the answers. I shake my head again, look at my dad through these tears I'm trying to blink away, and tell him honestly, "I don't know when that picture was taken. I don't remember a thing."

CHAPTER 3

"It's okay, Mimi. It's okay." Dad is running his hand over my hair, and I can't remember the last time we've had any sort of physical contact like this. Usually it's a half-second hug before bed. If he's even home by the time I turn in for the night. I used to like to kiss the scratch of his cheek, but that was when I was younger. I can't remember the last time I kissed him.

Can't remember ...

"What was I doing in the hospital?" I'm trying not to get hysterical, but I feel the panic welling up inside me. It's like I've lost something but can't even remember what it was so I can properly mourn.

"You had an accident, baby." I hear the strain in his voice, the tension, and yet the words come out so rehearsed. Have I heard them before? "You lost some of your memory."

I'm crying. Sniffling. Trying hard not to sob. Wiping snot on the sleeves of my pajamas. I don't understand. *This isn't funny, Dad.* That's what I want to tell him. *This isn't funny, and I want to talk to Mom.*

Now.

He points to the picture in the hot-pink album. "This was taken the day after graduation."

I shake my head, forgetting that each time I move my brain feels like it's getting slammed into ice picks the size of dinosaur claws. "That's next week." I'm desperate to make him understand. Make myself understand. "Graduation is next week," I repeat. "Today's the class trip. Chris is supposed to be here …"

And then I hear it. A sound I've never heard from my dad in the eighteen years I've been alive. A pained, tortured, tormented sob. "There was an accident," he repeats. "Mimi, I'm so sorry."

I can't take my eyes off the photo. I remember my friends. I know all their names, how long we've known each other. I haven't lost all of my memory. So why don't I recognize the hospital room?

Dad's trying hard to keep his composure. I might be mistaken, but I think I feel his body tremble once from the effort. "You were in the hospital for a week."

"I don't remember any of that," I whisper, wishing my dad was lying, wishing he possessed the kind of sick and twisted sense of humor it would take to prank someone in such a grotesque way. But I know my dad. And I know he's telling me the truth.

An accident? Took my memory? Why do I remember my own name? Why do I remember my room? Why do I remember that I was supposed to go on my senior class trip today?

"I need to call Chris," I tell him, and immediately I realize I've once again said the wrong thing. The thing that makes Dad grimace, that makes the raw pain even more evident in his expression.

"You can't," he croaks. I've never heard him talk like this.

I wonder if someone my age can die of panic. My heart is racing so fast it's making me even dizzier. I force each gulp of air in deliberately, fearing that if I stop, I'll forget to breathe entirely.

"What do you mean I can't?" Why is Dad telling me this? He may not be Chris's biggest fan in the world, but he knows how much my boyfriend means to me. Knows how much I'd need to talk to him at a time like this. Need to hear his voice.

I have to know what happened. I know Dad's probably worried about giving me too many details too fast and making me feel overwhelmed, but there's no way to feel any more confused than I already do. The only thing that's going to help me now is answers.

Lots of them.

"Tell me what happened," I beg. My voice is whiny. I can't mask my terror.

"I think you should get dressed. I'll make you breakfast." What's Dad talking about? Does he seriously think I'd be worrying about my wardrobe or my appetite right now? At the mention of food, my stomach sloshes with nausea. I wonder how fast I can race to my bathroom in my condition if I have to throw up.

"I need to call Chris," I tell him again, glancing around the room, desperate to locate my phone. Tears streak down my cheeks. I can hardly breathe. Is this what it feels like when your body goes into shock? Is the strain going to give me a heart attack? "Where's my phone?"

Dad turns his face away. I can't see his expression. Have no idea what he's thinking, what he's going to say next. A terrible question grips me. What if we've done this before? What if we've had this exact same conversation in the past, only I can't remember it?

I touch Dad's arm. We're not used to being physical with each other. Not in years. But he has to understand what I'm going through. Has to realize that it's the uncertainty that's going to kill me, not the truth itself.

"Please," I repeat, barely able to raise my voice beyond a whisper. "Please tell me what happened. I need to know everything."

***

Ready for more? Grab this heart-gripping, page-turning Christian suspense novel that has been called "intense," "life-changing," and "impossible to put down." *Forget Me Now* will keep you reading ... and guessing ... late into the midnight hours. If you like intense psychological dramas, surprising twists and turns, and a powerful message of faith, then you'll love this riveting thriller.

For a fast-paced adrenaline rush you'll never forget, download your copy of *Forget Me Now* today.

Made in the USA
Columbia, SC
08 October 2024

43298252R00224